PENGUIN BO

Swim

Jackie Davis' first novel *Breathe* was published by Penguin Books in 2002. Her short fiction and poetry have been widely published, both in New Zealand and internationally. She is a registered nurse and a full-time mother and holds an MA in Creative Writing from Victoria University in Wellington. Jackie lives in Gisborne with her husband and two sons.

Swim

Jackie Davis

PENGUIN BOOKS

PENGUIN BOOKS

Penguin Books (NZ) Ltd, cnr Airborne and Rosedale Roads, Albany,
Auckland 1310, New Zealand
Penguin Books Ltd, 80 Strand, London, WC2R 0RL, England
Penguin Putnam Inc, 375 Hudson Street, New York, NY 10014, United States
Penguin Books Australia Ltd, 250 Camberwell Road, Camberwell,
Victoria 3124, Australia
Penguin Books Canada Ltd, 10 Alcorn Avenue, Toronto,
Ontario, Canada M4V 3B2
Penguin Books (South Africa) (Pty) Ltd, 24 Sturdee Avenue, Rosebank,
Johannesburg 2196, South Africa
Penguin Books India (P) Ltd, 11, Community Centre, Panchsheel Park,
New Delhi 110 017, India
Penguin Books Ltd, Registered Offices: Harmondsworth, Middlesex, England

First published by Penguin Books (NZ) Ltd, 2003

1 3 5 7 9 10 8 6 4 2

Lines from an adaptation of the song 'I Saw a Taniwha' are reproduced
by kind permission of Linda Adamson.

Designed by Mary Egan
Typeset by Egan-Reid Ltd
Printed in Australia by McPherson's Printing Group

ISBN 0 14 301856 6
www.penguin.co.nz

for Billie
and for my boys,
Michael and Simon

One

Black or white. She couldn't decide. She walked along the quiet aisles and her fingers trailed behind her, rustling the hangers and making them shiver. She closed her eyes. She would be daring or demure; she would trust the process. Her arm reached out over the racks. She allowed her hand to stop when it was right. It came to rest on the cool throat of a plastic hanger. It slipped the hanger off the rack. She opened her eyes.

Black. Maya blushed. She glanced around. She'd never bought a black bra. They were for women who still went out for drinks after work, for women who woke up on Saturday mornings at eleven, or later, with sheets and clothes and limbs tangled. Black bras were for fast women. God, I sound like Gran, she thought. She stood there in the middle of the lingerie shop and the black bra with its straight shoulders and perfect posture teased her with its lace and its dark and slippery shine. She couldn't help passing it between her fingers. How soft, how smooth it was. Not dangerous at all.

Suddenly, there was Charlie in front of her. His small face poked out from a rack of big white bras, for women with ample bosoms.

'Cool colour, Mum.'

'Really?'

'Yeah.' He stepped out and thrust his hands into the pockets of

7

his cargo pants. Little man. 'Do you know that black is my favourite colour?'

Maya smoothed his hair down, instinctively.

'I thought green was,' she said.

'Nah. Green's for wusses. Black. That's the best.'

'Well, then,' said Maya. 'Black it is.' She held the bra to her, hiding it with her hand.

She laid it on the counter. Its perky, softly padded breasts pointed upwards.

'Nice choice,' the shop assistant said as she ran her laser gun over the price tag.

'Thanks,' said Maya.

'Forty-nine ninety-five. Will that be cash or charge?' The girl smiled with her lipstick mouth.

Shit. Fifty dollars. She hadn't even looked at the price. Could have gone down the road and got three for that price. Still. This is my birthday treat, she reminded herself.

'Eftpos,' said Maya. She handed her card to the girl, watching the computer screen as it looked up her balance, her available credit, in a neatly ruled-up ledger somewhere. Please let there be enough, Maya said to the man who filled in the numbers, with his quill of black ink that went scratch scratch as it added up the money in her account.

The machine beeped. *Accepted*, it flashed.

Thank you, Maya whispered to the man.

'Come on, Mum,' said Charlie. 'This is boring.'

'All right. Nearly done.'

The shop assistant pushed a paper carry bag with stiff rope handles across the counter. *Dangerous Curves*, in flowing emerald script, slid towards Maya. There were no thin plastic bags destined to line her rubbish bin at this shop. She ran her hand over the bag and remembered when her mother brought the groceries home in big square paper bags from the Four Square. You could make a mask with one of those bags. You would pull it over your head and draw with a crayon where your eyes were. You'd cut out the eyeholes and paint the face, add hair – any colour – and look, you were someone else.

Maya took the bag and headed out to the hubbub of the street.

'Where shall we go to eat?' she said to Charlie. 'McDonald's?'

'Yeah,' said Charlie. He kicked the heel of one shoe with the toe of the other. Then, 'But it's your birthday. We'll go wherever you want to.'

Maya kneeled down. She put her arms around the slight frame of her son. 'You're so thoughtful,' she said. 'What did I do to deserve a boy like you?'

'Oh Mum,' said Charlie, and he squirmed out of his mother's embrace. 'Gross.'

They licked around their ice-creams. Skinny rivers of hokey pokey and goody gumdrops ran down the orange cones.

'You wouldn't think ice-creams would melt so fast in winter,' said Maya.

'Is this okay?' said Charlie. He crunched into a nugget of hokey pokey.

'What?'

'Ice-creams on the beach. I thought you'd want to go to one of your proper cafés or something.'

Maya scooped out a raspberry gumdrop with her tongue. It left a hollow in the blue ice-cream.

'Are you kidding?' she said. 'There's nothing better in the whole world than to sit with you on my birthday –'

'Eating ice-creams on the beach,' Charlie joined in.

Alto and boy soprano.

They sat there, side by side. A man walked along the beach, holding hands with a boy about Charlie's age. They wore matching blue padded jackets. Surfguy was embroidered across their backs in red and gold. Maya saw that Charlie was watching them. She felt his hand find hers.

'Do you miss my dad?' he said. He worked around the edge of his cone.

'Yeah,' said Maya. 'How about you?' She tried to sound casual.

'I'm not sure. I guess I do. Mostly on birthdays and Christmas and stuff. And sport, you know, when all the other dads are there.'

'So mothers don't count?' She flicked sand away from around her.

'You know what I mean.'

'He would have loved you. Your dad.'

'Yeah?'

'Absolutely. He did love you. And he was so proud to have a son. He couldn't believe it when you were born. He walked around in a daze for ages.'

'Yeah?'

'He chose your name. Did you know that?'

'No. Really?'

A shiver of ice-cream ran down the cone and onto Maya's hand. She licked it off.

'He loved your name. He said you were destined for something great with a name like Charles.'

'Cool.'

'But do you know, the funny thing was that it wasn't until we were filling in your birth certificate details that we realised that you were Charles and he was Philip. You know, like Prince Philip and Prince Charles.'

'True?'

'He called me Queenie for ages after that.'

Charlie poked dents in his ice-cream with his finger. They were craters on a white mountainside.

The man jogged back along the beach. The boy ran beside him, working his legs hard to match the man's stride.

'Did he have to die?' said Charlie.

'Oh, buddy.' This is too hard, thought Maya. She watched the man get smaller and smaller.

'Did he have one of those breathing machines? Did they zap him and everything like on *Shortland Street*?'

'They did everything they could to save him,' and she realised she was talking exactly like someone on *Shortland Street*. Except it was true and those were the best words. 'He was too badly injured. But we're okay, aren't we? You and me?'

She was tired now. This wasn't how she wanted to spend her birthday. She'd been burying this for seven years. Not today, buddy.

She looked down along the bay. The beach was deserted now. The man and his dog had gone. The coast stretched, in a lazy yawn, from the piles of logs stacked into pyramids at the port, under Kaiti Hill, to the White Cliffs, where slices of the land had once fallen into the sea.

'Isn't it funny how nothing is original,' said Maya. She was grasping for neutral territory.

'Eh?' said Charlie, taking tiny bites from around his cone. It looked like an orange frill, thought Maya as she watched him. All those small teeth jags. He seemed unaffected by talk of his father's death. How resilient kids are.

'Sorry. Thinking out loud again.' The tips of their shoes touched as they sat on the sand. 'I was just thinking about the White Cliffs there' – Charlie followed the nod of her head – 'and how they have the same name as the White Cliffs of Dover.'

'What's that?'

'It's a place in England. It's a huge cliff. Like that one.' She pointed to the edge of the land. 'And that made me think about Waikanae. And how our beach, in little old Gisborne, has the same name as that beach just out of Wellington. You know the one. We stopped there once, after we'd been to Te Papa. And you wanted to swim out to Kapiti Island.'

'Oh yeah,' said Charlie. 'And we brought home heaps of shells.'

'Nothing is original, you see,' said Maya. This was a big point. She wanted Charlie to understand. 'Or new. It's all recycled.'

'That's good, isn't it, Mum? Recycling. You're always moaning when people don't recycle their bottles.' Charlie poked the end of his cone into his mouth and it disappeared like a pointy tongue.

Maya laughed. 'I guess so.'

They sat in silence. Winter waves fell onto the sand. Maya counted them. Was it true that every seventh wave was bigger than the rest? That's what she'd been told. She remembered her mother standing next to her in the surf, her frilled and shirred swimsuit clinging to her, and as the waves slapped her on the back, and the salt water fanned up around her head, she called out *Count to seven, Maya. After the next big one*. And she would, waiting with her yellow flutterboard in her small fingers. Six, seven, go. And she gave in and the wave picked her up and carried her to the beach, and for a moment she was weightless, a paper boat bobbing down a flooded drain. *Yes, yes*, she heard her mother shouting. *You did it*. She picked herself up off the wet sand and turned and her mother was standing in the sea up to her waist with her arms up over her head and she was clapping and cheering for her daughter, for her, for Maya.

'You're a very cool mum, you know,' Charlie said. He picked up a stick, smooth and white as bone, and drew circles in the sand.

'Why is that?' Maya threw the tip of her cone, now soft and soggy, out towards the sea. A gull swooped, snatched it up in its beak. It tipped its head back and flipped the cone into its throat.

'Letting me have the day off school when it's your birthday.'

'Well, you're my best buddy. And anyway, you're a good excuse. I'd feel a bit stupid coming down here and eating ice-cream by myself.' She grabbed at him, tickling him, and they fell onto the sand laughing and hugging and the seagull squawked and flew away and Maya suddenly thought how good it was to be thirty-seven.

'What about a movie?' she asked once they had brushed the sand off their pants and coats and shoes, and they were back in the car with the heater on.

'Are you sure it's not really *my* birthday?' said Charlie.

'If you're happy, I'm happy,' she said, and she couldn't help reaching over and smoothing his hair down again.

But there was nothing on, of course. It was the middle of the day in the middle of the week. School holidays were still a while away. There were no movies they could both enjoy.

'Not to worry. We'll do movies at home.'

They stopped at the video shop. When she came back to the car Maya had a bag of popcorn, a bottle of Coke, a box of Jaffas and two videos. 'Don't peek. It'll be a surprise.'

'It's a double feature,' she said when they were home and settled on the couch. She put her arm around Charlie. He snuggled into her, and even through the layers of sweatshirt, vest and skivvy she could feel his breath, warm and soft, like a baby's.

They ate all the popcorn. They drank the Coke out of the bottle, passing it from one to the other the way Maya remembered doing with bourbon in a hip flask with her friends during her training days. A lifetime ago. They ate all the Jaffas and by the time they began the second movie they both felt sick. Their tongues were candy red.

Charlie made it through the first video but he was asleep before the next one was halfway through. His small head fitted into the hollow of Maya's shoulder. She picked up strands of his pale hair, let it fall and watched it settle exactly where it was supposed to. She rested her cheek against the top of his head. He smelled like shampoo and butter. She pulled back his fringe and kissed his forehead.

He was warm in her arms as she moved to pick him up. She remembered him as a baby, a smaller bundle to be tucked into bed. He opened his eyes as she carried him. He smiled the drunken grin that is a sleepy child, and tightened his grip around her neck. He sighed.

'Boys of eight and a half shouldn't need to be carried to bed by their mothers,' Maya whispered as she lowered him into his bed. She took off his shoes and socks and pulled the bedclothes up to his shoulders.

Charlie opened his eyes again. 'Hug,' he said, and he raised his arms. She leaned down to him, filled the space between his arms with her body. She felt his fingers imprint onto her back.

'Love you,' she said.

'Love you too,' Charlie answered, and his voice slid effortlessly into sleep.

Maya went back to the lounge and turned off the video player. She picked up the empty Coke bottle and a sweatshirt with holes in

13

the elbows. Tidying up. Tomorrow. It can wait until tomorrow. She went into the kitchen and poured herself a glass of wine. It was as dark as lipstick and its oily surface lapped against the sides of the glass. Happy birthday, she said. The house was silent. It was as if she was expecting someone to answer. The walls, maybe? The furniture? Her birthday drink? Felicitations. And many happy returns, Maya. She downed her wine and put the glass in the sink. Maybe senile dementia is setting in, she thought. An early onset. Goodnight, Mister Zebedee, she said and she turned off the light.

She went in to check on Charlie, as she had done every night of his life. He lay on his back, arms outstretched. His mouth was open. He breathed silently. He snorted, then rolled onto his side and snuggled into Honey Bear. The bear squeaked as Charlie pressed into his furry tummy. Maya smiled. That bear was bigger than you once, she thought. She stood there for a moment longer. Stupid sentimental woman. Is this what happened when you turned thirty-seven?

She lay awake for a long time. She was hot with the winter weight of blankets and a thick and feathery duvet, but when she moved under it all she got cold again. Winter. Ha. Who needs it? But spring was just around the corner.

In fact it was spring already. If you counted off the months in groups of three, four seasons fitted neatly into each corner. December, January, February. March, April, May. June, July, August. September, October, November. September. See? Spring had already started. The daffodils were flowering, with their fleshy stems and narrow nodding faces. The branches of the kowhai outside Maya's bedroom window were heavy with their yellow velvety flowers. A tui had made the tree its home, sipping the nectar there, and singing to them each morning.

Spring. And yet it still felt like winter.

Two

*I*n here it was its own community, with its own rules. Keep to the right of the lane. Let quicker ones past. Fold up your clothes neatly, bra and undies tucked inside.

And there were the rules she'd learned as a girl. Don't stare. Don't make too much noise. No jumping. Don't run. Don't pee in the water.

It all applied, still.

The chlorine made her eyes sting as soon as she pushed open the door. She could almost taste it.

'Hi,' said Maya as she passed her concession card across the counter. The receptionist clipped it and a tiny keyhole-shaped piece of card fluttered onto the desk. As Maya watched it land she was suddenly reminded of when she was at school – intermediate – and she caught the bus from Gran's house every morning. Clip clip. Different shapes stamped out of her ticket by the bus driver in his blue jacket. What kind would it be today? A tiny bird, a star, an angel? She was sure that's what they'd been. Did each bus driver get to choose his own clipper, or did they get issued with any old one each morning? Maya decided she'd have chosen a dolphin clipper. With a swishy tail.

The receptionist held the card out for her. 'Thanks very much,' Maya said.

'Have you had a good day? You look happy.'

Maya leaned forward, as though this were a secret. 'It was my birthday yesterday,' she whispered. It felt good, this public (yet quiet) declaration. You only got to say it once a year.

'Well, happy birthday for yesterday.'

Maya took the card and headed off to the changing rooms. She slipped off her clothes. Underneath, she already had her togs on. Silly getting changed at work, from her uniform into street clothes, and then having to take it all off and put her togs on at the pool.

She snapped on her yellow bathing cap, goggles with dark lenses. I'm like an underwater creature, she thought. Something out of *Stingray*.

She stood at the edge of the pool, stretching, pointing her fingers to the ceiling, warming up her after-work muscles.

The diving block was wet and cold. She shivered, then bent over, flexed her knees. Go.

This was her moment of freedom. The split second between thrusting off from the block and slicing through the water. She wished she could freeze it. She was airborne, disconnected from earth or sea.

Her body slid under the tight surface. The water was warm but Maya shuddered slightly as her body was surrounded by it. She was propelled forward, felt herself slow and began to stroke through the water. Left arm right arm breathe. Left arm right arm breathe. Again and again until her hand contacted the rough concrete of the wall. She looked up at the clock. Not bad. Not bad for thirty-seven and one day.

She set off again, from one end of the pool to the other. Again and again. It was effortless, yet it was hard work. When she was finally done and had pulled herself out of the water her legs were trembling.

Get dried. Get dressed. Get Charlie.

The alarm buzzed her awake. Her hand slapped it quiet. Ten more minutes.

Then the every-morning madness started. Coffee and toast and do you want Weet-Bix or Coco Pops. Have you got your homework and don't forget soccer practice at lunchtime and I'll see you tonight. You're going to Jacob's after school today. No, I won't be late. Have a neat day. Love you. Love you too.

They went in opposite directions at the gate. Charlie, left, to school; Maya, right, to work.

She zipped up her jacket and put her hands in her pockets. Spring indeed. And yet it was everywhere, in every garden she passed, every tree holding its breath for the perfect moment to burst into leaf or blossom.

The sky was the colour of milk.

Once she stepped inside the hospital Maya was caught up in the commotion of people all with somewhere to go. It truly seemed to be another world. Centrally heated, with the air circulated and recirculated according to industry standards. Here, things were done to people's bodies that they would never permit anywhere else. Sometimes the patients knew the outcome, sometimes they didn't. And even the people who worked there – the doctors, the nurses, the cleaners, even the guy in the laundry who scraped shit and clots of blood off the sheets before they were washed, had no control. Over anything, really.

Morning. Hi. How are you? Happy birthday for the other day.

Everyone was a friend in a small hospital.

Maya paused at the double doors under the sign that announced Operating Theatre Staff. No Admittance without Authorisation. She paused as she did every morning. She took a deep breath, held it in her lungs and slowly expelled it through a tight mouth. Routine. Habit. Toast and marmalade. Fish on Fridays. Episodes of Coronation Street.

She pushed the doors open and walked through. This place made her stand straighter, taller. She knew she belonged.

'You're cutting it fine, aren't you, birthday girl?'

Maya hung her jacket in her locker. 'Shh, Kathy. You're not supposed to notice. Did you have a big night? You look like shit.'

'Well, thank you very much. You can always rely on your friends to be straight up with you.' Kathy sat down, pulled off her clogs and threw them into her locker. 'We've just done an aortic aneurysm, if you must know. That'll keep you busy for a while.'

'I know you think all we do in recovery is sit around reading magazines.'

'And drinking coffee.' Kathy laced up her sneakers. 'And all we do in theatre is laugh at the surgeons' jokes and make ourselves available to them for private consults.'

'Exactly what I was going to say.' Maya pulled her green scrubs tunic over her head.

'Hey, nice bra,' said Kathy. She dropped her uniform into the linen bag. 'Are you trying to impress someone?'

'Hardly. It was my birthday present to myself. Cost a fortune. But God, I'm worth it.' She finished in a soap opera voice.

'Well, you'd better go and show it off to the aneurysm who's waiting for you.'

'Sleep well.' Maya hung her stethoscope around her neck, slipped into her clogs and headed off for work.

She took the handover from the night recovery nurse, then checked the patient lying on the recovery bed, beeping and flashing. She measured his observations and outputs, recording them on the red vinyl chart on the end of the bed. Then she went to the desk to read over his notes.

She scratched at the place where the wire on her bra met the seam. New lace. Admitted to the Emergency Department at 0040 with shortness of breath, pallor, sweating and back pain. Scratched again. Assessed by house surgeon and transferred straight to theatre with ruptured aortic aneurysm. Should have washed it before wearing it. Stupid. Estimated blood loss 3 litres. Aneurysm repaired. No complications. Charted pain relief, antibiotics. Transfer to ICU.

Her hand reached in under her top to itch at the place again.

And there it was.

As neat and round as a bead. Like a dried pea seed from the jar in Gran's shed, secreted out and slipped under the soft flesh of her breast. And left there.

Her fingers stopped. Snatched themselves away as if they had been burned. She swallowed. Breathed. Remembered to. Told her hand to check again and felt her anxious fingers fumble inside her bra. They pressed against the place. Once more. There.

The man in the bed lay still. His pulse oximeter beeped along with his heart. Fluids dripped into his flaccid arm.

Maya withdrew her hand and held it out in front of her. She turned it over. Look, they were fingers. Hers, and they were as soft and pink as they had ever been. No blood, nothing to implicate them. Just fingers. Straight pink fingers. And yet the imprint of the lump was on them still. She wiped her hand across her sleeve. The sensation remained. An indentation on her fingertips, surely. She brought her other hand up and brushed it over the smooth hillocks that were the pads of her fingers. They touched her so lightly, and yet the sensation was overwhelming.

'No,' she said. How calm she sounded. In control. She shook her hands at her sides as if she was shaking off pins and needles. She looked at the floor around her, as if she might expect to see fragments of herself, pinhead-sized pieces of her flesh, but there was nothing.

She stood up, but her legs were weak and her head was light. She felt drunk, hung over, anaesthetised. Her legs walked her to the man with the sewn-together chest. She pulled her stethoscope from around her neck. She was sure she could feel the lump grow, push against the soft of her breast. Stop it. His blood pressure had dropped. She increased the rate of the intravenous fluids. Her hand, that hand, reached out and shook the man on the shoulder.

'How are you doing?' she heard herself say. 'It's all over. Everything went well. You're going to be fine.' Her voice echoed around the smooth walls of the recovery room. It reverberated in her ears, inside her head.

Somehow morning became afternoon and the aneurysm patient

was replaced by a circling list of young men having had arthroscopies on one knee or the other. Men who should have known how to ski, or play rugby. They, in turn, became small children whose tooth decay was so advanced that their tiny teeth had to be extracted in hospital, under anaesthetic. Their mothers should have cleaned their teeth. They should have taught them how to do it. Thoroughly. Two minutes. Or one minute at least, if they were late for school or it was past their bedtime.

Maya picked up a plastic specimen jar from the end of a theatre bed. The girl at the top of the bed was four. A trickle of dried blood stained her cheek. She sucked her thumb. Maya rattled the jar. Twelve dead and discoloured teeth rattled back. Will the tooth fairy visit you tonight? She smoothed the girl's hair back from her face. Sweetheart. She went to the nurses' desk, found two dollars and dropped the coins into another jar. *From the tooth fairy*, she wrote on a sticky label. She smoothed it onto the cheek of the jar and tucked it under the girl's pillow.

She caught herself, at odd times during the day, resting her hand on her left breast. As though she had to protect it, as though she had to hide it. Had she imagined it? Her hand slid under her shirt, inside her bra. But her surreptitious fingers found it every time. Traitors. And every time they did, her breath caught in her throat, which was suddenly sclerosed. The air was forced from her in a whistle.

Her fingers fled. To a pocket, a pen, a patient. To somewhere it was safe.

It became evening and the five-till-eleven nurse was asking about the patients in the beds. They'll be all right, thought Maya. They've had their operations. They'll go home tomorrow or the next day or the day after that, to their husbands or wives or mothers and fathers, and they'll be looked after until they are better.

IV fluids, catheter drainage, wound ooze, blood pressure. What did it matter? They'd get better with or without her telling the five-till-eleven nurse a whole lot of information that she could see for herself.

She sat on the bench in the change room until everyone else had gone, with her hands clasped in her lap, as if she might be at church. She was numb, disconnected from her self. More than anything, she was tired.

Finally, she opened her locker. She pulled out her skivvy. Striped and stretchy. She slipped off her green scrubs. She looked down at her new bra, soft and smooth and dangerous.

'Fuck you,' she said, and she began to cry.

Three

She couldn't decide whether to get marigolds or petunias. Or maybe pansies with blue and yellow faces. Black-whiskered like fat-cheeked cats, and they would lie by the front door and watch her house and watch out for her visitors and watch over Charlie and her. It was hard to get enthusiastic. It didn't really seem to matter any more.

'I don't like the smell of marigolds,' said Kathy.

'Neither do the flies,' said Maya. 'That's why I like them.'

'Because the flies don't?'

'I plant them in pots around the front door. And the back. Then the flies don't come inside.'

'I'll take your word for it,' said Kathy.

Maya ran her hand over the soft mat of petunia seedlings. Which colour? Why was she bothering with this anyway? She rubbed her fingers across her forehead. Why were there so many decisions to be made? Why couldn't she be a kid again, like Charlie, for whom the hardest decision of the day was which sweatshirt to wear to school? Or what he wanted on his sandwiches? 'It's too hard being a grown-up,' she said to no one in particular. To herself. To the universe.

Kathy took her arm and guided her to the garden centre café. 'I think we need coffee,' she said.

They sat in silence. Maya stirred the froth of her cappuccino into a whirlpool, around and around. The teaspoon clinked against the edge of the cup but still the milky cloud spun until it was marbled, mixing with the hot liquid. Then it disappeared.

'When do you get the results?' Kathy asked. The silence shattered like best crystal.

'I have to go and see the surgeon tomorrow.'

'Would you like me to come with you?'

Maya nodded. She smiled a wobbly-lip smile. She could not speak.

It had happened in a blur. In a hurry. Like waiting at a level crossing, watching a train go past. You tried to count the carriages but the train was going too fast and you lost where you were up to and then you couldn't remember and it was no use starting again.

Discovery. Rediscovery of the lump that day and the next.

Standing in the shower with a soapy hand, feeling like the picture in the self-examination brochure. Staying there until the water ran cold.

Making the appointment with the GP. Sounding so grown up on the phone but sitting on the floor and crying after hanging up.

Seeing her. Saying it's probably nothing. You know how us nurses are – overdramatising everything. Watching her lips as she rang the surgeon, right there, wondering what shade of lipstick she was wearing.

Waiting eleven days to see him. Driving past his rooms so she'd know where to go. On The Day. Thinking she might not survive until then.

Saying nothing to Charlie but wanting to tell him everything, wanting to explain about the world, about death and being born, about astronomy and how to make muffins, about what songs they should play at her funeral.

Pulling up outside his rooms. Wiping her hands down her skirt. Wearing a skirt. A suit. Somehow hoping that if she looked as if she was a professional, a together kind of person, it would all work out okay.

Taking off her blouse. And her bra. Wanting to cover herself. Pointing to the spot. Here. Before he touched her.

Turning away as he readied the syringe. Reading the charts on his wall. Watching fish in a tank swim in and out of a pink and orange castle. Wondering if they knew it was a castle. Thinking that fish and castles didn't really go together.

Pressing her nails into her palms as the needle bit into her. Blinking. Breathing.

Thanking him as she buttoned up her blouse.

Kathy reached across and rested her hand on Maya's. 'Drink up, girl. We've got plants to buy. And I'll be forced to choose for you if you can't make a decision.'

The leaves of the tiny petunia seedlings were soft like moss. Silver green. You couldn't tell what colour the flowers would be. They kept their secrets hidden.

Salmon, primrose, white, scarlet. Maya walked along the length of the seedling display. She closed her eyes. She would trust the process. Her fingers barely touched the plants. Just the fine hairs on their leaves. Along and back. Along and back. She would know when it was right.

She opened her eyes and read the label of the petunia her hand had claimed. 'Primrose,' she said. She put three punnets into her basket. She wiped her hand across the front of her sweatshirt. Tiny sparks of potting mix fell around her.

Kathy peered into her basket. 'Pale yellow?'

Maya shrugged.

'Is that okay? It's not very exciting.'

'I know. It'll do. They might get a bit lost in my garden, but pale yellow it is.' She led the way to the counter. 'You can come and help me plant them,' she said as she paid for them. 'Only if you want to.' She made herself smile.

'The coffee's better at your place than anywhere else,' said Kathy. Maya watched her uncross her feet and cross them again on Maya's sun lounger.

How many cups of coffee had they shared over the years? How many bottles of wine, more to the point, she thought. Best friends since they began their nursing training, when they were partnered together for practical exercises.

'I'll be the patient,' Maya had said, and she had lain on one of the hospital beds lined up in rows in the nursing school pretend ward. She pulled the sheets up to her chin. 'Nurse, nurse!' she croaked. 'I need my bed bath!'

Kathy had seemed sure and confident. It was as if she had been doing it for years, Maya thought.

'All right, Mrs Wimple,' she said.

'Mrs Wimple?'

'Just shut up and be the patient.'

She'd lain there, under the stiff covers, in her white uniform.

'You must treat your pretend patient like a real patient,' the tutor had said. 'Turn them, change the sheets under them, pretend to give them a bed sponge.'

And so Maya lay there, her uniform skimming her knees, while Kathy rolled her from side to side like a log of wood, jammed clean sheets under her and rolled her again to pull the sheets flat. She pretended to wash her, with a dry flannel that she dunked into an empty sponge bowl.

'Wash and dry only one part of the patient at a time,' the tutor announced. 'Don't expose any of the patient's body unnecessarily.'

'One arm, uncover, soap, rinse, dry, cover up. Then the other. One leg, then the other. Front, back, genitalia,' the tutor said, speaking in capital letters. 'But we'll just do arms and legs for the purpose of this practice,' she laughed, sounding slightly hysterical.

Maya offered her limbs, first one, then the other. They may have belonged to anyone.

'Anybody home?'

Maya shook her head, bringing herself back to the present.

'You okay?' said Kathy.

'Yeah. I was a million miles away. How's the coffee?'

'Excellent,' said Kathy. 'But finished. I suppose that means we have to do gardening now.'

'I suppose it does.'

They worked side by side, poking the petunia seedlings into gaps between orange and red gerberas, lavender, thorny rose stalks that were about to sprout brick-coloured stems and heady flowers that would be Iceberg, Sexy Rexy, Tess, Whisky. They planted between the legs of a corrugated iron goat, beside a concrete sheep, a smiling scarecrow.

'I'm going to have to admit it,' Maya said after a while.

She watched Kathy out of the corner of her eye. She froze, her trowel deep in the rich earth. 'Admit what?'

'That I'm getting old.'

'Oh,' said Kathy. She laughed – much louder than was appropriate, Maya thought.

'Who would have thought I'd be gardening with a foam knee-pad?'

'Whatever it takes, girl,' said Kathy. She slid a soon-to-be-primrose petunia into the ground beside an alstroemeria – apricot with a narrow red throat.

Maya sat back on her heels. She pulled off her gardening gloves and rubbed her fingers across her forehead. 'Do you think they'll be nice for summer?' she asked.

'I think they'll be awesome,' said Kathy. 'Now don't you think you'd better go and get that boy of yours from Jacob's, before he starts to think that his mother's forgotten him? Or before he forgets you?'

'I don't think there's much chance of that,' said Maya. 'His stomach would bring him home eventually.' She pushed the last seedling into the ground, beside a smiling green pottery cactus.

'Would you hurry up and finish your breakfast.' Maya slammed her mug down. Coffee sloshed over the edge and made mud-coloured splatters on the white formica. She gripped the edge of the bench. 'I don't know why you have to muck around so much in the mornings.'

Charlie was motionless at the table. Milk and Weet-Bix sludge dripped off the spoon. 'I'm going as fast as I can, Mum,' he said into his bowl.

'Every time I've got something on. Every second blimmin' school day. I spend half my life waiting for you.' She ran her finger across the bench, joining up the tiny dots of coffee. Skinny finger-shaped bridges between the splashes.

'I'm not very hungry anyway,' Charlie said, and he carried his bowl to the sink.

Maya turned around and went to say something to him. She went to apologise. To say, I'm sorry. I've got a lot on my mind. On my plate. I can't do it all. Something's got to bear it. Someone. The point of least resistance. And right now it's you. She went to say all that, but Charlie had already gone upstairs to clean his teeth.

She hugged him when he came down again, held him against her. How fragile, how temporary his small body was. His shoulder-blades were like plates under his clothes. The points of his shoulders jabbed into Maya's soft belly.

'Skinny boy,' she whispered, and she smoothed his hair. 'I'm sorry. It's just –'

She stopped. It was just – what was it? She couldn't, wouldn't identify it. It was too hard. Today. That day. Any day. She shrugged, rubbed her hands up and down Charlie's arms as though she were warming him up. Rubbing life into him. 'I dunno,' she finished. She reached for her jacket and handbag. 'Come on,' she said. 'I'll race you to the gate.'

He seemed so little, his backpack almost wider than he was, and yet so certain, as he strode off down the street to school. He turned and waved. A small salute. 'See ya,' he called and he turned away. His hair fanned out around his head, then settled flat and straight again.

27

A yellow Mini pulled up. Kathy leaned across and opened the passenger door. 'Wanna ride, cowboy?'

'Good timing,' said Maya. She folded herself into Kathy's car, clicked her seatbelt in. 'You just saved me from getting maudlin.'

'Exactly my purpose in life,' said Kathy, and she pulled out into the street.

Maya watched the houses dash past. She wasn't used to being the passenger. 'Everything looks different from this side,' she said to the window.

'Why do you have to whisper in doctors' waiting rooms?' Maya whispered.

Kathy flicked through a magazine. 'What I want to know is why all the best recipes are always ripped out.' She held up a copy of *Next*. 'Censored,' she said. 'Maybe the chocolate and cream cheese police have been in. I mean, they're supposed to promote healthy lifestyles in doctors' rooms, aren't they?'

Maya smiled. Good old Kathy. She tried to think of a clever retort but nothing came. It was as if her brain had been taken over, invaded by fear, dread, breast lumps.

Her fingers reached for her forehead, for the furrow that had appeared between her eyebrows. Overnight, it seemed. She ran her middle finger up and down the deepening channel.

'Maya,' she heard from the other end of the waiting room. From a hundred miles away. Another continent, even. She looked up. There was Mr Gaskin, with a manila folder tucked under his arm, standing there, his head cocked to the side, like a bridegroom at the head of the altar. 'Come through,' he said, and he stepped back, swept his arm to the side and waited. Maya felt as though the orchestra should start up and they should dance and she should be Ginger to his Fred. Stop it.

Her legs pushed her up out of her seat. She turned to Kathy. I don't know what to do. I've changed my mind. Tell me what happens next.

'Shall I come in?' Kathy asked in a quiet, standing-to-the-side voice.

'Yes please,' Maya said. How needy, how pathetic those words sounded. And yet if she were offered a hand to hold, she would gladly grasp it.

'Well,' said Mr Gaskin, because this was how all surgeons began conversations. Warming up, edging towards the centre.

He put Maya's folder down on the desk. Hardly more than the cardboard cover, she thought. There's not much of me in there. That's a good thing, surely. She stared at the folder. She closed her eyes. She tried to imagine the test results. She looked across at the surgeon with his face that fell into soft folds around his neck. She looked at his hands. Ordinary, unremarkable hands. But so still. They lay quietly on his legs.

The room was silent. Empty. All sound and thought was sucked out. They were in a vacuum. Nothing existed. Everything mattered.

'Well,' he said again. The seal was broken, the vacuum gone. Maya breathed, breathed again.

'Yes,' she said. She leaned forward. She sensed Kathy lean towards her, move her body closer, as if she was shielding her from the wind.

'I'm sorry to have to tell you this –'

And that was all she heard. His voice carried on, his mouth continued, but she couldn't hear him. She retreated. She shrank into herself, was absorbed by her own body, felt herself get smaller and smaller as time and matter fled backwards. She was a child, a needy baby, she was inside her mother's uterus and she could taste the cancerous cells that were searching for her own mother's breast.

'So we've got some decisions to make.' Those words pushed themselves into her ears and she shook her head to scatter them, to send them away.

How many cups of coffee will it take? Maya thought. The spring sun was weak and insipid. It hardly warmed them as they sat at a wooden table in the courtyard of a coffee shop. The nearest one they came to. She shivered.

'You'd think the sun could at least do its job,' she said.

'What do you mean?'

'It's freezing here. Look, I've got goosebumps.'

'You'll be okay,' said Kathy, and there was her hand again, strong yet soft. So full of life. 'You will.'

Maya looked at her friend. She couldn't read her face. Couldn't tell if it was just getting warm that she was talking about, or something much more.

'Can you tell me what he said?'

'What who said?'

'Mr Gaskin.'

'Weren't you listening?' Kathy laughed, a shallow tinkle.

Maya rubbed her hands together under the table. She pressed them between her knees. She could barely feel them.

'It kind of all went blank. I thought I'd remember, but it's funny, I couldn't tell you a single thing he said.'

'It's shock.'

'I know that. I'm not stupid, you know.' She looked down at her hands. She was sure they were part of her. 'God, Kathy, give me a break.'

She turned away and stared out onto the street. Everything looked so normal. A woman pushed a pram along the footpath. A dog barked somewhere. The wind ruffled the trees around them. This is like a tableau, Maya thought. All this suburbia and ordinariness has been arranged here, for my benefit, to make me think everything's normal. It feels like *The Truman Show*, she thought. But even they wouldn't be so cruel as to manufacture a breast lump into the plot line. Would they? Think of the ratings.

'So, do you want me to tell you what he said?'

'Yes, please.' Her voice was that of a child lost in town.

'I'll just order the coffees.'

Maya watched Kathy walk into the café, so sure, so in control. A sparrow landed on the table in front of her. Its tiny beak tapped at the wood, searching for crumbs. It hopped closer to her, tap, tap. Maya bumped the edge of the table. 'Bugger off back to your nest,' she said.

'Two cappuccinos,' said Kathy and she sat down again.

'Oh. It's got chocolate.' Maya said.

'You always have chocolate.'

'I might have wanted cinnamon today.'

Kathy said nothing.

'Okay, then,' Maya said quietly. 'Tell me what he said.'

Kathy took a sip of coffee. Her cup trembled as she placed it back in the saucer.

'All right. The gist of it was that the needle biopsy came back looking suspicious. He had hoped it would just be a cyst or some other inflammatory process. But it looks like it might be malignant.'

Maya nodded. They might have been discussing any unconscious patient in theatre.

'Do you want me to carry on?'

She nodded again.

'Okay. What he wants to do is get you in for a lumpectomy. They'll do a frozen section and if that confirms it, then he'll do a mastectomy straight away.' She paused. 'Given your family history,' she added.

'Well,' said Maya, 'let's hope the outcome turns out better. Given my family history.'

'So that's all, really. You're booked in on the urgent list. They'll do it as soon as they can.'

'Thanks,' said Maya. What else was there to say?

'You're welcome.' Kathy banged her palms on the table. 'I'll be back in a minute,' she said, and Maya watched as she went into the shop. The morning was quiet, still. As if it was holding its breath. Waiting for permission to move. She looked around, crossed her arms, tucked her fists into her armpits. Her right hand pressed against the place. The lump. It was covered with a Bandaid. Such a trivial plaster. The spot ached where the surgeon had done the

31

biopsy. Sucking out deforming cells with his skinny syringe.

She wanted to shout. She wanted to scream. She wanted to swear. Instead she remained silent. She sat in the sun.

'Da daah.' Kathy's voice sang out from the door of the café. Maya turned around and laughed. Kathy held out a huge plate, on which sat a chocolate gateau, covered with cherries and chocolate shavings. Three sparklers, the kind that she and Charlie spun circles with at Guy Fawkes, sizzled on top of the cake. 'I decided our lives needed more sparkle,' she said, and she placed the cake in front of Maya.

'You're incredible,' Maya said. She watched the sparklers burn down, like fizzing incense sticks. Kathy handed her one that was freshly lit and she found herself writing her name in the air. M-a-y-a. Joining up the letters to make golden script in the morning sky. M-a-y-a. You had to write your name. That was the rule with sparklers. Imprinting yourself on the air. Defining yourself with a temporary dazzle.

'This was the best part of Guy Fawkes,' said Maya, drawing circles in front of her. 'Writing my name in the air. Or the name of a boy I liked.'

'You had an exciting childhood, didn't you, girl?'

'Shut up, you.' Now she made zigzags, sharp corners and straight lines that cut the sky in two. 'Didn't you do that kind of thing?'

'Not really,' said Kathy. 'I did have a game where the next day I'd count how many beer bottles I could find around the house.'

Slash slash. Maya's sparkler sliced the day into blue and yellow slivers. It spluttered, coughed and died.

'Not with a bang,' she said and she dropped the spent sparkler on the ground. 'Let's have some cake,' she said. 'Shall I be mother?'

Charlie would be home soon. Precious minutes ticked by. They flew off the clock on the kitchen wall in sixty-second lots and leaked outside, under the gap in the back door, and out the high skylight

32

window that was jammed half open, the wooden frame swollen and buckled.

Maya went from room to room, scanning everything she saw. She had to remember it all. The hospital corners on her bed, cutting the blue and white stripes that ran the length of her bed into sharp points. Her slippers kicked off at the foot of her bed, waiting for her feet to fill them out. The jumble that was her dresser top: lipsticks, perfume, a box of tissues. Charlie's birthday card was propped up there. Happy Birthday, each letter a different colour, the H, A, P, neat and even, but Maya could see that he had got bored, and the colouring in was scribbly and rushed by the end. He was always in such a hurry. He'd drawn himself, yellow hair radiating from his head, and her, brown hair in long straight lines from a point at the top of her head so it fanned out around her. They were holding hands, his fingers drawn over the top of hers, or were hers over his? Charlie's smile was pencilled in, Maya's was thick red felt. He'd drawn a border of pink hearts around the edge of the card, tidy, coloured in at the top and just the outlines along the bottom.

She crossed her arms.

In Charlie's room Honey Bear was in bed, his furry face poking out from under the duvet. He looked so calm. A Lego construction was in progress on the floor. A pile of books was stacked up on the bedside table. *The Hobbit, How Things Work, Horrible Histories.* He was reading them all.

She went downstairs. Charlie's pyjamas lay in the middle of the floor where he had stepped out of them that morning. The legs were inside out, at awkward angles like fractures. The morning's chaos felt like a hundred years ago. It seemed all so trivial.

Coffee, she thought. Coffee always helps. While she was waiting for the jug to boil she wiped down the bench. She scrubbed at the toaster, the breadmaker. Maybe she would make some bread. Steam billowed up and crawled along the ceiling like fog, tiny droplets of water clinging to one another, moving in a pack. They cooled and separated. Eventually they disappeared.

What would Mum have done? At a moment like this?

If she could only pick up the phone and ask her (just once), then she'd be able to deal with this. Even hear her voice – hello, are you there? (just once) – then she'd manage. She would.

What *had* she done?

Maya didn't know. Couldn't remember.

She spooned coffee into her mug, a thick-sided cup that she'd got free with coupons from the supermarket. The daisies that were stamped on the sides were starting to fade. Bugger it. Why did she always use those mugs? She had nice ones – thin china, hand-painted – that she kept for when she had visitors. She would use one of those. Why should she keep her good things for other people? Was it that she was trying to make a good impression on her friends? Or was it really that she didn't think she mattered enough? Second best would do?

She reached up to the top cupboard for one of her good mugs. The place where she'd had the needle biopsy pulled as she stretched up. Spooning fresh coffee and pouring in the boiling water, she heard Gran's voice.

Second best is good enough. Best china, good towels, are for company. Why would we want to use our good things? Gran's voice followed her outside. We make do, don't we?

She sat on the step and sipped coffee from her good mug. Second best is good enough for us, Maya. When it's just you and me.

She looked up at the kowhai bursting into flower all around her. The petals made a velvet skirt for a fairy, a tiny nymph. The seedpods that would soon hang down from the branches were like Christmas decoration icicles. Kowhai. She remembered the kowhai by the front gate, at home, when she was little. She had thought the seedpods were like necklaces: beads strung together, with golden, polished pearls inside. She would hold a long pod against her wrist. It could have been a beautiful bracelet. The dry bark-like seed case had scratched her skin.

'Do you know that each seed can grow into a whole kowhai tree?' her mother had said.

'Wow. Really? Every single seed?'

Her mother had smiled and nodded, and her hair bounced like a fluffy cloud.

'We could have a whole forest of kowhais,' Maya said.

'They take a long time to grow.'

'That's all right,' said Maya. 'We can wait, can't we?'

Maya wiped her hands on the teatowel. Everything had changed, and still there were dishes.

'Let's go to the beach,' she called.

'But it's a school night,' said Charlie from the lounge.

'I won't tell if you won't.'

It was something they did on Friday or Saturday nights. Not every week, because part of the magic was deciding to go and doing it without even thinking about it. Sometimes they went to the beach, sometimes they stopped at the railway line, got out and sat right by the train tracks, on the grass verge, close enough that the rush of the train stole away their breath and whipped their hair about their faces.

There's something exciting and kind of naughty about going to the beach at night, Maya had said the first time they'd done it. They crept down to the sand, holding hands, and they sat with their backs against the sharp kukuyu grass, their toes digging into the cold sand. Sometimes they talked, sometimes they were silent.

They told each other jokes and Maya always laughed at Charlie's. Sometimes his jokes were funny. She told him about her family, his history. They pretended they were shipwrecked, and Waikanae beach was a deserted island and Gisborne was paradise.

When they went to the train tracks they imagined who the passengers were and where they were going. They made up stories together.

There's a family who have escaped from deepest darkest Siberia and they're carrying their entire belongings in an old suitcase. They're eating cheese sandwiches as they look out the train window and they wonder about their new life in New Zealand.

There's a knight and he's just killed a dragon and he's got its wings wrapped in a velvet cloth as proof of its slaying. He has to kill a whole army of dragons before he can marry the princess.

The stories in the trains always had happy endings. The characters always lived happily ever after.

They got into Maya's red hatchback, grabbing coats and hats at the front door as they left. The beach of course was empty, but still the waves splashed the shore, dumping salty water and sand, taking some away. The waves were louder at night, as though the still of the darkness gave them more energy. Permission to shout. They sat in their usual place. Maya put her arm around Charlie. He rested his head against her breast, close to her heart. She winced as his head found the spot.

'Hop on the other side of me, buddy,' she said, and his slight body squirmed over her and nestled into her right side.

The moon was a skinny smile in the sky. It hardly made a shimmer on the sea. Norfolk pines stood on silent sentry along the road that hugged the coastline. Behind them the macrocarpas and copper beeches shivered.

'Are you okay?' Maya asked, after a while.

'Yep.'

'Happy?'

'Yep.'

'Sure?'

'Yep.'

'Good.'

More silence. It was currency these days, a precious commodity to be fought for. It was the language between them. What they both understood. Maya's face was warm where she rested against Charlie's head. Her other cheek was cold and tight. It ached. She moved her head and kissed him on the top of his head, the top of his fleecy blue beanie. He stirred and slipped his hand into her jacket pocket. He wriggled it under hers. She enclosed his small hand with hers.

'You're awesome, Mum,' he said. He was looking out to sea.

'Thanks,' said Maya. A wave slapped the beach, higher and louder than the others. The seventh wave, she thought. She started to count them, but her thoughts, like the mist of salt spray that threw itself up out of the water, disappeared into the night and were lost somewhere above the swell. 'Do you know how much I love you?' she asked.

'Oh, Mum,' said Charlie. He pulled back and looked up at her. 'I should,' he continued. 'You tell me all the time.'

'It's nice to hear the words, though, isn't it?'

'Yeah, I spose.' He looked away. He fingered her keys in her pocket, under his hand, inside hers and then suddenly he pulled his hand away. He crossed his arms over his chest, puffed up with the thick fabric of his coat. He yawned, the wide uninhibited yawn of a child. His head became heavy against Maya's shoulder.

'I'd better get you home, buddy,' she said, but she didn't move. The space in her pocket where Charlie's hand had been was a cavern. 'School tomorrow.'

'Is it very late?' asked Charlie.

'It is, actually.'

'Cool.'

Work carried on. The days came and went. Operations continued. Patients woke up and there was Maya, checking, listening, recording the functioning of their quiet bodies. They were pleasant and belligerent, laughing and in tears, recovering and in shock. They snored, coughed, vomited.

It's funny the things you get used to, Maya thought one morning as she leaned over an elderly lady who had had part of her bowel cut away. As she breathed out, a cloud of garlic breath puffed up and over Maya's face. I used to hate that smell: anaesthetic. It made me feel sick. Like the smell of congealed blood. Gangrene. Infection. But you get used to it. Wait for it, even. And one day you find that you miss it if it's not there.

The lady blew her shivering breath out through papery lips.

And suddenly Maya's hand reached up and touched the spot on her breast, her left breast, that one, and it found the lump and there it was and it was getting bigger, creeping over the healthy tissue of her, invading it, suffocating her.

No. Maybe it was shrinking. Shrivelling. Suffocating itself, consuming itself. Maybe it had gone.

But they found it, those fingers. Every time.

Four

*G*oing private would have been automatic if she'd had health insurance. But that – like getting a more reliable car, or painting the roof – meant money. She would have said in a strong and confident voice, yes, I have health insurance, when Mr Gaskin, across the gulf of his shiny desk, had asked. And she would have been an entirely different kind of patient then. A priority patient. Maybe one with a star on the corner of her chart.

But the corner of Maya's chart remained bare. If she wanted to go private she'd need to win Lotto. Ha. What a joke. She had as much chance of coming up with that kind of money as – what? Her mind was blank. Emptied of thoughts. She scrambled for the words she needed. Reached for them, stretched out her arm to grasp them, catch them before they disappeared like dandelion fairies. But they were gone.

It was happening a lot. Forgetting things. Not remembering things. You've got a lot on your mind, she told herself. Then why does it not seem able to contain a single thought? It's like a pot on the stove with the lid left off, and my thoughts are boiling away.

It's just temporary. Once everything's organised and we're back on track, I'll be okay, she thought. Maya found herself talking, thinking even, in cliché. The banalities of language insulated her. I'll be right as rain. Fit as a fiddle.

So, public it was. Mr Gaskin's nurse, with her pencilled-in eyebrows and leaking lipstick, said it probably wouldn't be before the last week in November. Do they realise it's urgent? Maya had said. A desperate tone had crawled into her voice, as it did a lot these days. Every day I wait . . . she said, and trailed off. She didn't want to articulate it. Because words, once said, cannot be unspoken. And how dangerous they are as they zip and spin around in the atmosphere, finding their place to settle.

'Why don't you talk to the booking clerk at admissions?' said Kathy. 'There have to be some perks for working here.'

'I've tried that,' said Maya. 'Things are flat out at the moment. All the surgeons are trying to clear their lists before Christmas, so they've double-booked all their sessions. She's going to see what she can do, though. Since it's me.'

'Good.'

'I don't mean to sound like a fatalist,' said Maya, 'but the time will be right, whenever it is. I'm sure of it.'

That had been in October still, when the last clutches of spring lingered.

Every day after work, after picking up Charlie from Jacob's, Maya thanked his mother and said I owe you, no really and she meant it. She felt that the wine and plants in pots and stalks of broccoli cut from her garden that she thrust at Rachael were inadequate gestures of thanks, but they were all she could do.

As they walked home she visualised her phone there on the bench. She imagined the message light blinking red on off on off and she saw herself pressing play and hearing the admissions girl telling her that tomorrow would be the day and would she report to the hospital at eight a.m. and to have a good day. She played this scene out every day.

But it made no difference to the hospital waiting list and Maya had to wait her turn.

And now it was November and how many cells inside her body had shrivelled and died and been replaced by firm and eager warriors? How many had mutated, taken over – mould spores that turn bread, forgotten about in the back of the pantry, into blue-grey dust? How many had broken off and were carried, like Pooh sticks, along Maya's blood vessels before cragging on a branch or a dam of river rocks, setting up camp, setting up home? Now it was November.

'Do you know we've only got thirty-three days of school left?' Charlie said. He put his empty lunchbox on the bench. The answer-phone light flashed, but today Maya had forgotten to check.

'Then the holidays,' she said. She opened the lunchbox, tipped a muesli bar wrapper and a scrunch of plastic wrap into the rubbish bin. The plastic had holes punched in it, where Charlie had sucked the taut film into his mouth, wound it in a circle to make a bubble, a pedicle, and popped it between his fingers like a cyst. 'We'll go away,' she said. 'Up north, or to Hawke's Bay. Somewhere nice.'

The Christmas holidays stretched out in front of them. Tantalisingly close, but teasing them with forty-something sleeps to wait. And what would happen between now and then?

It was always there, below the surface of every thought, every decision. Bubbling underneath the everyday things, it was threatening to come to the boil.

Waiting, waiting.

Like when you paused a video and there was Meryl Streep or Nicolas Cage or Christina Ricci caught in mid-gesture, an arm raised in a wave, or eyelids half shut (half open) in the middle of a blink.

Like watching the second hand of a clock sweep slowly – exquisitely so – to twelve and past twelve, and wondering if seconds really were this slow.

Like being nine months pregnant and everyone else on the street was able to walk so quickly, so effortlessly. You were struggling, shuffling, wide-legged, and thinking you would be pregnant forever and this baby would never come out, but at once aware of (and terrified of) the inevitability of its delivery.

Like waking up every day with a cancer inside you, and knowing that the very fact of waking meant you were one day closer to its

41

removal, and yet this growth was therefore one day more advanced, and which would win out in the end?

Waiting, waiting.

Maya turned to flick the switch on the jug, to reach for a can of tomatoes from the pantry, to get cheese from the fridge. Something.

She saw the phone winking at her with its one red eye. She knew it was the hospital. The admissions girl with her brown lipstick and jangly bracelets and her smiley, too-quick voice.

'Go and check the mail, would you, Charlie?' Maya asked. Her own voice trembled, was weak at the knees. Her mouth was dry.

'Didn't you already look when we got home?' said Charlie.

'Go and check again. The paper might have arrived. Play outside. Take your soccer ball.' She was grabbing at air, trying to hold on to nothing.

'You look weird,' said Charlie, and he dribbled his ball down the hall and out the front door.

She saw her arm reach out. Her finger was extended and it looked straight and sure but it could not have been more uncertain. It touched the flashing button and now her finger was lit up, haloed red, on off on off. The button was cool, curved. She pressed it slowly. Play. She heard the tape start.

'Hi, Maya. It's Jenna from the hospital here.' She spoke too fast. Slow down, Maya wanted to say. People want to hear what you've got to say. Especially me. 'I'm just ringing you with the good news that we've got you booked in to come in on Monday for your op on Tuesday morning.' How dare she have such a sing-song voice? 'So I'll put a tick by your name. You don't need to get back to me unless you can't make it, or you've changed your mind,' Giggles there and the jingle of bracelets. 'So seeya, and have a good day.' How dare she be so casual, so offhand, talking so quickly as though this was just one of a dozen phone calls she had to make before she went to lunch, or went home?

Maya punched erase. The tape whirred as those foolish words were wiped away. Her hands were shaking, trembling as though she was an alley drunk looking for her first taste of the day. She

42

crossed her arms, thrusting her fists into her armpits. Her right hand, balled tightly, grazed the lump on her breast. She began to cry. She walked from room to room, arms still crossed, sobbing. When she got to her bedroom she crept under the covers, still with her shoes on, still with her arms crossed, still crying.

'Could I come in for a moment, Rachael? I need to talk to you about something.'

'Sure thing. I'll put the jug on.' Maya followed Rachael's wide bottom into her kitchen. She sat down at Rachael's breakfast bar. It was a jumble of accounts, receipts, letters half written, school notices. She looked out the window to where Charlie and Jacob were bouncing on the trampoline.

'Funny, isn't it? It's not that long ago that I wouldn't have let Charlie go on a trampoline.'

'Is that right?' It was a muffled statement as Rachael filled the jug from the tap.

'I guess it's the only-child-of-a-solo-parent syndrome.'

Rachael turned. Her bottom followed half a second later, shuddered and settled into place. 'Do you think there is such a thing?'

'Maybe. I don't know. Probably not.' She stopped. She breathed deeply, so much that it hurt at the base of her lungs. 'I think I have to let him take risks now.'

Rachael switched the jug on, then leaned against the bench. She crossed her ample arms.

'Well, they're nearly nine. Gotta let them leave the nest sometime, eh?' She picked two bananas out from the fruit bowl. Their skins were dark streaks and smudges on the yellow. Maya watched her run a long thumbnail down the length of the fruit, then slip the bananas out of their coverings. She laid them down, side by side on a plate, then mashed them with a fork till they were sludge.

'We've got to let them spread their wings,' Rachael said, and she plopped the banana into a big china bowl, half full with sticky yellow batter. 'You know, let them fly on their own.'

Stir stir with a big silver spoon. She dropped spoonfuls into twelve muffin trays. She sprinkled chocolate chips on their doughy peaks. 'Into the oven,' Rachael said. 'We can't stop them growing up. They'll do that while our backs are turned anyway.'

Maya smiled. 'It's more than that, Rachael,' she said. She sucked another mouthful of air inside her, as though it would give her courage. 'It's more than just knowing that they don't need us as much as they did when they were little.' She watched the muffins glisten behind the oven door. 'It's just that I might be needing you a bit more, for a while,' she continued. 'You see, it's just that, I'm not sure. It's, well – '

Words were tumbling over one another, stumbling, tripping. They would not come out one at a time.

Rachael's hand was on her shoulder. The touch revived her, splashed cold water on the face of her thoughts. 'Rachael, I have to go into hospital on Thursday. I found a lump. I might have to have a mastectomy.' Her eyes looked up at her, from the safety of her downturned face. She was a child admitting to having broken a window. She felt ashamed, as though because her body had let her down, it meant she was weak, needy. Their eyes met briefly. Maya was the first to look away. From outside, in rhythmic puffs, as Charlie and Jacob bounced up and down on the trampoline, she heard two boy voices.

One day a taniwha
Went swimming in the moana,
It whispered in my taringa,
Oh won't you come with me,
There's such a lot to see,
Underneath the deep blue sea.

Their song was off key, mistimed. How beautiful they sounded.

'Maya, honey.' She was jolted back to Rachael's kitchen, there among the dirty dishes, the baking smells, the chaos that was being a mother. 'What can I do for you?'

Thank you. Thank you for not saying you are sorry, Maya thought. For not pitying me. Everything was spinning above her head, and even when she lifted up her arms to grab at substance, her hands came away empty. She was connected to nothing.

Deep breath. Again. Air was giving her bite-sized pieces of energy. Clarity. Courage.

'Can Charlie stay with you while I'm in hospital? It's a big ask, I know, and please say if it's not okay. I don't want to burden you. I don't want to put you on the spot. I'll only be there for a few days. Then I'll be fine.' She smiled with her mouth.

'Look,' said Rachael, and she slid a mug of coffee across the bench. 'It's fine. Really. The last thing you need is worrying about Charlie. He can stay here, honey. As long as it takes. It'll be like having another son.'

Maya shivered. Someone's just walked over my grave, she thought. Ha. Maybe it was Rachael. Maybe it was Charlie.

'Are you sure?'

'He'll be just fine. He fits in so well. Look at them out there.'

And she did. She turned with her coffee cup supporting her hands and she watched the two boys playing, laughing, singing, and how comfortable they were with each other.

'They'll be like brothers. I think Gordon was planning on taking Jacob fishing this weekend anyway. He'll enjoy having Charlie come along too.'

Maya felt an ache begin in her belly. It smouldered like a flame trying to catch. She put the cup down and rested her head in her hands. She sighed, filling her lungs with air, and because oxygen is what fuels fire, now it was alight inside her, leaping, licking, alive, and the flicker that had been a doubt was now fear and it was burning out of control. She had to move or be engulfed by it all.

'I'd better get Charlie home,' she said and she was standing up and going outside. Shouting now. 'Would you get off that trampoline this minute and get over here. I'm not going to wait another second. Pick up your shoes. Hurry up. We have to go home.'

She turned and fled to the front door. She stood on the step, tapping her shoe against the concrete. She jammed her sunglasses on top of her head. She crossed her arms. Charlie scuttled after her, his school bag flung over his shoulder, shoes and socks under his arm.

'Thanks, Mrs Allen. Yeah, I'll see you after school tomorrow. Bye. Bye, Jacob.'

They walked down the driveway.

'Why haven't you got your shoes and socks on?' Maya said. 'God, you look like a homeless child. You look like an orphan.'

She felt Charlie staring at her, at the back of her head, the back of her marching feet. She couldn't think of anything to say.

'Have you taken sick leave?'

'Yes.'

'Have you told them when to expect you back?'

'Yes.'

'Is Charlie all organised?'

'Yes.'

'Are you ready for this?'

'Yes.'

'Are you sure?'

'Yes. Of course I am.'

There was Kathy's hand again. The lightest touch, a feathering of fingers across the fabric of her shirt. Nothing more than a stranger brushing past you in a crowd, a shop assistant helping you out. Four fingers and a thumb. Joints, nerves, muscles, fat, blood roaring in and out without making a sound. You could ask almost anything of your hands. Maya had taught her hands to sew, to clap, to play the piano, to colour in her lips, to dress wounds and her baby, to bath him, to comb his fine hair, to hold him. And now here was Kathy's hand, as real as the Motu River, resting on her arm.

She shut her locker. It clanged. Ominously, she thought. Like in a soap opera. A bad movie. But now it was closed and now she was on sick leave. She resisted the urge to turn and take in a sweeping gaze of the change room, stamping the sights, the smells into her mind. That would be way too much. So she picked up her bag, gathered her handful of keys, smoothed her hands down her front and left.

'Train tracks, Charlie,' said Maya. He sat in the passenger seat, his skinny legs stuck out the bottom of his shorts. His knees were bulbous growths in the middle of his legs.

They pulled up beside the level crossing sign. She slammed her door. The sound of it bounced off faraway hills and scuttled back to her. She jammed her hands into her pockets.

'Mum, you left the keys in the ignition.'

'Don't worry about it.'

'But someone might come along and steal the car. A robber.'

Maya laughed. 'It'll be okay. We're right here. But take them out if it makes you feel safer.'

'Cool.'

'Just don't start the car and drive away.'

Charlie rolled his eyes. 'Mum.'

She sat on the bank, where the grass skidded down to the railway lines. It was dry, still warm. Early summer. As quiet and new as a bud. A moment later, there was Charlie beside her, her keys overflowing from his fists.

Their bodies huddled together. She could feel the warmth coming off him. If she believed in auras, she would see one around his head. A halo, yellow, or blue.

They said nothing. Behind them a row of macrocarpas swayed silently, asleep on their feet. Maya could hear the sea. The grass around them was still. The parallel lines that snaked all the way to Napier, Wellington even, groaned as they cooled, settled down for the night.

'I'm not sure if we'll even see a train tonight,' she said. Her voice drifted down the tracks in a straight line. 'So,' she said. Because she knew it had to be said, all of it, and there was no other way to begin. The words erupted from her then, bubbled up and spilled over, like the volcano that Charlie's class had made, pouring vinegar into a baking soda crater lake in a pile of sand and watching it froth up, expanding, full of chemistry and magic, and pouring down the sides of the wet sandy mountain.

And eventually she had nothing more to say. The moon drifted lazily across the sky, in and out of fat clouds.

Maya sat there. She stared at the grass, at the gravel piled up in channels either side of the railway lines. She wanted to sleep. She found Charlie's hand. It was so small inside hers. So soft. She pressed her hands either side of his.

'Are you going to die like Nana did?' he asked. 'And Dad?'

Maya stretched out her arm. It fell flatly against the crisp sheet stretched over her bed. Sometimes she thought Philip would be there, snoring softly, just as he always had been, as he should be now.

This was like the period of time after he died, this waiting. Like being in limbo. Undead, between two states of being, holding your breath, waiting, not experiencing anything, not living certainly, and not even being dead, because even in death you *are*, things happen, your body is acted upon, it is dressed and draped, coloured and camouflaged, contoured, and then it collapses, implodes, and you deconstruct. But in the state of limbo you are nothing. Nothing at all.

Maya would wake two, three times in the night, sometimes so often that she wondered if she had even been asleep at all. Philip, are you here? Where are you? And thinking (for a second) that he was working late, or away on business, or asleep on the couch downstairs, the TV on its endless nocturnal infomercial loop. And then she remembered (how could she not?) and she was once again in that state of suspension.

She lay there, forcing herself not to move, even though her muscles cried out to her. As she stared at the wide daisies that were cut in two by the folds of her curtains, she thought about Philip in A and E, pale and still on the trolley in the resus room that was full to overflowing with equipment and machines to keep people alive and how she had left him there, and how that had been the hardest thing she had ever done.

Let me take little Charlie, a nurse had said, but with him gone, Maya's arms were bare and empty and she stood beside Philip with her arms folded and she knew she had to stay like that or the insides of her would surely spill out onto the shiny, shiny floor.

She willed him to breathe, to open his eyes. Something. She dared him to, but he was surely dead because his heart was quiet, his lungs were flat and the house surgeon had told her and doctors don't lie do they? and she could see for herself how it was.

A sheet had been placed over him. The edges hung down over the sides of the skinny trolley and Maya stared at the hem of the sheet. She thought that Philip should be tucked in – he likes the sheets tucked in – and she almost bent down to do it, to tuck them under the thin mattress, but she didn't move (couldn't) because her arms were glued over her chest, and you don't tuck in the sheets of the dead now, do you?

With the sheet over his face, over his head, past his head and off the top of the trolley, Philip couldn't breathe (even though he was dead). What if he opened his eyes, just for a moment, to find out where he was and all he saw was the white of the sheet, then he would undoubtedly believe he was dead (or maybe blind, but he would know he was seeing white, and don't the blind live in a world of darkness?) and so he would just close his eyes again, think, Well, that's that then, and really truly positively become dead.

Maya couldn't risk it and so she unfolded her arms from her chest and peeled back the sheet from Philip's face. Back and back until it lay straight and smooth across his shoulders. He didn't move. She waited for him to, begged him; she stared at his mouth that hung open but he just lay there, dead.

She searched his face for injury – a scratch, a bruise, a graze. None. And then she lifted up the sheet that covered him to look down the length of him. He was naked, his clothes having been cut off him to get clear access to his flesh, his organs underneath, in order that he might be saved.

All there was was a bruise down the left side of his chest: a curve, an outline, part of a circle, a strip of apple peel thrown over a shoulder to land in the shape of a letter, a whorl, a finger painting, the mark of a steering wheel, a skinny moon.

That was all there was to indicate that Philip had been in an accident. Maya stared at the mark. Surely there had to be more than that? Where were the open fractures of tibia or femur where the snapped bone jagged out of the limb? Where was the head injury, the scalp or facial lacerations that peeled away the skin to expose the skull or the soft of the cheek? Where were the spat-out teeth, the red and bubbling saliva, the quiet moans, the flailing arms and yawning breath of the brain injured?

All she could see was a muddy bruise on her dead husband's chest.

She let the sheet drop and it fell in slow motion, it seemed, as a balloon of air puffed it up and back, up and back, before it settled again over his body.

She turned the top of the sheet down so it was again at his throat.

She reached out her fingers but stopped them before they contacted. She did not want to touch Philip's empty body.

We're ready to go, she'd said to the nurse who was in the staffroom with Charlie on her knee. She had his fingers splayed open and was tracing a circle over his palm with her finger. *Round and round the garden runs a teddy bear*, the nurse said, in time to her finger. *One step*, and her fingers walked up Charlie's wrist, *two step*, further now to his elbow, *tickle him under there*, and Charlie chuckled as her fingers disappeared into the softness of his side.

Stop it, Maya said. He doesn't like that game, and she snatched him up and held him to her and walked out into the night with him in front of her, like a shield.

She was protecting him, wasn't she, because that was her job. That's what parents were supposed to do.

And later, once Charlie was back in his cot, kissed and tucked in, Maya lay in her own bed waiting for sleep. Her bed was as big as the ocean. It was as cold as July. She stretched her arm out and it flopped against the half of her bed that was Philip's. She reached for his pillow and held it to her and later, much later, she went to sleep (gave in to it) and when she woke up to the sound of Charlie babbling, she knew things were changed forever.

So this was like then. There was the same rock in her belly, heavy and dense, there was the same quietness about the house, and there was the same empty feeling inside her and outside of her.

It would all be resolved in a few days, one way or another. The waiting (often the hardest part) would be over and she would be dealing with it. Whatever it may turn out to be. Surgery, definitely, but the extent of it, and therefore the consequences of it, were unknown.

But Jesus, Philip, it would all be so much easier if you were here. There were the mundane aspects to be dealt with. Who would look after Charlie while she was in hospital and recovering afterwards? Who would hang out the washing and bring it in again?

And then there were the big issues, never confronted unless you were facing your own mortality. What if *she* died?

There, it was said, she thought, and it wasn't as frightening as she had expected it to be. What if I die, she repeated.

Then Charlie will be alone. An orphan. Like she was, like Philip had been. She was suddenly short of breath. She could feel her heart thumping in her chest, there, resting under the cells that were dividing, multiplying, growing exponentially. A sense of panic was building inside her: it was desperation, urgency.

She had to have everything sorted out. All her ducks in a row, Rachael would say.

In her bedside cabinet was a pad of writing paper, yellow, with purple tulips across the bottom. She pulled it out and clicked on a pen.

My will, she wrote.

Charlie's guardian.

The house.

This can't be real, she thought from the sludge of her unconscious, as the sensible, rationalising part of her made out a What Will Happen in the Case of My Premature Death list.

It must be pretend, or practice, or something. This can't be me, planning for a time that I won't be alive to experience. Maybe it's part of being a grown-up, she thought. Planning for the inevitable and the unexpected. For the possibles and the probables. For the what ifs and the whens.

They'd been the perfect team. Maya, Philip and Charlie. A complete set. They set one another off, enhanced one another. They were the three sides of a triangle – no matter which way up it stood, it was solid, stable, perfect.

History demanded trinities, trios. The three little pigs, three little maids from school, three bears (and there was Goldilocks disturbing the balance), Father, Son and Holy Ghost, the three muses, three, three, three.

It was so right.

We'll always be the three of us, Philip had said.

But then he'd gone and ruined the symmetry by dying, damn him. Fuck him.

And now it seemed that Maya was edging closer to leaving Charlie as a solo. They'd somehow filled up the gaps that Philip had left. Like spooning out a section of pudding batter (a third, of course) and you know that if you leave the bowl on the bench, the remaining batter will spread to fill in the space that is left.

Maya and Charlie had become a duo. Batman and Robin, Hansel and Gretel, Starsky and Hutch, Laurel and Hardy, Persephone and Demeter.

But there was one thing that all the solo figures in history had in common. Spiderman, Cinderella, Charlie Chaplin. When you saw them, you always felt sorry for them. And when you looked in their eyes, you saw sadness.

Fivε

The atmosphere seemed heavier. The humidity was almost tangible. Maya sat on the side of the pool, legs dangling. The other swimmers were faster today. The roar of the water as they churned through it was louder, angry somehow. Everyone looked so determined.

She slipped under the surface. Tomorrow she would be going into hospital. She brought her hands up to her breasts, wet fingers touching the slippery fabric. What would happen? Maybe Mr Gaskin would just need to wrench out the lump (like pulling dock from the garden) and then smooth the gash together, sew it shut (tight) with fine nylon stitches.

That's what would happen.

She opened her eyes, there, under the water, and the vision in front of her goggles was flooded. Her legs were pale under the surface, dead white. Bubbles of trapped air clung to her skin. She brushed them away with her hand. She felt as if she was moving in slow motion, an astronaut. She was being restrained by the press of the water against her. It was all there was holding her together. She was surrounded by it.

The events would scoop her up, race her along, not allow her to stop, think, act for herself. She knew this was how it would be. Hospital did that to you. You went in with a problem that needed fixing (a condition, a cluster of symptoms) and you found yourself taken hostage. Days or weeks later you were let go, pushed out into the sunlight. Sent on your way, clutching a handful of pills to counteract the effects of what had been done to you. Thank you, you said, and you went home and back to bed, but this one was *your* bed and it fitted the shape of you.

Maya pushed off from the side of the pool, arms pointing and pressing her forward. She opened them wide apart, open across her chest. Her legs kicked in a quiet rhythm, open, out, open, out. She slid through the water. As she approached the far wall she turned, tumbling, not sure how her body knew to spin her around like that. She might have been a fish or a foetus. She swam back, foaming the water behind her.

She knew this would be her last swim for some weeks. I should go home, she thought. There was so much to do before tomorrow.

Maybe just another hundred metres. Things could wait.

'Hey, you behave at the Allens', okay?' Maya zipped up her small black suitcase.

'Yes, Mum.'

'Don't you let Jacob get you into any trouble.'

'No, Mum.'

'Make sure you eat everything Mrs Allen puts in front of you.'

'Yes, Mum.'

'Don't stay up all night talking.'

'M-u-u-m!'

'Sorry, buddy, but, you know –'

'Yeah, I know.' And he was tight around her, his head pressed against her. He squeezed and squeezed with his thin arms. 'You're going to be okay, aren't you?'

'Absolutely,' said Maya. 'Now come on. Kathy'll be waiting.'

And she was, her yellow Mini trembling in the drive.

'All aboard,' she called out as Maya and Charlie came outside, hand in hand. 'In you get, Charlie,' she said, and he climbed over the front seat that was bent over like an old man and he settled in the back seat, Maya's suitcase next to him. He held on to its scuffed corner.

Maya pushed the seat back into position. 'You've got to get a bigger car,' she said as she clicked in her seatbelt. 'What do you think, Charlie?'

'I dunno,' he said. He stared out the window. His small fingers stroked the suitcase.

'It'll be okay,' said Maya and she reached over and took his hand. He struggled free and crossed his arms tightly. 'Kathy will make sure I'm all right. She's going to look after me all the way through.'

'Now you should be really worried,' said Kathy. She changed down through the gears, jammed on the brakes and slid around the corner.

'Shut up,' said Maya. 'You're not helping.'

Kathy looked at Charlie through the rear-vision mirror. 'You know I'm only kidding, don't you?' she said.

'Yeah, I guess,' he said. His arms stiffened.

'Here we are. Your school, I believe, sir,' Kathy announced. Maya sprang out of the tiny car and pulled her seat forward to let Charlie out. He scrambled over her suitcase. She knelt down to him and took his hand. It was limp inside hers.

'It'll all be okay,' she said. 'I promise.'

'Yeah, whatever.' Charlie blinked, looked away, blinked again.

'Kathy will pick you up after school and bring you in to see me, then she'll take you to Jacob's. Okay?'

'Will you have had it done then? The whatever it is? The thing you have to have done?'

She smiled. 'No, buddy. That's tomorrow. Today I just have to have a whole lot of tests. Just to make sure I'm in good shape. See, they take care of everything. I'll probably be really bored waiting around. I can't wait to see you after school. Hear about your day. You know.'

She gathered him into her and held him – held on to him until she felt him unstiffen, soften against her. She kissed his hair, his forehead.

The school bell jangled. Nine o'clock. Suddenly she was ten

years old, scrambling among all the other ten-year-olds in the cloak bay outside her class. It smelled of wet raincoats and bananas. The bell was ringing. It was three o'clock. She was sitting on the floor doing up the laces of her shoes (and how she would always remember the sensation of cold lino through her nylon pants) and there was Mrs Insley, who lived next door but one, in front of her, with her thick stockings the colour of calico and her gloved hands clutching at the pearls at her throat.

'Maya, dear,' she said and she'd never sounded like that before. So quiet, reverent almost, as if they might be in church. 'I have to take you home. It's happened. Your mother.' And she picked up Maya's school bag, a small, hard-sided suitcase that went click click when you opened it, and she strode off and all Maya could do was follow her. She thought her feet weren't quite touching the ground. She couldn't feel them as she hurried after this woman, but she said to herself heel toe heel toe, just to make sure. She rested her head against the side of Mrs Insley's car as she unlocked the door and looked out the window as Mrs Insley drove her home. She had never actually said that her mother was dead.

'Maya, Charlie has to go in for school, now,' Kathy was saying. The bell had stopped ringing. The playground had cleared. The swings were coming to rest.

'Okay, buddy,' she said. She drew away from him and crossed her arms as she stood up. To fill in the space where he had been. 'Bye,' she called brightly.

'Bye, Mum,' said Charlie. He dragged his backpack behind him. It bounced and butted against the ground. 'See you after school.' And he was gone. Swallowed up by the wide school doors.

'I'm not going to cry,' said Maya as she got into Kathy's car.

'You're allowed to,' said Kathy. 'In fact, I think it's compulsory.'

The day scurried by, filled up with X-rays, blood tests and measurements. Maya sat on the edge of her hospital bed. Kathy sat on the straight-backed chair beside her. They ate chocolate and grapes. Every so often, after a moment or a week of sitting there eating, not

56

talking, Maya was summoned by a nurse or an orderly with a blood test form or an X-ray request.

She walked down to Radiology in dressing gown and slippers. She felt completely vulnerable like that. I hope I don't see anyone I know, she thought. But this was Gisborne Hospital. She worked there.

She undressed in a small white X-ray cubicle and sat shivering in a backless gown.

She was ushered into one of the radiology rooms and told, Stand here. Arms around, like this. Chin up. She hugged the cold X-ray plate, held her breath and was subjected to invisible particles of energy that stamped her lungs and ribs and the diseased parts of her onto film.

At the laboratory she offered her arm and watched, bravely, bravely, as blood was drawn out of her. Into one tube, two, three and they would be spun around, left to settle and the contents of her counted.

She ate a hospital lunch and afterwards Kathy took her to the café for hot chips and coffee.

She waited.

She thought about Charlie, what he might be doing at school right now. Reading silently at his desk, painting the face of a papier mâché puppet, playing cricket, his face bright with the adventure of it all.

Two-twenty.

'I'm sorry, Maya, but you have to go back down to X-ray. They didn't quite get the image they needed.' A nurse handed her another form.

'Didn't get your best side, huh?' said Kathy.

'I can't go now,' said Maya. 'School will be out soon.'

The nurse glanced at her watch. 'You'll be back in plenty of time.'

'Away you go, sweet pea, and I'll go and get that boy of yours.' Kathy picked up her keys. 'Don't forget to smile.'

Maya huddled in the tiny cubicle again, waiting for her turn. Waiting. It was all about waiting. Being patient. Ha. She flicked through a magazine, hopelessly out of date. Flicked through it again. Read a couple of articles.

Waited.

And then it was all happening in a hurry. She was bustled along, swept along as if she was one of a concert crowd surging forward to the stage. Stand here. No, this way. Hands here. Yes. Here. Breathe in when I say. Keep still. Now. Hold it. Keep still. Yes. Done. You'll have to wait while it's processed.

The big white envelope that she carried back to the ward contained the insides of her. She dropped the X-ray packet on the nurses' desk and hurried back to her room. And then she heard him, sobbing. She heard him before she saw him.

She ran in and there he was, a fragment in Kathy's arms. She was rocking him like a baby. Maya knelt down before them. 'What is it? What's wrong?'

Charlie crawled onto her. His face was in the hollow of her shoulder. His tears splashed onto her breast. His arms circled her neck. She thought he would never stop crying. She thought he would never let go.

'Shh, shh,' she cooed, and she stroked his hair, his back. Shh, shh. It would be the rhythm that would save him. Shh, shh. She settled back on her knees.

'I'm sorry,' said Kathy. 'When we arrived you weren't here and no matter what I said, he thought –'

'Oh, buddy,' Maya whispered, and she kissed his hair, because that was all she could do. Shh, shh. 'It's okay.'

She collected him up and they lay on her narrow metal bed together. It clanged like a diesel train when she moved. Eventually Charlie stopped crying. He gasped, drawing air into his lungs in spasms every now and then, and then he let his body soften as he breathed out. Shh, shh.

'I didn't know what to do,' he said. 'I got to your room and you weren't anywhere. I didn't know what to do. You weren't anywhere, Mum.'

Maya closed her eyes. She wanted to put her hands up over her ears. She wanted to put her hand over Charlie's mouth to stop his words. But she closed her eyes. Maybe they wouldn't get in, that way.

'We brought you Honey Bear,' said Charlie. 'He wanted to look after you while you're here.'

On cue Kathy passed up the bear. Maya pressed him against her. He smelled exactly like Charlie.

'Can I come and see you tomorrow?' His words were clear and even again. His face was dry.

'If you like, sure. I'll be attached to lots of drips and things, though. Will you be okay with that?'

He sat up.

'Will there be blood and stuff?'

'I hope not too much. But I'll see if I can arrange a little bit for you.' She ruffled his hair, smoothed it down again.

'Right, you,' said Kathy, and she pulled herself up from her chair. 'Let's get you to Jacob's.'

'Bye, little man,' Maya whispered, and she held Charlie to her. He hugged her back. Tighter, tighter, until she thought one of them might burst.

You need your sleep, Maya told herself as she lay in the bed. As a mother might tell her child, a nurse might tell her patient. You've got a big day tomorrow. She listened to the night nurse with her squeaky shoes and whispery voice. She listened to the traffic. To car horns, ambulance sirens. Someone cried out in pain. Someone was sick in a bowl in another room. Someone rang a bell. Help me, nurse. Help me.

A ribbon of sky hung down through the not-quite-closed curtains. Just a ribbon of it. Long and black and glittering with stars that swam in the sky. Orion's Belt, Alpha Centauri, Taurus. She had known them all once.

Eventually her hand made its way down to her breast. How neatly it fitted. She thought about Philip, how he used to say more than a handful's a waste. And then with his eager lips: more than a mouthful. Her hand stayed, as though it was comforted there, above her beating heart, but there above the lump too. How could that be? Good and evil residing within the same breast?

More than a handful's a waste. Why should she suddenly be thinking of Philip? She closed her eyes, tried to bring up his picture. Blond hair, blue eyes, a smile as wide as the Poverty Bay Flats. She could see pieces of him in isolation, as if they were police identikit features. Yes, officer, those are his eyes. His mouth? This one? No, fuller on the top, rounder, yes, these are the lips of my husband. But she couldn't match them all up so he became a whole, her husband, her Philip.

What else did he used to say? Maybe she could conjure him up, pull him out of her magician's hat that way.

Wouldn't that rip your nightie?

Life's a bitch and then you die.

Yes. And yes.

But still he was elusive. Just out of reach.

'Bugger this.' Maya's voice filled up the silence in the room. She drew her hand away and shivered as her breast was uncovered. She got out of bed and went down to the nurses' station.

'I can't sleep,' she announced. 'I'm going to make a coffee.'

'You're nil by mouth, aren't you?' It was the whispery nurse. She had been on nights too long. Her skin was sallow. Grey circled her eyes.

'It'll be all right. It's hours before I go to theatre. Look, it's only one o'clock.' She felt like Charlie trying to justify why he needed another new toy.

The nurse sighed, as all night nurses must do. 'Oh well,' she said, and she ran her finger down the operating list. 'Since it's you.'

'Thanks. Do you want one?'

'No thanks. But nothing after that, okay? Do you want a sleeping pill? You've got one charted. It wouldn't do any harm.'

'Why not?' Maya said. 'I'll take whatever's going at this point.'

The night nurse looked up at her. Her eyes went straight into her. Maya shivered and thought how she would have to get used to looks like that.

The patients' lounge was cold. What an uninviting room, Maya thought as she looked around at the vinyl-covered chairs all backed up against the walls. A fruit salad plant with two lone leaves struggled for its life by the door. *Reader's Digest* condensed books, three abridged novels per leatherette-bound edition, stretched along a bookshelf. Old copies of *Woman's Day* and *Boating World* were scattered on a low table.

Maya sat down and held her coffee between her hands. Down the hall a patient's bell rang. A nurse's quiet footsteps followed it.

This isn't right, she thought. This, here, now, it's not supposed to be like this. No, no, no. Wasn't it supposed to be that if you don't think about something, it won't happen? The avoidance technique. If I don't allow something (a thought, a fear) into my life, it doesn't exist.

When she went to live with Gran after – (don't say it or you'll have to believe it, accept it) – they'd never talked of Maya's mother. Never spoke her name again. Never referred to her. Never looked at a photo, never remembered her. It was as if she had never been alive.

At first Maya held on to the image of her mother, her beautiful billowing hair, her strong arms pushing through the surf, see, this is how you do it, love, left arm, right arm, breathe, her soft fingers smoothing down Maya's wet hair, helping her into her clothes again afterwards, doing up her buttons, counting them as she did. Singing, laughing.

But the overriding image was turning out to be that of a bald, red-faced woman, her cheeks tight and shining, puffed out by the drugs she had to take to quieten her cancer. It was of whispering, tiptoeing, would you shut up, Maya, your mother is trying to sleep. It was of standing at the end of her bed after school and telling her, lying in bed, coughing, clutching a handkerchief in her weak fingers, what had happened at school that day. Often she made something up. It was of taking shallow breaths in that room, not wanting to inhale the smell of her mother dying. Of staring at the bedpan that sat under the bed. Sometimes it was empty, sometimes it contained wees red with blood.

Of kissing her mother's cheek every morning before she went to school. Not wanting her lips to touch her mother's, so pulling them

61

in against her teeth and only allowing the skin around her mouth the kiss. Walking home after school and opening the front door, not knowing if today would be the day.

After a while she began to forget her mother, because she ceased to exist in their lives, hers and Gran's. This was the rule. If you don't think about it, it isn't true.

So why hadn't it worked now? With her cancer? She'd spent a lifetime avoiding it. Skirting around it, sidling past it with her eyes closed, should she be confronted by it at work, in magazines, in public health promotions. She'd been successful so far.

She had buried the possibility under a job where she could help other people who were suffering and hurt. Her actions could even make them better. Cure them. And weren't people so grateful when they were healed? It filled her up, this career, with a sense of belonging, of purpose. But most of all, she thought, there in the shivering dark of the patients' lounge, it meant there was no room for grief, disease, death to reside in her.

Until now.

A yellow beam of torchlight stood at the door.

'Are you okay?' it said.

Maya nodded. She couldn't trust her voice.

'You should get back to bed.'

She allowed herself to be led down the hall like an old woman, demented and dribbling, who gets into the wrong bed in the geriatric ward. She watched as her bed was straightened and the sheets were turned back for her. She slipped into bed. Look how well behaved she was.

She closed her eyes, screwed them tight like a child. She turned onto her side and brought her knees up to her chest. Her arms circled her legs. She felt herself begin to fall, to succumb, but as she did, she pulled herself awake again. She wanted to sleep but she wanted to stay awake. Her conscious mind was a much safer companion.

She wanted to be at home.

She wanted to be drunk, deliriously so.

But most of all, she wanted her mother.

The sleeping pill eventually began to work. Maya drifted, afloat. She bobbed about and the rhythm of the waves that she heard and felt inside her head began to lull her to sleep. But then the caffeine began its dance. It wasn't enough to jolt her fully awake, just enough that the rhythm pounded behind her eyes, fighting with the soporific effects of the sleeping pill. She was caught. Suspended halfway between drug-induced sleep and drug-enhanced wakefulness. Finally the pill won out and she fell into a dreamless, motionless sleep.

When she woke in the morning she felt unrefreshed. It was as though she had been running all night.

It's like I'm pretending, she thought as she stood under the shower. This is a dress rehearsal. She slid back into bed in her backless white theatre gown. She was so calm. As though she had done this a thousand times before. She held her hands out in front of her. They were still – barely a flicker from her fingers.

Any moment now they'll jump out from hiding places, her friends, the doctors and nurses here, from beside bedside lockers, under her bed, behind the door, out from the curtains, and shout well done, Maya. Good job. Maybe hold up score cards with marks out of ten. And then Mr Gaskin will amble in, with lattes and small pastries and sit on the side of her bed. And how was it pretending to be a patient? he'll say. You did so well. You had everyone fooled (laugh). Especially *you*. Look, you've even talked yourself into believing it. And how they'll joke about this later on, at morning tea or in the theatre change room. Really, they will.

'Maya.' A nurse appeared beside her. She spoke with apology.

'Yes?' A shiver ran down the length of her. Was it time already?

'Here's your pre-med. They're nearly ready for you.'

Maya smiled foolishly. 'It's too late to change my mind, isn't it?'

Six

'Left or right?'

'Pardon?' Through the fog of her pre-med, taken forty minutes before on an empty stomach, Maya was sure Mr Gaskin was standing beside her asking which side he should operate on. Him, with his calm hands and quiet smile. Left or right. Shouldn't he know? Wouldn't it be written down somewhere, on her chart, on the theatre list, on a scrap of paper in a nurse's pocket? Somewhere? Am I going to be one of those medical misadventures you read about, where you wake up and the wrong leg has been amputated, the wrong lung, the wrong eye removed? The wrong breast.

Or worse. You are awake the entire operation. Every inch of you, except your brain, is paralysed with drugs. You can hear everything, feel every scalpel cut. Every time a retractor spreads the insides of you, you are certain you will die with the pain of it. More suction please, and you feel your blood, pieces of tissue being sucked away. You can hear him and his scissors that cut through you, and he mops up the blood that pools inside you, with gauze-tipped forceps. They are sandpaper grating over your cut and bleeding interior. And you cannot do a thing except breathe and scream inside your silent self and wait for it to be over.

Of course it was written down. Her operation was documented

in a dozen places. But the surgeon had to know that the patient knew what was going to happen. The patient had to know that the surgeon knew, too.

'Which side, Maya?'

'Left,' she said.

'Thanks. Just double-checking. You know.'

Maya smiled, a half-drunken loping grin. Left. Or had she meant left, but really said right? Had her mouth betrayed her, let her down at this most crucial of moments?

Her eyelids were heavy. She had been awake for weeks, it seemed. All she needed was sleep. Left. Or right. Either one. It really didn't matter. She would just sleep. Worry about it later. That's what she would do.

They were wheeling her into theatre now. How different everything looked from this angle. The lights were mirrors: she could see repeating images of herself, a stick figure in the bed, as pale and still as fog. There was noise, a machine being turned on behind her. It sounded like a tractor, she thought. There was the clang of metal on metal: instruments, bowls, dishes in which to place the diseased and unnecessary parts of her. Talking, laughing from another room. Getting ready.

In an instant her head cleared. This was no dress rehearsal. This was no dream. Mr Gaskin's words came back to surround her. We'll start with a lumpectomy (and what an absurdly childish name that was for a surgical procedure such as this), and a frozen section. If the section comes back unfavourably we'll proceed right away with a mastectomy and lymph node clearance. I'm fairly certain that's what we'll need to do, given your family history and the clinical picture. So let's prepare for that outcome.

Let's.

Cold hands picked up one of hers. They were Mr Jayasurya's and they were long and thin. He rubbed her hand and to anyone else he may have been soothing her, and he was with his smiling eyes, but he was bringing up the veins on the back of her hand, ripening them for the needle.

'All right, Maya?' Mr Gaskin asked from behind his paper mask.

He hovered behind the anaesthetist.

She nodded.

'Ready?'

'I suppose so.'

Mr Jayasurya flicked air out of a syringe of anaesthetic. Just like they do on ER, Maya thought. Just like they do in real life.

'You're a brave girl,' Mr Gaskin said, and he laced his gloved and sterile hands together. Platitudes did not fall comfortably from his lips. But maybe this was part of the charade too.

You're a brave girl, Maya. Don't cry. Your mother wouldn't want you to cry. Show everyone how strong you are. How brave you can be. That's enough now. No more tears. Here, hold the hymn book for me. Shh, now.

And because Maya didn't want those to be her last thoughts before she was anaesthetised, she made herself think of Charlie. Charlie, awarded Player of the Day at cricket. What a game that had been. He'd never played like that before. Took a catch. Got his highest score with the bat. And all with a look of fierce determination. Determination, she said to herself.

'Here we go,' said Mr Jayasurya, and the needle's sharp tongue licked her hand.

If I was going to die during my operation, I would never know. How odd, she thought, and the bright circles of light above her faded and shrank until they were pinpricks, and then they were black.

She struggled with her eyelids. They refused to stay open. Weighed down with lumps of concrete, they slid shut just as she began to focus. There was talking around her. Whispering: not behind-the-hands schoolgirl whispering, but that of people who are practised at it, who do not want to disturb the patient in the bed. The whisperee. She could almost make out the voices.

Again she tried to open her eyes. This time they sprang up easily. The anaesthetic was washing away. She looked around. She was back in her narrow hospital bed in her narrow hospital room.

Hibiscus and banana palms swayed on the curtains at the window and bunched at the foot of her bed. On the bedside locker, in perfect symmetry, stood a water jug, a glass and a small plastic bowl covered with a flannel. Like Gran's sugar bowl, over which was draped a circle of crochet, radiating from lemon at its centre out to peach and lilac. The endpoints were weighted down with glass beads. No flies could land on Gran's sugar.

At the end of the bed she could see Charlie and Kathy. They were playing cards, hunched over Maya's tray table. They could have been a million miles away. It was like looking through the wrong end of binoculars.

They were slapping cards down, slap slap as they landed on the formica-topped table. The sound shattered inside Maya's ears. The cards were huge and they changed shape like Silly Putty. They were yellow, blue, the orange of sunset. Diamonds, clubs, smiling knaves with curling moustaches slipped off the cards and lined themselves along the foot of Maya's bed. Here was a Queen of Spades. She threw off her crown and it clattered to the floor. Maya was certain she heard it. The Queen of Spades pulled a brush from the bodice of her red and yellow dress and began to pull it through her thick black hair. Each time she passed it through, her hair came away at that place. She pulled the clumps of hair from the brush and stuffed them down the front of her dress. There, she cried at each handful, each stroke.

There.

Slap, slap, more cards hit the table. Charlie and Kathy laughed, mouths like hyenas.

Cards fanned out into circles, stacked themselves into piles and turned themselves into multi-storeyed houses, with windows, chimneys, narrow balconies on which tiny climbing roses grew.

The King of Hearts blew Maya a kiss. She felt it hit her cheek, wet and warm. Maya, Maya, he whispered. She shivered as his breath cooled against her ear. I love you. I love you. And now he was Philip and he was holding her, till death do us part, Maya, did you remember that bit? he was saying. Were you paying attention? She had been watching his face, his marvellous mouth, and maybe she hadn't been listening, but was that any reason? Was it?

And thinking that each decision, every single one, steers your course. Not just the big ones, but the trivial choices – pizza or Chinese for tea, whether to put the washing out or not, these shoes or those ones. Not being aware, but knowing innately that it was the polarities that determined your future.

If Maya hadn't been paired up with Kathy that day in class, if they hadn't struck up a friendship, if Kathy hadn't said, laughing, oh, you're an orphan too, isn't that a weird thing? If Maya hadn't joined Kathy and her brother for a drink after work, if he hadn't asked her out, if they hadn't got married, if Charlie hadn't been born, if Philip hadn't died. If if if.

Fifty-two cards rained onto Maya's face, sticking in her hair, in the folds of the bedclothes.

'Snap,' she heard Charlie call out and he slammed his hand down. The cards vanished.

Maya swallowed. She blinked, trying to work out what was going on. Was the operation over or was she still waiting for it to begin? It didn't feel as if any time had passed. Maybe they'd put it off. Maybe she didn't need it done after all.

Beside her, a nurse watched drips of fluids falling into the tubing that ran into her arm. Watched and counted. Regulated the flow. Maya's body could not be trusted to take care of itself.

Hi, guys, she went to say. Look, I'm back. I guess I've had some sort of operation. I must have because they don't give you a drip just for the hell of it, do they? What are we doing? But as she moved her lips to speak, a surge of anaesthetic or pain relief or something from inside her washed over her brain and her eyes and her throat and her mouth and she sank back into the hollow of her bed, and slept.

Minutes, then hours, then whole sections of the day slipped and slid by like sheets of ice. They hardly seemed real. Things were done to Maya's body that she had no control over. She was injected or measured or aspirated at increasing intervals.

Sugar and water and salts were dripped into her arm. Fine plastic tubing stretched across her face and around her ears, feeding oxygen into her depleted body. It was a wide clown smile. And more tubes: a catheter draining urine into a bag that was hooked, hidden under the blue hospital bed cover, onto the frame of her bed, out of sight, as all body fluids should be. Alongside it, a thick transparent tube emerged from under the bedclothes to a plastic concertina that expanded as it filled with blood. And it did. Dark blood slipped through the tubing into the container and there in her quiet white room, time was measured by the filling of that bottle.

She woke intermittently and went to lift her arms, pinned under tucked-in sheets, to find out. It seemed she had had an operation. In that case, had they just taken the lump, or was her whole breast gone? Sliced off like the White Cliffs and tossed into the sea. But her arms were too tired and the sheets were too tight and it really didn't matter, she thought, and then sleep overwhelmed her again.

Sometimes she woke up and heard Charlie. Laughing, playing I Spy or cards again and there was Kathy, guessing. Throwing down her cards. Sometimes she heard Mr Gaskin and she felt his soft fingers on her. Sometimes she heard Philip. Maya, honey, how are you? You look like shit. Do you mind me saying that? I'm sorry but you do.

But Philip was dead. She had buried him. She had kissed his cold face, surrendered his sliced-apart and sewn-together body, held up her infant son so he could wave goodbye to his daddy before Philip was dropped into the ground and covered over with Kaiti silt loam. He was dead, wasn't he?

Did that mean she was dead too? Was this what it was like? Would she be stuck, post-operatively, for eternity, being a witness to the people who mattered the most?

And now it was all tumbling – the phone call, the desperate drive to the hospital with Charlie in his yellow pyjamas with planes on them and sheepskin booties that didn't match, but what did it matter, who would care that she hadn't been able to find a pair, being ushered into the visitors' room in A and E, and knowing what the house surgeon would say because there was only one reason for the visitors' room, and as he was speaking with awkward words, watching him twist his wedding band round and round and thinking how young he was to be married and how his wife would be at home alone for so many nights while he patched up and sewed up the sick and the dead.

And thinking fuck you, Philip, for being out on the road at night. Everyone knows that nights and streets and cars are dangerous things and together what fatal synergy they make. Why couldn't you have had a safer job? A better car? Faster or slower – one that wouldn't have been hit at that instant by an unlicensed driver in an unregistered, unwarranted, untrustworthy car.

Life's cheap for that kind, Philip used to say, and he'd whistle 'The Time Warp' as they drove in their sturdy, seatbelted, safety-featured company car past such hoons. Dammit, Janet, I love you, and he'd place his hand on the inside of her knee and how his touch thrilled her, like electricity.

But he was dead and Maya had buried him. She remembered that. She made herself open her eyes and focus on the hibiscus and their orange tongues and she made herself listen to Charlie and to the jumble of hospital noises outside her room.

There was that whispering nurse again, beside her, smelling of Red Door and soap.

'Open your eyes, Maya. It's all over.' And she tried to, but she was so tired again. The nurse was shaking her arm, talking into her face. Her voice was firm but at once kind. 'You're all right now. Open your eyes. It's over.'

She wished she could believe the nurse with her coffee breath and neat fingernails. She wished it was over. But she thought it was really just beginning.

Now there were flowers. They were filling up her room, invading all the spaces in it. Crinkly cellophane, huge red bows, brown paper and raffia. Nurses filed into her room in an absurd procession, a string of badly dressed bridesmaids. Bunches of gerberas, gypsophila, straw grass, tiny slipper orchids, carnations. They each carried a bouquet and placed it in a jar (Agee, or Craig's jam, family size, were best) on the windowsill, a ledge, Maya's bedside locker, on the paper towel holder above the handbasin. 'Look, Maya,' she heard. 'You've got flowers. Look who these are from.' Or she thought she heard their voices.

Maybe this was part of the dream, the trick of anaesthesia. Maybe this was her lounge instead, with Charlie's playpen in the corner, his nappies and baby wipes in a cane basket, fluffy blue and yellow stretch-and-grows, domed overalls and tiny sweatshirts waiting to be folded and put away. Maybe she was sitting on the couch, rolling and rolling Philip's death certificate in her fingers, rolling and rolling it, stark and spare as cold meat and salad, somebody's signature making it real and the doorbell ringing (and Charlie waking from his afternoon sleep each time it sounded). She went to the door and there was a courier with a bouquet and would you sign here and have a nice day and whistling as he went down the driveway back to his van because he didn't know if these were celebratory flowers or thank you flowers or I'm sorry flowers.

Maya filled her everyday vases, her wedding present vases and finally preserving jars, even a plastic ClickClack container that she usually used for cornflakes. The house sagged with flowers. But still she felt nothing. She was numb, frostbitten.

Maybe this was Gran's kitchen and still the doorbell was ringing. Yellow chrysanthemums, proteas, flax wound into curls. Gran saying, Maya, get another vase out, would you. And wanting her own kitchen and her own bed and most of all wanting her mother. And knowing somehow that she would never recover from this.

Look, Maya, these are from theatre, and opening her eyes drunkenly and seeing bird of paradise stems, their sharp beaks sticking out through narrow grasses and fluffy thistle heads and thinking they looked like pukekos that ran out from the swampy verges onto the road at Patutahi, Manutuke, Muriwai.

This time she wanted to wake up. It was like she'd had a hot bath, got into fluffy pyjamas and slept between fresh sheets until her body told her it was time to wake up. She looked around and there were Kathy and Charlie. Still. My two best friends, thought Maya. Kathy was in the same straight-backed chair, her feet propped on another chair, her head tipped back and resting against the window frame. Her mouth had fallen open. She was snoring softly. Charlie was wedged beside her, his limbs thrown about her. He too was asleep.

Maya smiled. They're here. Was this the same day? Had she slept through a whole day and a night and this was tomorrow? How would she know? She swallowed but her mouth was dry and her throat was scratched and swollen. She thought they were wearing the same clothes as before. Charlie in his sweatshirt with *Skate Star* across the chest. It must have been the same day. She ran her tongue over her lips. Dry, dry. She was like a dried-up riverbed, just dust and crazy jigsaw cracks.

A drink. She looked across to her locker. A glass of the clearest, coolest water stood there, enticing her with its freshness. Aah. She would just prop herself up and reach over, take the glass and drink through the straw. She wriggled her arms free from the sheets and went to pull herself up. A jolt of pain cut her in two. Like lightning, an electric shock. Sweat sprang out on her forehead. She gasped and fell back onto the pillow. She had only tried to sit up. She lay there, breathing deeply, waiting for the tearing across her chest to subside. It ebbed away slowly, like an outgoing tide, every splash of it a little more distant. Finally it was gone.

She would ring the bell. She would summon a nurse. But there it was, looped neatly around a hook on the wall behind her bed. Out of harm's way.

'Kathy,' she said, but her voice leaked out, spreading under her skin. It crept through the dissected resected parts of her chest and was lost there, absorbed by the tiny white blood cells that had massed there to defend her against infection. No sound came out. She licked her lips and went to speak again. Kathy. Charlie. Skate Star. Nothing.

She was stuck.

Maya looked up at the bag of IV fluids that dripped into her. The bag was three-quarters empty. Someone would be in soon to change it. She would have to wait. Someone would come in soon.

When she next woke, what she saw was yellow and red. And a swathe of purple. And a blond head behind. Two hands clutching a fistful of flower stalks wrapped in purple paper.

'Mum,' said Charlie, and he dropped the flowers onto the bed and flung his small self onto Maya's chest.

'Don't –' Maya began, but again her voice failed her and he was there before she could do anything, and how could she save herself from her son anyway? It was as if she had been hit by a train. The air was pushed out of her lungs. 'Oh, oh,' she managed through her screaming throat. It felt as though the wound across her chest had been ripped apart, sutures tearing through the edges of her. The pain was paralysing her.

Charlie sat up. The burning eased. She sucked air in greedily.

'Are you okay?' he asked, pulling back, unsure of this gaping, gasping stranger.

She nodded and tried to smile. Her dry lips split and she felt pinpricks of blood spring to the surface.

'Hey,' she heard from the doorway. Kathy dropped her bag, an armful of magazines, a bottle of juice and a punnet of strawberries. She dragged Charlie off the bed. 'You can't touch your mother.'

Sudden silence encompassed them. Kathy stood with Charlie in front of her, her arms down, crossed over his body, as though he needed to be restrained. Charlie stared at his mother. Fear and disbelief and something else, like distrust, washed over his face.

'Mum?' he said.

Maya went to smile. She went to raise her hand to say it's okay, buddy, really. She went to speak. But her mouth was stuffed with cotton. She couldn't say a thing.

What should she do? This wasn't the time, the place for making decisions or being a grown-up. She wanted to pull the covers up to her chin, roll onto her side and go to sleep with her mother's soft fingers stroking her cheek. This was a time for being nurtured, for being cared for by someone older and wiser. Someone who could tell her what to do. Surely.

But things don't always work out the way they are supposed to, Maya thought. She counted off her losses: Mother (dead), Father (dead), Grandmother (dead), Husband (dead). Why, in the middle of my life, should I be surrounded by so many people leaving me? she thought. The weight of so much sorrow pressed down on her. She shook her head to disperse it. It settled over her anyway.

'Mum?'

'Hey, buddy,' she said, and how cheerful she sounded, in spite of the tearing in her throat and the weight on her chest. 'It's okay,' she said, smiling with cracked and bleeding lips.

'That's what I like to hear,' she heard from the doorway. Mr Gaskin stood there holding a chart against his belly, flat like a tray. He smiled. 'How are you, Maya?' he said, and he moved towards her.

'I don't know,' she said. 'How *am* I?' She tried to laugh and tasted blood from her lips.

'Come on, Charlie, let's go and get some lollies from the machine,' said Kathy, and she backed out to the door.

'Can I press the buttons?' he asked.

'Sure.'

'Can I put the money in and everything?'

'Absolutely,' Kathy laughed. 'We'll see you later,' she said to Maya and to Mr Gaskin, who was hovering like a nervous suitor beside Maya's bed.

'Thanks, Kathy,' Mr Gaskin said. He knelt down so he was eye to eye with Charlie. He ruffled his hair as though he knew how to connect with small boys. 'How are you, young Charlie?'

'Fine,' he said defensively. 'Come on, Kathy.'

They were gone then, down the hall. Maya's small room suddenly felt like an ice cave, white, crystalline, freezing.

'He's a lovely boy,' Mr Gaskin nodded to the doorway. 'You're doing a great job with him.'

'Thanks,' said Maya. The pain she had felt moments earlier was going. Simmering. She searched the surgeon's face for signs of diagnosis. Stared at the chart that pressed into his belly. Looked for clues in his face, the tone of his voice, the way he raised one eyebrow at the end of each sentence. She knew he was standing there with her future between the covers of that chart.

This was going to be one of those defining moments. Like coming to a fork in the road. Left or right. Everything after this would be measured in relation to this instant. But she was powerless. Her life was not going to be dictated by something *she* was to do. She was being acted upon. And she knew that everything would change. One way or another.

'Well,' said Mr Gaskin, settling into that surgeon-speak way of explaining. Smoothing his voice over the unsettled and frightened parts of her. 'I won't beat around the bush, Maya,' and she suddenly thought of Rachael in her kitchen, so full of clichés. And how they fell so easily from Rachael's full lips, yet seemed out of place here. 'The operation itself went very well,' he said, 'but things don't look so good, I'm afraid.' She watched his fingers stiffen over the edge of her chart, as though he was containing his fear there.

He stumbled on, tripping over sharp rocks left in his path, catching his sleeve on the jag of a branch. 'The lump was malignant, I'm afraid.' (He was saying it again. *You're afraid*, Maya thought. Can you imagine how it feels on this end of the conversation?) 'It was more invasive than we had thought. We had to do the total mastectomy and clear the axillary nodes. It looks as if we got everything, though. We'll get you up and about and aim to have you home the day after tomorrow. Christmas Day's next Wednesday, so you'll be back and well settled by then. That'll be something to look forward to, won't it?'

She watched Mr Gaskin's lips and how busy and animated they were when he spoke. There was a crumb of something, a muffin or a cheese scone maybe, hanging off his bottom lip and every time he spoke it flapped dangerously, threatening to dislodge itself and be lost on the floor.

'We'll need to start chemotherapy and then radiotherapy as

soon as the wound has healed,' he continued. Where was the Mr Gaskin that Maya knew? The one she could have a conversation with, the one to whom she was a colleague. The one who spoke with compassion about all things, the one who was real. This man was an imposter, a stranger, protecting himself behind the shield of his white coat. Was that what would happen from now on? People would become clinical and talk in complete sentences? Chatter was for earlier times.

'So, let's take a look at the wound,' he said, and he laid her chart on her locker. She wriggled down the bed as best she could so she was supine and accommodating. With an effort she lifted her bottom and pulled her gown up. God, how it hurt, but she had to look as though she was managing, recovering. Mr Gaskin folded her bedclothes down to reveal her pale blue hospital gown. It had Hospital Property stamped across its front. As if anyone needed reminding. He turned the sheets back in crisp layers, as though he might be folding a flag or a map. He placed a cuddly, a fluffy white blanket, over her legs and belly.

'Right then,' he said. 'Okay?'

She nodded and smiled through a closed mouth. She was a little girl sitting on her mother's knee, waiting for the bee-sting to be pulled from her foot.

She watched his hands wriggle under the cuddly and lift up her gown. Every part of her that was not directly related to this examination had to remain covered. How odd, when this man had squeezed and prodded and touched every centimetre of her breasts and had scalpelled her, seen her bleed and had cut out and cut off and cut away parts of her.

'Ready?'

She nodded, still the aquiescent child.

He drew the cuddly back flat against her belly. Maya watched his face, concentrated on his eyes as he examined the wound. She felt his fingers brush across her chest, although it didn't feel like herself – it was like running your hand across a graze: the sensation was there, but diminished. Now he was lifting up her arm and it sent waves of pain over her. She groaned. She couldn't help letting the sound escape her. He pressed into her armpit, felt down her ribs and onto her back, his fingers sandwiched between the hospital sheets and her skin.

'Good,' he said, and he pulled the cuddly back over her chest. He washed his hands at the basin, splashing water vigorously over the wall. Still the surgeon, Maya thought. He turned back to her and picked up her chart again. Protection. He opened it up, pulled a pen from his breast pocket and began to write.

'Any nausea?' he said.

'No.'

'How's the pain?'

'Not bad.'

'Are you managing anything to drink yet?'

'A little bit.'

'Good,' he said, and he snapped the cover of the chart down. 'I'll come back tomorrow. Just ask one of the nurses if you have any problems, won't you. In the meantime,' and he shrugged his shoulders as if all was hopeless and what else could you do?

'Thank you,' said Maya, and now she realised the balance had shifted. She was The Patient. The CA Breast in Room Five (and what a neat abbreviation CA was for the word cancer. You didn't have to say it at all).

'Right then,' said Mr Gaskin, and he tapped the fingers of one hand on the edge of her bed, turned away and was gone.

She stared at the door for a long time. It was as if her head and her eyes were too tired to move. I didn't look, she said to herself a thousand times. I will, I will. I'll just pull down the cuddly and lift up my gown. Pull down and lift up. It'll be so easy. Have a quick look and cover it all up again. That's what I'll do.

Seven

'School breaks up on Friday,' said Charlie. He tipped his head back and drained the last of the Coke from the can into his mouth.

'Great,' said Maya. She swished a mouthful of water around in her mouth. It seemed to be sucked into the surface of the inside of her cheeks, her tongue, the soft insides of her lips. She swallowed and followed the water as it cooled and moistened her throat. She was sure she could feel it splash into her stomach.

'Do you know how many sleeps there are till Christmas?' he asked.

'No. Do you?'

'No.' He crunched the can in his fists. 'Jacob's mum will know.' He jumped off Maya's bed and opened the lid of the rubbish bin by pressing on the pedal with his foot. He threw the can in and took his foot away. The lid clanged down. He pressed the pedal again, pulled his foot away. Open shut open shut. The noise was fingernails down a blackboard inside Maya's head.

'Buddy,' she began. Open shut open shut clang clang. 'Charlie,' she said, firmer now. He stopped and sat back on her bed.

'Do you know Jacob's mum has cleared out two of his drawers for me to use? Cool, eh?'

He slid off Maya's bed and stood by the door. He flicked the door handle. Up down up down. 'I'd better go,' he said. 'They'll be waiting for me.'

'Okay, buddy. See you tomorrow. Be good, eh.'

He slips away so easily, she thought. Like water through my fingers.

Maya was now an 'up-and-about' patient, in spite of the drip stand that she wheeled around, and from which a plastic bag of salty water dangled and dripped into the needle in her arm.

Ah, to be mobile. To feel the hot shower on her shoulders and back. To sit beside her bed for Mr Gaskin's round, instead of in it. To be wheeled outside into the hard Gisborne sun, feeling, with a rug over her resting legs, like a soldier from the Great War suffering shell shock or gas gangrene (smelling sulphur or beef tea or the stench of rotting limbs, black and swollen). But the smells here were hospital food, delivered on a plastic tray, all compart-mentalised; a sharp cleanser that stuck in the back of your throat and seemed slowly to burn it away; and resignation.

Maya's first steps after her operation had been after Mr Gaskin's first visit, after Kathy had taken Charlie home (to the Allens'). She had slept and rested, eyes closed, eyes open, sipped water, rested some more. She had gathered up all her courage and strength so they fitted in her hands and she had opened the neck of her pale blue Hospital Property gown and looked down at her chest.

It wasn't the experience she had expected it to be. Not earth-shattering at all. The left side of her chest was covered with a large square white cotton pad, over which a transparent adhesive dressing had been placed. As neat and tidy as you like. No blood, no ragged suture line with black stitches like spiders' long legs poking out. Just a white pad covered with plastic. Her right breast, flaccid and soft, fell away down the side of her, against her armpit, as usual. And because of the padding her left side looked the right size. So that wasn't so bad. But it wasn't enough. She lay on her back and looked down at her body, at the gravity-assisted fall and slide of her, but she needed to see herself in her entirety.

So she swigged on the last of her water and made herself sit up. God or the Devil dragged on her chest, trying to push her back down again, but she stayed upright, breathing through an open mouth until the pain went away and she could move some more. She swung her legs over the side of the bed and stayed there for several minutes, waiting for her brain to equalise and stabilise her. She slid off the side of the bed into a standing position. The floor was cold under the soles of her feet. She shivered, breathed in and out, pushing pain and nausea away, and she held on to the drip pole as though her life depended on it. Maybe it did.

She unhooked the plastic drain from the side of her bed and held it in one hand, still gripping the drip pole with the other. She shuffled to the door. It was the hardest thing she had ever done. She rested at the doorway, leaning back and feeling the cool of the door against her shoulders. Go away, she said through a tight mouth to the God of Post-operative Pain. She pushed one foot, then the other across the hallway to the bathroom.

And then she was there, under the glare of fluorescent lights, in front of the mirror over the handbasin. She could not hide from herself: her lank greasy hair, her sallow face, the dark shadows under her eyes, her bloodless lips.

Okay, she said to the person inside her head, the one who had thought this would be a good idea. She gathered up her gown into her hands and raised it up, up, over her chest, over her face, over her head. Out through her 'good arm' first – one of the first lessons a nurse learns – undress the good arm first (as though the other arm has been bad and must wait, as punishment). Then over her left arm, next to her wound and her dressing and carefully over the place where the drip went into her arm. It bunched at her wrist there, where her left hand still held on to the drip pole. It was all that was keeping her up.

Maya concentrated on that gown, on the removal of it, so it wouldn't snag on any tubing or dressing or corner of her. And then she was naked. And she had to look.

She began at her face, which contained memories of her but had somehow morphed into the face of someone else. She could see her

80

bare torso in the edges of her vision but she wouldn't drag her eyes down yet. She shivered as she stood there, naked. The bag of IV fluids swung on its hook. Her wedding ring chattered against the shiny metal pole. Her head spun, thumped; it became disconnected from her body. She breathed. Always breathe. If you don't know what else to do – breathe. It had always worked up till now.

And then, by accident almost, although Maya knew things never actually happened by chance (there was always design involved), her eyes slid down to her chest and then she was looking and she was transfixed by what she saw.

Her right breast hung there like an abandoned birthday balloon, looking like the empty vessel it was becoming. The nipple was tight and puckered. No surprises so far. But the left side of her. Her chest there was flat, her breast had indeed been sliced off and although the wound was covered up, the shapelessness of that side made her shiver uncontrollably. And as she did, her right breast shuddered and she found herself laughing at the sight of it.

Do your boobs hang low,
Do they wobble to and fro,
Can you tie them in a knot,
Can you tie them in a bow,
Can you throw them over your shoulder,
Like a continental soldier,
Do your boobs hang low?

How funny that song had seemed to giggly schoolgirls.

How glamorous they thought boobs would be. How they longed for them, balling up socks and shoving them down the fronts of their white skivvies, admiring their absurd profiles in the mirror.

And here she was now, a one-breasted, flat-chested freak. Half woman, half prepubescent child. Confused, afraid, tired. So tired.

'I think we'll have to postpone Christmas this year,' said Maya. Charlie sat on the edge of her bed playing with the Gameboy that Jacob had lent him.

'Hang on a second, Mum. I'm so close to wasting the enemy on this level.'

Be calm. He's just a boy. Suddenly he leapt off the bed and thrust one arm up in the air. 'Yes,' he shouted, and he danced on the spot like a cartoon character. 'Look, Mum, I *wasted* him. He – is – toast!'

When did my baby turn into a trend-following, cool-talking boy? It's my job to protect him from the dangers of pop psychology, thought Maya. And what about alcohol, drugs, diseases, driving too fast with a car full of friends he wants to impress? She pressed her hands against her forehead. It was just too hard. And what if –. She shook her head and focused her vision on Charlie, his thin arms skyward. His shorts were low on his narrow hips. There was a band of belly exposed under his teeshirt. She suddenly wanted to kiss him on his flat tummy, blow raspberries like she did when he was a baby and he had laughed with the pleasure of it. And she had laughed too, at his throaty chuckle, his round bald head and his wide smile that was all gums, no teeth.

'I can see what I'm going to have to get you for Christmas.'

'What, Mum?'

'A Gameboy. Yellow, or silver, or whatever the best one is.'

'Jacob said I can keep this one. He's got a new one. Cool, eh?' Charlie stood very still then, the game between his hands.

'We're going to have to postpone Christmas this year,' Maya repeated. Am I becoming redundant? she thought. Invisible? Are you listening, Charlie?

He sat down on her bed. 'What, not have Christmas because Jacob's giving me his Gameboy? That's a bit weird, isn't it?' He kicked his legs out. Left right left right.

'No, buddy. It's just that I don't think I'll be properly well enough. I'm sorry. We might just delay it. Till January. When I'm back to normal.'

'How will Father Christmas know to come then?'

Quick. Think. 'We'll leave him a note on the mantelpiece. Like we did the year we went camping, remember? He knew to come and find us in our tent. He's very clever, he'll know when to come back.'

'Okay, then,' said Charlie. He pressed a button on the Gameboy and tinny music started up. 'Just so long as he knows.'

'We'll have you well and truly settled by Christmas.'

As if it made any difference. Christmas was just a day. A benchmark with which to measure time. But in a way, it made all the difference in the world.

The touch on the back of her hand was firm and certain. Maya opened her eyes. She'd been asleep for only a few minutes but this touch said wake up, take notice. She hated the fact that she was so tired. She felt like Gran, who had 'a rest' every afternoon, slack-jawed and snoring in her lavender-smelling room. Still, Maya thought, it's only day two. I'm allowed to be this tired. And hospital makes you so; it hypnotises you into complacency and you find that after breakfast and a shower you are ready for a sleep.

'Hello,' she said.

'Good morning. How are you?' The woman spoke with that edge of pity and resignation to her voice that had become common. She wore a crisp cotton shirt, collar turned up and captured by a string of pearls. She sat next to Maya's bed, knees together, and smoothed her hands over her linen skirt. 'I'm Charlotte, I'm one of the social workers.' She smiled widely and pulled an A4 pad out of her leatherette satchel.

Maya didn't recognise her. Everyone knew everyone here, and being a patient meant she had more visitors (I'm just popping in on my way to morning tea, thought I'd call in before I go home/go on duty/hit the wards) than she wanted or needed. It was all so exhausting. Smiling, being sociable, chatting, listening to the goings on of the hospital and being strangely unenthused by any of it. Detached. I'm tired, she wanted to say. Leave me alone. I'm grieving, I'm sad, I'm overwhelmed, I'm trapped, I'm drowning.

'Are you new?' she said. She tried to sound interested.

Charlotte laughed. She shook her head and her shiny hair

bounced around her face. 'I'll have to get used to being in a small town, won't I?'

'I suppose you will.'

'I imagine you're wondering why I'm here.'

'Yes I am, actually. I'm quite tired.' Not caring that she sounded rude.

'I'm sorry. This won't take long. I'd like to organise whatever help you might need once you go home. Out into the real world.' She twittered again.

'Help?'

'You know, housework, sickness benefit, insurance payouts. That type of thing. My job is to ensure everything goes as smoothly as possible.'

'Oh.' Maya shifted her feet to where the bed was cool. She looked away, to the window and outside; the sky was empty. You could almost see through the blue of it.

Help? Maya didn't want help. She wanted to get out of this bed and this room, get dressed and go home. She wanted to drink coffee or wine (get drunk maybe), decorate the Christmas tree, make fruit mince pies from the recipe her mother had used (glued into the back of an exercise book and it was in her mother's own handwriting and every December Maya would sit at the table, open the book and run her fingers over the page. My mother's writing. It was all she had) and plan her holiday with Charlie.

'I really appreciate you coming to see me,' Maya said, and she made herself pull her eyes back from the window. 'But I can do this on my own. I don't need any help. We'll manage just fine.'

It was Gran's words coming out of her mouth. We'll manage just fine, and you could see her lipstick leaking into the lines around her tangerine lips. We don't need anyone's help, thank you. Charity. Maya couldn't help the words escaping her.

Charlotte's mouth was tight. 'You don't need to decide now. I know it's all a bit hard at the moment. You've got lots of things to think about. I'll come back just before you go home. You might have changed your mind by then.'

'You never know your luck.' Maya watched Charlotte clip clop out of her room and she heard her walk down the length of the ward. We'll manage, she told herself, and she turned back to the window. The blue of the sky went on forever. We'll be just fine. She almost had herself convinced.

'Why on earth didn't you accept that social worker's help?'

'I'm not sure, Kath. It's something about giving in, I think.'

Kathy placed a glass of water beside her. Maya watched a skinny slice of lemon floating on the surface.

'That's what you pay your taxes for.'

'Yeah, I know. But this is something I want to do on my own. As soon as I have someone doing things for me, I might as well curl up in a dark cupboard and give up.'

'So does that mean you don't want my help?'

Tiny teardrop-shaped cells of lemon sank to the bottom of the glass.

'No, that's different. I appreciate you more than anything. But it's when someone gets paid to help you with everyday things. That's where I draw the line.'

'It's a shaky-looking line from where I sit, Mrs Wimple.'

Maya smiled. 'You an' me against the world,' she sang, her voice feeble and faltering. 'Hey, didn't Helen Reddy have breast cancer, too?'

'I think it was Olivia Newton-John.'

Maya reached for her glass. She took a sip and set it down on the bedside table again. Her fingers left clear marks on the condensation. 'Still,' she said. 'It's a sign, isn't it? Don't you think?'

'Maya, are you decent?'

She looked over to the door, from her chair by the window. She had been looking out at the garden for hours, it seemed. Visitors had come and gone, nurses, delivery vans. She had watched a man pull a pair of secateurs from his back pocket, cut six roses off the sagging bushes, tie the stems together with a ribbon (from his front pocket) and go into Maternity.

'Hi, Rachael. Come in.'

She pulled a chair over in front of Maya and sat down, wiping at her top lip, pulling her skirt over her knees. 'Phew, it's hot out there.' She fanned her face with her wide hand. 'How are you?'

'Good, thanks. It's lovely to see you.'

'I wanted to wait until you were on the mend before I came to see you. There's nothing worse than having to entertain visitors when you're not feeling up to it.'

Good old Rachael. She always knew the right things to say. The right way to act.

'I've brought you some goodies.' She thrust an ice-cream container across to Maya. 'There's nothing better than home baking when you're a bit under the weather. Charlie likes my baking. My word, that boy can eat.'

Maya smiled. She felt a tingling across her chest. It was an old response, a fading memory of the let-down reflex, from when Charlie was a baby and thinking about him would produce milk from her heavy breasts. She would always be a mother.

'How's he been? I really appreciate your help.'

Rachael waved her hand between them. 'He's no problem. He's fitted in so well. Like another son. And I know he's loved mucking around with Gordon. You know, helping him fix things.'

'Oh.' The tingling was squeezing now, constricting into a fist inside her chest. 'That's nice,' she managed. 'I'm going home tomorrow. Did you know?'

'Oh, honey, I didn't. That's wonderful.' They sat there, saying nothing, comfortable with the silence, but even so, there was a slight unease between them. Maybe it was the hospital room, Maya thought. 'So, what's in here?' she said after a while. She prised the lid off the container, gasped. 'Railway biscuits.'

'What?'

'Railway biscuits. Are these railway biscuits?'

'They're hokey pokey biscuits. Caramel. I don't know – they've probably got lots of names.'

Maya found herself blinking, swallowing, pushing back sudden tears. 'My mother used to make these,' she said, and she brought the container close to her face. She breathed in. Sweet, buttery, the smell of warm golden syrup. 'We called them railway biscuits because when you flatten them on the tray with a fork, the pattern looks like train tracks.'

'That's a nice story.'

Maya leaned back in her chair. As much as she needed Rachael, they were a world apart. 'And we had bleeding eggs for poached eggs.'

'Eh?'

'The yolk – when you stab it, it bleeds onto the plate. And Titanic soup for potato chowder.'

'Now you've really got me, Maya.'

'The chunks of potato – like icebergs. You know.'

'But why Titanic?'

Maya sighed. 'Because the *Titanic* hit an iceberg.' She shouldn't have to explain these things. Wasn't it obvious? It was just as well she was going home. She'd have Charlie back. He'd be home again, where he belonged.

'What did I tell you? I knew we'd get you home well before Christmas.'

True enough, thought Maya. She zipped her small black case shut and stood it by the door. Her discharge letter, prescription and follow-up instructions were inside.

She sat in a chair by the window in shorts that had somehow got too big for her and a teeshirt that screamed out her disfigurement.

Kathy's voice boomed down the corridor.

'Anyone wanna get outa this joint?'

She smiled. A person could learn a lot from someone like Kathy. Then she heard Charlie's voice, whispering, certainly, but unaware of acoustics, sound tunnels and a mother's acute sense of hearing.

'Do I have to go home, Kathy? Why can't I stay at Jacob's? It's awesome there.'

Hi, Charlie, she practised in her head. Ready to go home?

Maya couldn't wait until Christmas morning. She was exhausted but she still couldn't wait.

'You know how I said we weren't going to have Christmas until January?' she said.

Charlie sighed extravagantly and paused the game on his Gameboy. He looked up. 'Yeah?'

'Well, I didn't think that was totally fair. I mean, Christmas is pretty special, isn't it?'

His finger hovered over the Play button. 'Yeah.'

'So if you go out the back, you'll find part of your Christmas present.'

'Cool.' He was off, still holding on to the Gameboy.

'That's all the Christmas there is until January, though.' Maya's voice followed him outside. She waited for the reaction, smiling in anticipation.

'Awesome, Mum.' His voice burst in from the back yard.

'Really?'

'Yeah.'

'Just don't break your neck on it, that's all.'

'This is cool, Mum. Thanks a million.'

She heard the thump thump of Charlie jumping on the trampoline's dark mat. Hey, yay, yeah, she heard. She smiled. Thank you, Rachael and Gordon, for putting it up for me, she thought. It was good to have friends who would do things for you. But it was hard to ask for help, breaking the habit of a lifetime. Be independent, girl, don't ask for charity. If you want something done – Gran's words were loud in her head.

Hey, yay, yeah. Charlie's voice was louder.

Eight

She held the appointment card between her thumb and fore-finger. She squeezed it until it bent, then it flicked away. It spun through the air as if in slow motion and she watched it flutter to the floor like one of those sycamore seeds – helicopters, Charlie called them.

Maya reached down to pick up the card. 'Aargh,' she grunted, as her knee pressed against her wound. Even though it was padded with a dressing (protected, hidden), the nerve endings there had been sheared off like poppies that had had their blooms cut, leaving the plants bare and bleeding, just stalks in the ground. Her hands moved to her chest, as though pressing against the place would stop the pain leaking out.

'Pick that up for me, would you, Charlie?'

He was sitting beside her, quiet and uncomfortable. He kicked his legs out, under, out, under, as though he might be on a swing.

'There you are,' he said. He resumed the kicking. Out, under, out, under. Stop it, Maya wanted to say. Sit still. She looked away to the opposite wall with its display of pamphlets and health warnings, but she could still see his legs moving. Stop it. She closed her eyes. His kicking was a rhythm that filled up his body, leaked out onto his chair, and onto hers, next to his in the long row of vinyl chairs. Out, under, out, under. Her chest prickled as the suture line damped itself down from the sharp pain of a moment ago.

A woman on the other side of the room jiggled her baby on her knee. *This is the way the lady rides, trippety trop, trippety trop.* The baby smiled and grabbed at the air with its fists. *This is the way the gentleman rides, gallop a trot, gallop a trot.* The woman's leg went higher and the baby began to laugh. Its fingers stretched out, then curled into themselves again. Maya smiled. Charlie had loved that game too.

This is the way the farmer rides, hobble de hoy, hobble de hoy. It was Philip's voice, warm and smooth as creamy soup. They were on the couch, Maya and Philip, close to each other like newlyweds. Philip held Charlie on his leg, his big hands encircling Charlie's tummy. Charlie's head bobbed around as Philip bounced his leg up and up and up. *Hobble de hoy, hobble de hoy.* Charlie laughed, no teeth, no hair. His smooth round face crinkled with delight. *Hobble de hoy, hobble de hoy.* And then Philip scooped Charlie inside his big arms and brought him up against him. He kissed his baby on the cheek, on his neck; he blew a raspberry on his bare chest.

Charlie squealed and laughed again. He balled his fists together and his open mouth found Philip's cheek and gave him a dry widemouthed kiss.

Maya brought her hand up to her face. She rubbed at the spot that tingled with the memory of how she imagined that kiss had felt.

'Maya?'

Hobble de hoy, hobble de hoy.

'Maya? Mr Gaskin's ready for you.'

'Mum.' Charlie was tugging at the leg of her trousers.

She opened her arms and looked down to pick up her baby and hold him close. How perfectly he fitted against her, his body against hers, one of her hands against his smooth head, her arm holding him in, in case he might slip away from her.

But this Charlie was slim, in cargo shorts and beach sandals and a teeshirt with a picture of a surfer on the chest. This Charlie had straight yellow hair, and his blue eyes were surely stolen from his father.

'Mum,' he said again, 'it's your turn.'

'What?' Maya shook her head. Memories and imaginings scattered around her and all that was left was reality.

She stood up, pressing the appointment card tightly in her hand. 'You wait here, buddy,' she said. 'I won't be long.' She smiled at him broadly – confidently, she was certain.

'Are you okay, Mum? You look weird.'

So much for looking confident, she thought, and she followed the nurse's quiet footsteps into Mr Gaskin's office.

The goldfish swam laps of their rectangular pool. Fluoro-green fishtank-sized palms swayed. The castle was still there, surrounded by coloured stones; it was still pink and orange, still absurd.

Mr Gaskin was probably finishing up with another patient, Maya thought. Delivering good news or bad or dictating a letter in another office. She sat quite still. She realised her hands were trapped under her thighs, pressing into the fabric of the chair.

The fish glided along like gulls that had caught a thermal. It looked effortless. You could barely see them move, not a twitch of their tail or a flutter of a side fin, and yet they slipped from one side of the tank to the other.

Maya closed her eyes. I'll see if I can swim like that when I get back into the pool, she thought. Flex my toes and I'll do ten metres. Stretch my feet out and I'll get halfway down the pool. She could feel the water on her skin. It enveloped her, warmed her yet at once made goosebumps on her arms.

This is the way the farmer rides.

She was at the deep end, her back against the smooth tiled edge. She watched Philip throw Charlie up into the air. Drops of water flew from his fat body as he flung his arms out. Would he fly? Did he know he couldn't? And then gravity was catching up with him and sending him down again and he would surely hit the surface of the water (*hobble de hoy, hobble de hoy*) and he was laughing. Charlie was always laughing, happy boy, danger baby, and what would happen when he went under? Would he inhale and fill his brand new lungs with water or would the sting of it force him to close off his throat, a reflex, the desire to live being stronger than the volition to drown? Down, down, falling in slow motion, laughing, gums pink and shiny, fingers stretched apart, the sensation of air across his palms, and there was Philip again, laughing too, catching this most precious of bundles, and slipping under the water with him, under with Charlie, and they were shimmery shadowy, disconnecting from her, from the surface, they were underworldly and she could see their hair float like yellow seaweed, like brown seaweed, and she wondered if they would ever breathe again.

They were still laughing when they broke through the surface, blinking, spitting out swimming pool water, Maya's merman and merbaby. Whee, she called out from where she stood, half crouched in the water, because she couldn't think of anything else to say.

The door opened then closed and Mr Gaskin sat down across the desk from her.

'Maya,' he said.

'Hello.' She blinked as if she was walking out from the movies in the middle of the day.

'How are you?'

'Fine, thanks.'

'I'm not just making conversation. I'd like to know.'

'Oh.' Mr Gaskin's soft cheeks wobbled. She blinked again. 'I'm tired, actually. But not too bad.'

'How long have you been at home now?' He picked up a pen and clicked the end of it, clicked it again. The nib shot out and retracted. Click click.

'A week, maybe. I'm not exactly sure. The days just race by when you're having this much fun.' She tried out a laugh. It was like a marble rattling inside an empty tin.

'Well,' said Mr Gaskin. Maya smiled. She'd been waiting for it. His first *well*. How long had it been? Two minutes? Stop it, she thought. That's not fair. It's just what he does. 'We'd better get these stitches out.'

He helped her onto the narrow bed in the office and covered her with a thin blanket. He folded it down to her belly, then turned to wash his hands. His shoulders had the roundness of a lifetime of bending over an opened-up body. He would hold out one hand and know that the scrub nurse (who had laid out a hundred shining and sterile instruments for him to use: scalpel handles onto which she would snap a fine blade, crocodile forceps, retractors like the head of a garden hoe) would place just the right one in his hand. All he had to do was apply it to the patient to crush, cut, separate, peel apart or burn away the body parts that had brought the person to him.

He might discuss the rugby or the cricket, depending on the month, may ask for the music (Vivaldi, Joni Mitchell, Dean Martin) to be played louder or more softly, more suction here please, may argue hospital politics or national politics, retract a little further nurse please, 3/0 silk on a curved needle if you would be so kind, he might think about the knots forming at the base of his neck, and although they hurt and he would dearly love to stop what he was doing and rub at the spot with the heel of his hand, clamp off that bleeder please, he carried on because this was what he did and this was his passion and the tightness between his shoulder blades was nothing compared with what the person in front of him had to deal with.

And afterwards he'd snap off his gloves (and they made exactly the same sound as the ones on ER as the doctors snapped them off wearily/triumphantly/in anger or desperation) and he'd stretch his spine back and his hand would reach to find the place and aah, that was better and a cup of tea sounded just like what the doctor ordered (ha ha) and thank you team for a job well done.

'Well,' said Mr Gaskin as he dried his hands on a rough paper towel. 'Not all my patients get their stitches taken out by the surgeon, you know.'

'Thank you.' Nervous, submissive, unsure whether he was trying to lighten the moment or making her aware of the widening gulf between them.

'These hands don't normally touch a patient unless there's a large amount of blood involved. Or money.'

'I hope that's not the case today.' Feeling braver now. Familiar banter.

'Oh, well, you never know your luck.' Mr Gaskin waved his fingers over Maya's body. 'Shall we?'

His fingers found her under the cotton blanket. They wriggled up her top and pressed here and here, either side of the gash where her breast had been. Maya turned to face the far wall over the top of Mr Gaskin's head. She could see individual hairs growing out of his scalp. She was sure she could count them if she wanted to.

Studying a poster there, fixed to the wall with yellow map pins. *Use it or lose it.* A picture of a cartoon man riding his bike, puffing and sweating, grinning, his hair sticking up around him. His shoes were untied and Maya could see that at any moment he'd get the laces caught up in the spokes of the wheel. That wasn't the point of the poster, she knew; it was just a humorous touch. But she could picture him pedalling pedalling and then the lace was sucked into the spokes, snatching up his foot, and now the wheel was jamming and he was falling to the side, tumbling onto the asphalt, grating the skin off his bare knees, his elbows, the side of his face.

He should have double-knotted his shoes, she thought. Two bunny ears, around and through the gap. Look at the trouble it would have saved.

Suddenly her breath caught in her throat. She gasped. She could see two white knees, skinned to the bone, just silvery fascia, and then pricks of blood appeared, as though they had been shocked momentarily and now they knew what they must do. The dots joined up to each other and the knees were now bathed in blood, swimming in it. It ran down his legs between the hairs there, becoming rivers, and the air that licked the wounds was electricity.

Mr Gaskin straightened up. 'Maya?'

She pulled her eyes away from the bleeding, broken man in the poster. 'Sorry. I'm okay.'

'Are you sure? Would you like a moment?'

'No, carry on.'

'Right then. The wound's looking good. You've healed well.' He opened up a tray on the trolley beside the bed. He folded back the fabric layers that both contained the tray and its contents, and kept them sterile. He poured saline into a dish. He peeled open a packet of cottonwool balls and they dropped onto the tray. As they hit the metal they may have made the sound of a mushroom expelling its spores.

Mr Gaskin, with his wide hands and neatly trimmed fingernails, dipped a wad of cottonwool into the saline and brought it cold and dripping up to Maya's skin.

She shivered as he ran it along the length of her wound, which was healed now, the raw edges snug against each other; they might have been sewn by machine.

A tag of suture material, nylon like fine fishing line, protruded from a knot at each end of the wound. The stitches themselves were under the surface, a magic trick whereby she was, indeed, sewn together but the stitches were not visible. It made a flat, fine suture line, as though Mr Gaskin had merely drawn across Maya's flat chest with a pink felt pen.

'Right,' he said, and he picked up a pair of fine-bladed scissors. He hooked one tip under the suture knot, and snip, it was undone. He held the inch of nylon in plastic forceps and snip, again, at the level of Maya's skin. The stitch was gone and now Maya was undone.

'Doing all right?' he asked. She nodded. *Use it or lose it*, she read from the poster. *Use it or lose it*. Loose. Sour. Tools. Trite. An old game, making words from the letters there. Making her brain play games, playing games on her brain. Giving it something else to think of, rather than the man who was kneeling over her, cutting away the line that kept her chest intact. Exposing her breast, and where her other breast had been. Dealing with it.

Sleet. Sour site. Trust.

And now her eyes were passing over the letters, white capitals against the green background of the hill that the man on the bike (still with his shoelaces undone) was climbing, flicking and flying, mixing up the letters and gasping and laughing and pulling herself up on their elbows as she formed the sentence: Loose tit ruse.

'Maya?'

Answering automatically, 'I'm sorry. It's okay,' and lying down again, against the hard bed and the hard pillow. Loose tit ruse.

There was just the problem of a spare 'I', Maya thought, but these were capital letters and you could pretend it was the number one, and so the sentence read: One loose tit ruse. Of course. Perfect.

One loose tit ruse.

Snip. Mr Gaskin cut the knot at the other end of the suture line, at her side under her arm. 'Right,' he said (again, again), 'I'll just pull this out and then we'll be done.'

Right. Maya glanced down and he was indeed pulling at the nylon tag. Tugging at it. Like when Maya had sat close to her mother on the couch holding the sewing basket while she unpicked the hem of a skirt or a pair of long pants that Maya had grown too tall for. See, dear, I just cut this end and the other end and then pull on the thread. Look how it's coming away, and it was, the hem magically separating itself. Look, we'll get another two inches from this. That'll see you through the winter. We'll use a false hem. And how remarkable that was. Bias binding sewn onto the bottom, turned over, pressed with a hot iron and, pffh, how it spat and snorted as it smoothed the fabric and creased its edge, and then the hem sewn by hand again with her mother's invisible stitches. All that work for a growing girl.

'Ow.' Maya looked down again. The stitch was caught somehow. It was taut in Mr Gaskin's forceps.

'Sorry, Maya, I'm going to have to pull a bit more. All right?'

She nodded, staring down at her flat chest, which was puckering now, gathering almost, as the suture material refused to give in, as it bit into her at every stitch. He pulled again, harder this time. Maya could see the effort in his face and in his hand as his fingers tightened against the plastic forceps.

'Ow,' she said again.

It would not budge. The nylon had somehow taken root in her, under the surface of her. Her healing wound had trapped the thread, as if to make sure it wouldn't come apart.

'Stop, please,' she whispered. Sweat tickled her top lip. She rubbed it away; her hand felt weak. Her flesh was burning as Mr Gaskin tried to tear the suture away from it. She was glad to be lying down.

'I'm sorry.' He sat back and wiped his brow with his forearm. He shook his head. 'You've healed too well, Maya. That's the problem. Shall we try again after a rest?'

That was all she wanted to do. Rest. Hide. Sleep. Wake up when this was all over, when she was better.

'Do you want some Entonox?'

Gas. To float, fly, be numbed, unconcerned. Not to recall the pain. For there was no problem with experiencing pain if afterwards you didn't remember it. Pain didn't matter if you had no memory of it.

'I have to drive home. And look after Charlie. No, we should just do it.' She smiled. 'But do you have a bullet I could bite on?'

'Let's have one more try and if we don't have any luck, I'll see if I can find one.'

He grasped the stitch with the forceps again and pressed against the wound with the other hand. 'I'm sorry,' he said. Maya dug her fingernails into her palms, squeezing each finger in turn, counting, one two three four one two three four. She pressed her tongue against the roof of her mouth until the muscles under her jaw ached. 'I'm sorry,' Mr Gaskin said again.

Maya thought the skin on her chest would be torn away, ripped from the flesh underneath, and that in turn would be pulled off her ribs. One two three four. One loose tit ruse. *Hobble de hoy, hobble de hoy*. The stitch screamed underneath her tender wound.

And then finally it was breaking free, separating itself from the scar tissue that was growing around it. It was a chain reaction, apart apart apart along its length like the climb of a rollercoaster on its first uphill, except that was the wheels catching, holding on, and this was the wound yielding.

Mr Gaskin's arm shot back as the nylon slid out of Maya's body and the thread arced up and back and it really might have been a fishing line and Mr Gaskin was in waders, thigh high in a quiet stream.

He rocked back, then righted himself. 'There,' he said, and he stared at the suture material dangling limply from the forceps. 'That wasn't so bad, was it?'

Nine

The clock on Maya's bedside table glowed its red numbers. 7:24. She couldn't make out what it meant. Three numbers in any order but right now they were lined up to read 7:24. Her brain, fluffy with the ragged edges of a dream and warm from sleep, clicked and whirred and began to work out the significance of the digits.

7:24. That meant either first thing in the morning (get up, get dressed, brush your hair, go downstairs, put the jug on, cajole Charlie into getting some clothes on) or evening (dishes done, Charlie in bed reading, sitting down with a glass of wine and reading the paper). But which was it?

How did it feel? Maya could rely on her body to give her the answers. Usually. Although it was starting to let her down, she thought. It felt like nighttime. If it was 7:24 p.m. it would still be light and warm (and how hot this Gisborne summer was turning out). But wait a minute. 7.24 a.m. would be light and warm too. Summer was a crafty player. Okay, body, are you ready for the day or ripe for sleep?

Her limbs were heavy, tingling slightly. Her mouth was dry. Her eyes itched. She felt a heaviness, an end-of-the-day tiredness settle over her. So it was evening. But that meant she'd been asleep all day. And all the night before. How could she have been in bed nearly twenty-four hours? What had Charlie been doing all day while she was lying there, cotton-pyjamaed, unconscious? Had he eaten? Was he safe?

She sat up with a start, a reflexive move that found her suddenly upright. 7:24. And then she realised it was morning. The sun was up already, at work with its yellow rays that had already heated up her bedroom. The TV was on downstairs. The air was silent; the birds had all gone out.

Maya looked over at her bedside table again. 7:25.

And today was the day she and Charlie were to celebrate Christmas.

'I'm starting chemotherapy on Monday,' she had said, 'so let's have Christmas before that.'

'What's chemotherapy?' They had been sitting on the sand, their small piece of Waikanae beach. There was noise all around them: dogs chasing seagulls, children shrieking as they jumped up in the surf to avoid the waves that slapped at their summer bellies, a car stereo thumping from the carpark. It pressed in around them, but Maya and Charlie might have been alone.

'It's special medicine that kills all the bad cancer in me.' It sounded so simple.

Charlie drew circles in the sand with a piece of driftwood. It was gnarled and knotted like an old man's finger.

'I thought they'd cut out all the cancer stuff when you had your operation.' Round and round, the stick that was a white bone mounding up a bank of sand.

'Well, they got everything they could see. But sometimes a tiny bit breaks off and travels around the body. It sets up camp somewhere else.' Maya looked out to sea. The horizon was a straight line between blue and blue. 'And the chemotherapy medicine kills it.'

Now Charlie drew lines out from the edge of the circle. Sand flicked up as he pulled the stick out.

'That's good, eh, Mum? So everything will be okay after that.'

'Well, that's the plan. Now, are you going to have a swim?'

'Okay.' He stood up and pulled off his teeshirt. His slight body was tanned. He ran down the beach and into the surf, running, running until the water was up to his chest, and then he let himself fall forwards, face down into the water. A second later he surfaced, his hair plastered to his head, waving back up the beach, smiling, laughing, and Maya thought her heart might break.

How did we get to this place? she thought. She looked down at the sand, at individual grains that sparkled and glittered among tiny fragments of crushed white shells. She felt a lump begin in her throat. It swelled, threatening to cut off her air supply. She swallowed, tried to push it down. I will not cry, she thought. She closed her eyes. There was glittering orange and red in front of her. I will fight this. I can I will I can I will.

But a voice in her head was taking over, pushing her to the edge of a cliff. She was burying her toes in the soft grass there and spreading her arms out wide. Sea wind gusted up the jagged wound of the cliff and fanned her hair around her face. She tipped her head back and opened her mouth wide. She tasted cold air on her tongue and salt and she heard a woman's cry. Long, low, like a moan, like the sound a woman might make as she expelled her child from inside her, out into the world. She was standing on the edge, right there, and she was swaying, groaning, catching herself in the wind, there, there and the voice was pushing her, urging her to step forward one foot in front of the other now now and she didn't know if she could stop herself.

Maya opened her eyes. There was the circle in the sand with straight lines sticking out of it like the sun's rays and the piece of driftwood discarded beside it. She picked it up. It was cool, smooth in spite of its knuckles. Where had it come from? she wondered. How many waves, how many grains of sand had softened its edges?

She drew two dots inside the circle, here and here, and a semi-circle underneath, a wide smile. It looked like a lion, and the sun's rays were its mane. She added a round body, four legs and a long swishy tail. And now a speech bubble. ROAR, she wrote with the stick. She tipped her head back and the heat of the sun, so many millions of miles and years away, hit her face.

She looked back out to sea and watched Charlie bodysurfing. Again and again he let himself skim onto the beach, caught on the edge of a wave, knowing how to carry his body in, and he came to rest, his face splashed with grainy sand and seawater, and then he ran out again to catch another.

Today they were having Christmas and Monday was chemo day. Day One. It was just like in a children's story, Maya thought. Everything began on Mondays. She stretched out, pointing her toes and reaching her right arm up over her head, fingers splayed wide. She rested her left arm across her chest where it protected and shielded her healing wound. She contracted the muscles in her legs, her belly, her shoulders and allowed them to relax.

She was almost pain free. Of course she couldn't hang out washing, or lift bags of groceries, or garden (and the weeds had become more vigorous, as if they knew her frailties), but she knew that every hour she was without pain meant she was improving.

Five minutes more and then I'll get up.

'Mum.'

Close your eyes.

'Mum.' Louder.

Pretend you're asleep.

Running up the stairs, sounding like a rabbit, or how you imagine a rabbit to sound as it hops to its burrow in its smart blue coat, furry arms full of lettuce and parsley.

Arrange yourself to look asleep.

'Mum!' Charlie landed on Maya's bed with a thump and bounced up the length of her bed. Her pain-free morning was over. She groaned and opened her eyes. There was Charlie's face, inches from her. She could smell chocolate breath. Push it away, she thought. The pain. (Just an ache.) I can I will. She smothered the stabbing in her chest with a blanket, stemming its oxygen supply.

'Guess what Father Christmas brought me?' His lips were lined with chocolate.

'Did he come?' she asked. Teasing, she knew.

'Yeah.'

'So he must have got our note.'

'Yeah.'

'I'm surprised he brought you anything. Doesn't he only give presents to good girls and boys?' Smiling now, blowing away the smoke of the pain.

'M-u-m!'

'What did you get, buddy?'

'Well,' Charlie began and he crawled in beside Maya and curled up against her. Don't ever grow up, she thought suddenly. Always believe in Father Christmas. Always be my little boy. And then the thought was gone, swirling away out her open bedroom window on a smudge of ash.

'I'll get you to help me,' Maya said. How quickly she tired. Anaesthetic, she told herself. It takes six months to clear itself from your body. It's stored in the fat cells. As if she was explaining it to a patient. But she was, and the patient was her. She sat down at the table. 'I'll give you orders from here,' she said. She put on her military voice. 'Orange juice, soldier.'

'Yessir,' Charlie shot back.

'Breakfast bowls, soldier.'

'Yessir.'

'Toast into the toaster, soldier.'

'Yessir.'

'Be careful, soldier.'

'Yessir.'

She watched him carry the breakfast things outside to the table on the deck. An old gnarled orange tree grew beside the deck. It had been there forever. Hairy green lichen splattered its trunk and winding branches.

'Fairy fruit,' Charlie called from the deck. He ran back to her, his arms full of oranges. Fairy fruit. He was nearly two when he had first discovered that oranges had fallen on the deck and table during the night. Fairy fruit, he'd called them. Except he'd pronounced it 'fairwee fwoot'. Maya smiled and felt that tingle across her chest as she thought of him, with his unsteady walking legs and an orange as big as a soccer ball between his fat hands.

He placed the oranges before her. She picked one up. It was warm. 'Smell it,' she said.

'Orangey,' Charlie said.

'Yeah, I suppose it is,' Maya laughed. 'Do you know that no one has seen inside this particular orange?'

'No one in the whole wide world?'

'That's right. So when we peel it, we'll be the first people to see the middle of this orange. Weird, eh?' She ran her fingers over it. Tiny pinholes puckered its surface. Ha. One of the warning signs of breast cancer, she thought suddenly, her student nursing notes there before her eyes. Signs and symptoms: palpable lump (and, absurdly, the word palpable made her think of bread dough and insects' sticky legs), discharge from nipple, orange skin appearance of breast.

It was all there in her own handwriting, on lined A4 sheets, ring-bindered and filed away. Why hadn't she remembered it? How had she let herself down? She should have picked it earlier. Any decent nurse would have detected the lump sooner.

But this was Christmas morning in January, and Maya was holding on to an orange from the tree in her back yard. Post-operative, but yet to begin treatment. One foot out of the water, the other dipping in, toes first.

'What next?' said Charlie, beside her. She jumped, suddenly aware of the drift her mind had taken. Her thoughts were like wind skipping over sand dunes, planting grains of sand at points of low resistance.

'Let's eat,' said Maya. 'Oh, wait,' she said as they sat down at the table. They were framed by the branches of the orange tree. It reached over them like an old man leaning on a cane. Lavender brushed the edge of the deck. Bees swarmed drunkenly. 'We need champagne,' and she was back with a bottle of sparkling wine and two long-stemmed glasses.

'Really?' said Charlie. His eyes were wide and disbelieving.

'You can't have Christmas breakfast without champagne. It's my new tradition.'

She filled one glass, waiting for the bubbles to subside before topping it up. She splashed just enough wine in Charlie's glass so he would be impressed with being allowed alcohol, then filled it up with orange juice.

She took the orange he had brought her and cut it into fine slices. It spat bitter oil into her eye as she cut it. She dropped a slice into each of their glasses.

'Is this okay?' said Charlie.

'Absolutely.'

'Cool, Mum.' She picked up her wine. Charlie watched her and did the same. They clinked their glasses together. How festive the sound was. How celebratory. How subtle.

'Cheers, big ears,' she said.

'Cheers, Mum.'

They each took a sip.

'What do you think?'

Charlie screwed up his small nose. 'It's a bit, I dunno, weird,' he said.

'Yes, I suppose it is.' She held a swallow of wine in her mouth. Tiny bubbles exploded over her tongue and the insides of her cheeks. It *was* weird, this sharp taste that made your words thick and your head wander.

'But it's okay,' said Charlie, as though he needed to convince himself.

'It'll just be a once-a-year tradition.' He looked relieved and his glass stayed there, on the wooden slatted table, untouched for the rest of the morning.

'Okay, then,' said Maya. She put down the magazine she had been reading. A Bumper Christmas Edition. Full of Festive Table Arrangements and Entertaining Ideas. She'd tried to read the articles, a short story, the gossip even, but her mind refused to stay in one place. It was a lost child, wandering aimlessly, calling out for help, looking for landmarks. 'Hands up who wants to go to the park,' she said.

'Can I bring my Gameboy?'

'I don't think so. I don't want you getting obsessed with that thing. It's not healthy. We could take your cricket gear, though, and I'll be Richard Hadlee.'

'Who?'

'Never mind.'

She packed up a picnic – a hasty combination of tomato sandwiches, Toffee Pops, lemonade and apples. She brushed her hand over a bowl of avocados on the bench, huge bulbous fruit from the tree by the garage. Bright green to purple-black, they were in all stages of readiness. She selected one and dropped it in the picnic basket, along with a packet of water crackers, and then they were ready.

'You used to love this park when you were little,' she said as they pulled up by the park's stone memorial gates. 'Especially the slide. You were such a danger baby.'

Charlie looked over at the red and yellow plastic slide. Maya wondered if he could remember climbing up the ladder in blue gumboots and knitted beanie with a pompom that bounced in time to his steps. He was so little, with his brand new legs and fat hands that gripped the rungs of the ladder. Wheee, he called as he skidded down the slide, and his small legs flew up in the air and he slid down on his back. Bump, he said as he landed on the bark chips at the bottom. Again, Mummy, again. Here, I'll help you. Not need you, he'd said, and he frowned, his mouth tight across his face. Not need you, Mummy.

But now he was nearly nine and the slide held no attraction. He ran to the climbing frame and grabbed the bars. He swung along, like Action Man, or maybe he was George of the Jungle.

'Let me know when you want to play cricket,' Maya called, and she unfolded her low beach chair and settled in, the warmth of the breakfast champagne still around her.

There's only so much of Hey Mum, look at this, and Watch me do this, Mum, you can take, she thought. She rummaged in her bag for her cellphone and keyed in Kathy's number.

'Merry Christmas,' Maya said into the little black phone.

'Eh?'

'Merry Christmas.'

'Look, Maya, I hate to tell you this, but Christmas was last month. You're falling behind.'

'Very funny,' said Maya. 'Charlie and I are celebrating Christmas today. We're at the park. I wondered if you'd like to join us.'

'That sounds nice. Shall I bring some wine?'

'You're the girl for me,' said Maya. 'See you soon.' She snapped her phone shut. It fitted inside the palm of her hand. She turned back to Charlie, who was hanging by his knees, upside down on the bars. She tipped her head back, placing her sunhat over her face. She closed her eyes and laced her fingers together across her flat belly. She felt like an old woman. Probably look like one, too, she thought.

She wanted to go to sleep. She could feel her body yielding, falling under the spell. I'll just doze. Just for a moment.

But what about Charlie? What if he falls and hurts himself? Gets stuck and can't get down? What if he is abducted? Kidnapped, left for dead in a ditch, held for ransom?

He was so little. He needed her to look after him for years yet. Needed her to be his mother for longer still.

Her head jerked forward and her hat fell onto the grass. I'll sleep tonight, she thought.

'Help is at hand,' came a voice from behind her, as fresh as an opened window. She turned around and there was Kathy.

'Hooray,' called Maya in a Famous Five voice. 'I hope you brought glasses.'

'I even remembered a corkscrew. Impressed?' She sat on the rug next to Maya's beach chair and nodded towards the climbing frame. 'What's monkey boy doing?'

'Just hanging around.'

They both groaned, then laughed. You are just what I need, thought Maya. She went to say it but stopped, afraid that the ease would be lost if it was articulated.

'Are you allowed wine?' said Kathy. Quietly now, serious.

'I think a glass for medicinal purposes would be all right. I am a nurse, remember.'

'All righty, then,' said Kathy. She opened the wine, a bottle of Gisborne chardonnay. 'A fine little local brew,' she said. She poured it into the long-stemmed plastic glasses. It was yellow, like Lemon and Paeroa, Maya thought. Straw tinged, like –

'Looks like a urine sample,' said Kathy.

'Did you know that Charlie doesn't know who Richard Hadlee is?' said Maya. They were halfway through their second glass of wine. The day was hotting up. She could feel her teeshirt sticking to her back. The tips of her fingers tingled.

'Is that a problem?' said Kathy.

'No. It's just that – I dunno.' Maya swirled her wine around in the glass. It lapped against the sides, then fell back. 'I want him to know everything that's important. You know, I want him to be able to have it all.'

'And Richard Hadlee is part of that?'

'Not really, but you know what I mean.' Why did Kathy so often take the opposite side? Devil's advocate.

'Look, with all due respect to Richard Hadlee, I don't think Charlie's education will suffer terribly if he isn't able to name all the famous cricketers of our generation. There are plenty of things we don't know from our parents' lives.'

'Yes, I know, but –' said Maya. She knew Kathy was right. But that was partly the point. Wasn't it her duty to impart all these things to Charlie? If Philip was alive, he would have explained who Richard Hadlee was, long before. The difference between a leg spinner and an off spinner. A googlie.

She should tell him these things. Being mother and father. Gatherer and hunter. Mender and carpenter. Cook and bicycle coach.

She remembered all those hours jogging alongside Charlie on his bike, holding on to the back of his seat. Round round round she said, and his thin legs pumped up and down, pushing the pedals round round round and she eased her grip but didn't let him know, round round, good boy Charlie you're doing well, and she took her hand away and there was nothing connecting her to him or him to her and still his legs worked up and down up and down, good boy you're doing it you're on your own.

She would be keeping Philip's memory alive if she taught Charlie all the things he would have. Ensuring he got the greatest opportunities. Opportunities she never had, spending Saturday mornings feeding sheets and towels through the wringer of Gran's fat washing machine and Saturday afternoons pulling weeds from her flower garden.

Marigold, aster, viola, portulaca. 'But I can identify any annual from its seedling,' she said. 'And tell you its ideal conditions.'

'Well, good for you,' said Kathy, emphasising each word. 'Now, let's eat.'

After lunch they played cricket. Charlie was the batter, stamping his bat into the ground like they did on TV. Maya threw the ball, keeping her left arm tucked into her chest like a bird with a broken wing. She had no run-up, but even so she was surprised how the ball flew from her hand, straight to Charlie. She was a girl again, skipping, playing hopscotch. Kathy stood to the side, running to the outfield to retrieve Charlie's hits. 'Four,' she called as she jogged back with the ball and passed it to Maya.

'Can't you bowl properly, Mum?'

'Sorry, buddy. This is as good as it gets right now.'

'I wish I had someone else in my team,' said Charlie.

'We could play something else,' said Maya, 'and come back another day with Jacob. I tell you what. I've heard about a group that's all women who have had the same operation as me. Maybe we could get together with all their families and have a picnic here one day.'

'A whole lot of sick people? That doesn't sound like much fun,' Charlie said. 'Can we go home now?'

Fun. That was the currency: the means of getting on in life when you were eight. Nearly nine. 'Good idea,' Maya said. She handed

Charlie the picnic rug and he ran to the car with it stretched between his wide arms. It flapped like a cape, like wings.

For a low-key Christmas, especially one in January, it had been a big day. Charlie was asleep in his bed, arms flung wide, his new radio-controlled car, fresh out of the box, on the pillow beside his head. The Gameboy rested at his side.

Maya sank into her bed. It washed over her, swallowed her up. She spread her arms out like Charlie. The sheets were cool against the backs of her fingers. Maybe she would sleep as freely as he did. She thought about the rectangular wooden planter box sitting by the back door. How perfectly it fitted in the space by the steps.

'I made it at Jacob's,' Charlie had said.

'It's awesome, buddy.'

'Jacob's dad helped me. When you were – you know.' And he wound a length of green ribbon round and round his finger. 'But I painted it all by myself.'

'This is the best present ever,' Maya said. 'You can help me choose what plants go in it.'

Should we get perennials or annuals? Maya wondered. Biennials? Rosemary for remembrance. Lily-of-the-valley for the return of happiness. Zinnias for thoughts of someone absent. Stop it. Just stop it.

Maybe tulips, she thought as she fell asleep.

Ten

It's time, thought Maya, although she didn't want to admit it. Wanted even less to have the conversation.

'Charlie,' she said to her son's straight back. He was sitting on the bottom step by the back door and his new radio-controlled car flew off a wooden ramp, a piece of timber left over from the planter box project, held up at one end by a cardboard box. It sailed through the air, small wheels whirring and spinning uselessly, then it was overcome by gravity and fell, front bumper first, onto the dry summer grass.

'Awesome,' said Charlie. He pushed the lever on the control box and the car bumped along the grass, spun a tight circle and stopped at his feet.

'Can I borrow you?' said Maya. Nice and natural.

'Okay.' The car skidded away along the edge of the grass.

'Can you put that down for a minute?' There was always competition.

Charlie shrugged. 'Okay.' He placed the control box on the step next to his foot. Maya saw him slide his foot along so it was touching the box. As if he needed the physical contact to know it was still there.

She sat down on the step. She pulled her knees up, rested her cheek on her knee and looked at Charlie next to her.

'You are unbelievably amazing,' she said.

'Oh, Mum.' He wriggled, rubbed his foot against the control box. I don't mean to be gushy, Maya thought. It just happens. She couldn't help her thoughts and when it came to Charlie she couldn't help the words that followed.

'Sorry,' she said, 'but you are.' She breathed deeply, blew it out. 'And I'm sorry about Christmas. You know, having to put it off till now.' Parenthood was jammed full of apologies. Always trying to make it right, kiss it better. Never quite achieving it though.

'That's okay,' said Charlie. 'It didn't matter.'

Breathe again. Blowing out the fear and trembling through pursed lips. 'You understand about me being sick, don't you?'

'Yeah, I guess.'

'You know I've got cancer.'

'Yeah.' Rub, rub, his bare toes against the smooth plastic of the control box.

'And I have to start chemotherapy on Monday.'

'Yeah, I know all this, Mum.' Rub, rub.

'Sorry, buddy.' (Another apology.) 'I just need to make sure you know what's going on. We're a team, remember.'

Charlie ran his fingers along the edge of the control box. 'So is that it?'

'Almost. I just need to tell you that the chemotherapy – the medicine that's going to gobble up any bits of leftover cancer – well, it's probably going to make me quite sick as well.'

'That doesn't make sense,' said Charlie. 'You're taking medicine to make you better, but it's going to make you sick?'

Maya smiled in spite of it all. Children were so wise. When did that wisdom fade into complacency? she wondered.

'You're right,' she said. 'It doesn't make sense. It's a bit like cough medicine. That doesn't taste very nice but it gets rid of the cough. And we don't mind taking yucky medicine if it's going to make us better, eh? Anyway, the chemo won't make me sick for long. I'll probably be mostly tired. But do you know what else it does?' She tried to sound light-hearted.

'What?'

111

'It's going to make my hair fall out. Funny, eh?'

'Why does it do that?' Charlie looked at her with narrowed eyes.

'Well, it's quite hard to explain. But as the chemo is going around my body gobbling up all the cancer, it happens to gobble up the cells that make your hair stay in your head.'

'Weird.' The radio-controlled car's windscreen caught the reflection of the sun. It glinted with yellow rays.

'So I'm going to lose my hair.'

'All of it?'

'Yep.'

'Weird.'

'I just wanted to warn you. So you don't get a fright when it happens.'

'Okay.'

'And I've decided to have Kathy come and stay for a while. How does that sound?' How cheerful she sounded and how trivial she made the treatment seem.

'Couldn't I go back to Jacob's? It's awesome there. He's got cool toys. And his dad lets me help him in his shed.' Charlie's fingers closed around the forward/backward lever on the control box. He nudged it forward. The car whirred but didn't move. Its wheels were stuck on a stone.

'That'd be a nice idea,' said Maya carefully. She could feel him slipping away from her. It was as though she was holding on to him as he dangled over a cliff edge. Their hands were sliding apart and he would plunge to the rocks at any second. Or was it *her* hanging off the edge, holding on by her fingertips? 'To tell you the truth, Charlie, I won't want to be by myself once I start the chemo. It'll be kind of like me needing a mother, someone to look after me.'

'I could do that,' he said. He looked up at her, the first time since the conversation had started. He still had the face of a baby. Firm soft skin, big eyes and dark eyelashes. She saw him as a baby, in his cot, following with his watching eyes the circus animals of his musical mobile, and as a toddler, kneeling on the grass, studying a worm.

'I thought of that,' said Maya. 'You're such a clever guy. But you need to enjoy your holidays. You don't want to be looking after your crook old mother. Anyway, Kathy's a nurse. She's used to sick people. And that's what aunties are for. Helping out in times of need. It's in their job description.' She paused, watching his face. How far should she go? How much should she tell?

'Okay,' said Charlie. 'Hey, watch what cool tricks this car can do.'

'Sure.' That was it, then: the conversation was over. He had taken as much as he needed, as much as he could handle. But did he really understand? She would have to trust him. We can do this, she told herself.

It felt like the night before an exam. School C, or State Finals. There was that fluttering, the beating of butterfly wings inside her. There was tingling that rose from her belly, up to her tight throat. There was her breath that shuddered from her mouth.

Maya licked her lips. Even her tongue trembled. She had the house to herself. It was so quiet. She was tempted to turn on the TV, the stereo, something. Resist the temptation, she told herself. Enjoy the silence. Face it.

Charlie had gone to Jacob's for the night.

'I don't want to have to be worrying about him on the morning of my first chemo,' Maya had said to Rachael.

'Of course not. One extra at teatime, another boy to tuck in; it won't be any worry. Fine and dandy. You need to nurture yourself at a time like this.'

'Well, I don't know about nurturing myself, but if I'm a mess, or I lose it or anything, I'd rather Charlie wasn't around.'

'Good as gold,' said Rachael.

She'd dropped him off at Jacob's mid-afternoon. 'I'll see you tomorrow afternoon.'

'Okay, Mum.'

'I love you to bits,' she said, and she hugged him as though her life depended on it. 'You'll be okay, buddy?'

'Yeah, Mum.'

'You've got Honey Bear, haven't you?'

'Yeah, he's in my bag.'

'Well, see ya, then.'

'See ya.'

She went to her bedroom window and opened the curtains. Rogue shadows streamed across her floor. The street was empty. The houses that lined the street were blacked out, asleep for the night. The streetlights, one here, one here, burned silently, patiently anticipating a car, a pedestrian, something.

This was the first night she'd spent in this house alone, she realised. And quickly thinking, how will it be tomorrow? She stretched out her arm and looked at the crisscross of blue-grey veins that ran from wrist to elbow. Good veins for chemo. She'd never liked giving blood, being injected. Never mind that she did it to her patients every day, but to have to experience the sting and drag of a needle herself . . . It's no worse than standing on a prickle, she told herself, or catching the back of your hand on a rose thorn. It just slides into the vein. Surely.

Think of the drugs finding every straying cancer cell and swallowing them up, drowning them with their harsh poisons. Think of that.

And the nausea. It will be like morning sickness, a side effect that means the baby is strong/the chemo is working.

What else? Tiredness. But Maya was tired already, had been for months, she realised. Ah, hindsight.

Hair loss.

She was suddenly nine years old, creeping across the cold wooden floor to her mother's bedroom. She had woken from a nightmare, where the faces of her friends were huge and distorted on tiny slouched bodies. It was instinctual to seek comfort from her mother.

She was a woman who rested each afternoon, from lunchtime

114

until Maya came home from school. Maya brought tea and short-bread on a tray to her room and sat on the end of the bed while her mother sipped the tea and asked about school.

She was pale, glamorous, like a movie star. Maya never saw her without lipstick, thick and red, right to the corners of her mouth. And her hair was silver curls, like clouds around her face.

Maya shivered with the cold of the floor. The lace around the hem of her flannelette nightie tickled her ankles. She would just creep into bed with her mother, curl up next to her, and the nightmare would stay away.

She pushed open her mother's door. She could see the shape of her, asleep, folded up in her bed. She took a step forward, and another, then stopped, still, frozen with a fear that was worse than any nightmare.

Her mother's head, with its billow of silver hair, sat on her dressing table.

Maya opened her mouth to scream but no sound came out. Her chest was slammed shut, she could feel it. She stared at her mother's head. She tried to drag her eyes away, but they, like her throat and her chest and her legs, were paralysed.

Eventually she found she could breathe, and that was when she began to scream.

It was all like a bad slapstick movie, Maya thought now as she looked out the window onto the quiet street.

Her mother had woken up with the sound of Maya screaming and had leapt out of bed. She had continued to screech, fists in tight balls at her side. Her mother was there now, behind her, with her arms pressing tightly around the small girl, pushing away whatever fear had struck her. She turned around because she had to and she hid in the warmth of her mother's misshapen chest. She could feel her mother's one soft breast against her head, spongy and warm, and if she moved her head just so, there were the hard lines of her ribs where her other breast should be. The screams became sobs, and then gasps.

She looked up, there in the dim of her mother's bedroom (but what would she see when she did look – her mother like the

115

headless horseman, shoulders and the beginnings of her narrow throat and then nothing?). She found she had more courage than she knew and she let her eyes slide up, up the fabric of her mother's nightie (tiny rosebuds, she could remember it still), up to the soft lace, to the sharp jut of her collarbone, to the hollow at the base of her throat, up, up to her mother's beautiful face.

It was miraculously there, attached to her body: her eyes, her marvellous lips that were stained with the colour of her daytime lipstick, her pale, pale skin.

And then Maya's eyes went up to the top of her mother's head, to her hair that was cottonwool, candyfloss, spiders' webs glittering with dew, but there was nothing. Her mother was bald. Her round head was shining.

This was almost as shocking as her mother's head on her dressing table. Confusing.

'Go to bed, now,' her mother whispered, and she squeezed Maya and then released her. Maya shivered and tiptoed across the cold floor back to her bed. She lay there for the longest time, trying to make sense of it all. Wondering if she had made it up, dreamt it. Was it part of the nightmare that had sent her to her mother's room in the first place?

Maya smiled, remembering her mother at breakfast the next day. Dressed, made up, hair done, immaculate. And the night before was never spoken of.

She went to the mirror. She pulled her hair back off her face, tight behind her head. Her eyes looked huge, child-like. She remembered when she was a student nurse in the oncology ward. Going into her patients' rooms and saying good morning and seeing the hair that haloed their heads around their pillows. Sometimes a few strands, sometimes handfuls of hair lay there and she was quick to brush them away with her hand and into the rubbish bin.

She watched the hairs settle among the paper towels and disposable gloves in the bin. And the patients were left with random tufts of hair; they were like Hiroshima survivors and some-how they always looked more desperate, more pathetic like that.

'Right,' Maya said to the woman in the mirror. She picked up her brush and ran it through her hair, again and again, until it rose up with static electricity and her arm ached.

'Right,' she said again, louder this time. More insistent. She pulled the scissors from the middle drawer of her dresser. Nursing scissors, from a million years ago, when she first began her training. M Bridgeman, engraved along the side. How many pieces of tape have these cut? she wondered. Shirt sleeves from broken arms, packets of bandage, bloodied hair. The tips were an open mouth where, after being sharpened so many times, they no longer met. Still, she thought.

She slipped her thumb and middle finger through the holes and raised the scissors to her head. She saw her hand tremble in the mirror. I can, she said as she steadied herself. I can do this. She picked up a handful of hair with one hand (which was it? In the mirror she couldn't tell) and positioned the shiny blades around it. She closed her eyes, held her breath. She could hear her pulse in her ears. She tightened her hand and the blades drew together. Schwoop as they cut through the strands of hair.

She pulled her hand away, the one holding her hair, and it came away easily. She held it in front of her and there it was, her disembodied hair falling across her hand like lengths of ribbon. She laid it on her dresser.

'Okay,' she said, and the sound of her voice and the sight of her hair lying there like a scarf made her strong. She picked up another handful. It would be easier this time, she thought, and of course it was.

Soon her head was all uneven spikes, like the sun's rays, and her dresser was covered with a cloud of soft hair. It isn't mine any more, she thought, and she swept it into the palm of her hand. She scrunched it down and pushed it tight, then she opened her hand and it sprang out like dandelion fairies.

Now what? She watched herself, this strange woman. She shook her head one way, then the other. How light her head felt. How cool. How free.

But the job wasn't finished. She went to the bathroom and filled the sink with hot water. She rubbed soap between her wet hands until they were slippery, then rubbed her hands over her head. A thousand ends against her palms. They were strangely soft. The soap was a thick layer on her head, like a bathing cap.

Was this how you were supposed to do it? She'd never shaved her head before. (Of course she hadn't. Why would she?) Legs, underarms, yes, and she had made smooth the surfaces of countless patients. Bellies, chests, genitals. But oddly, she'd never shaved a head.

She picked up her razor. A few thick underarm hairs clung to its dangerous blade. She swished the razor in the sink and made small waves that slapped against the sides of the basin.

'Okay, then,' she said, and she raised the blade to her head.

Under the shower, with the water too hot, she let the spray of water pound at her face. She breathed through an open mouth. I am like a fish, she thought, and the water was on her eyes, her cheeks, her lips, yet she breathed still. She made small noises huh huh as a defence against the hot, hot water. She tipped her head forward. The water was on her newly bare scalp, raining down on her head. The sensation made her gasp. She grabbed the shower curtain to steady herself. Stinging, stabbing, a million burning needles pierced her head. The water was less than an inch from her brain.

Eleven

They turned into the hospital carpark in Kathy's yellow Mini.

'Are we staff or patients today?' said Kathy. She pointed to a sign at a fork in the driveway. This way for staff, that way for patients.

'Patients,' said Maya. 'It's closer.' The garden between the carpark and the hospital buildings, tucked at the base of a brown and barren hill, was bursting with pansies. Their huge faces, yellow, brick, purple, blue, pressed against one another, cheek to cheek, petal to petal. A tight edge of trimmed buxus bordered the path to the entrance.

'Nice scarf, by the way,' Kathy said as she manoeuvred into an empty park.

'Thanks.'

'Any reason for it?'

'No,' said Maya. 'None that I can think of.' She got out of Kathy's small car and stood beside it, waiting for Kathy to lock the doors. She held her bag to her chest.

Outpatients.

This was where a thousand bleeding and broken patients came to be treated in the emergency department. Where a thousand more came to be seen, examined, diagnosed and advised at clinics. And where another throng came to be treated on chemo day in the day ward.

The hospital smelt different when you were a patient, she thought. Sour. It was noisier, too, brighter. The nurses laughed louder, their mouths stretched across their faces. Their badges were garish ornaments. Doctors' coats were as white as snow blindness; their beepers squealed constantly. The staff all knew where they were going, what they had to do.

Maya stopped at the day ward door. Kathy nudged forward.

'Hi, Jane,' she said to the nurse sitting at a desk lined with patients' charts. Red vinyl-covered stories, lined up in order.

'Hello, guys.' She stood up and took Maya's arm, guided her to a bed. The covers were stretched tight across its belly. Maya dropped her bag beside the bed and sat down in a La-Z-Boy chair that was covered with a thick drawsheet – a stiff thick sheet usually tucked under a bed-bound patient in case of a wet bed, or worse. Here, it would stop tiny particles of her invading the fabric of the chair and being transported to the next person who would sit there. Her microscopic sheddings would, instead, be bundled up and dropped in a dirty linen bag.

'Cosy,' she said with a forced smile. The unit was otherwise empty. She was the first to arrive.

'I booked you in to get under way, first,' said Jane.

Had she known her thoughts? Don't be silly, Maya told herself. Nurses just know what to say.

'I know how you must be feeling,' Jane said. She leaned against the bed, holding her chart in the same way that Mr Gaskin had done, Maya realised. 'Well, I don't really, but . . .' She shrugged.

Maybe they didn't always have the right words.

'It's okay,' said Maya. Why was she comforting Jane? Making her feel at ease? 'So,' she said, trying to sound matter of fact, 'when do we start?'

'I'm just waiting for the last of your bloods to come back.' Jane opened her chart and stared at the top page. 'Shouldn't be too long,' she said to the chart. 'And then we'll be under way.'

'Good,' said Maya.

'Good.'

Kathy was at the window, arms crossed, studying the garden outside.

Jane snapped the chart shut. 'Right then,' she said, and she stood there as if she was waiting for permission to leave.

I should say something, thought Maya. To ease the tension. But she didn't have the energy and so they stayed there, three players in a mime of the absurd.

As if on cue, the phone rang.

'I'd better get that,' said Jane. She turned away. Maya and Kathy were left to wait.

'Are you going to tell me about the scarf?' Kathy asked after a while. She split the silence in two with her words.

'What do you want to know?' Maya touched her hand to her head, covered with blue and green swirls, like reckless waves.

'Well, you're certainly looking like your traditional chemo patient with that thing wrapped around your head. Getting into character, are we?'

Maya rubbed her thumb along the hem of her baggy linen shorts. 'I am, actually,' she said quietly. She could see the weave of the fabric of her shorts, over under over under, thousands of fine threads being held together by one another. 'Are you ready?'

Kathy turned to face her. 'What for?'

Maya's hands went up to the base of her head. They loosened, undid, and she was pulling away the scarf that had been covering the brand new nakedness of her head. The smooth fabric slid over her scalp and she shivered at the feel of it. She gathered up the scarf in her hand, held it there as though its complicity was something she had to hide. 'What do you think of the new me?'

Kathy stared. She was like a child staring at the burns victim, the amputee, the hunchback. 'Fucking hell,' she whispered.

'Is that a good fucking hell or a bad one?' Maya asked. She was beginning to enjoy this. She felt strong and powerful. If she had this effect on her best friend, how would other people react? She could be like someone that jumps out of the bushes to frighten small children and then runs away laughing, overflowing with power. Bigness.

'It's just fucking hell,' said Kathy. 'What on earth possessed you to do it?'

'A pre-emptive strike.' That sounded clever.

'Well, you've struck me speechless. Bloody hell, Maya. You're a dark horse sometimes, aren't you?'

'It's funny how something like starting chemo makes everything else seem tame. It focuses the mind.'

'Like execution.'

'Exactly.'

'Are you planning on scaring the snot out of your lovely chemo nurse?'

'I suppose not.'

'I would have thought you'd want her to have a steady hand. And an even heartbeat.'

'Good idea.' Maya laid the scarf out flat over her legs. The colours swelled like the tide at the mouth of the Turanganui River. There was resistance before the colours, the waters, settled into place. She wound it around her head and knotted it again at the base of her neck.

'Done like an expert,' said Kathy.

'Thank you.' Maya patted her hands over her head as if she was pressing down scone dough. 'Not bad for a beginner.'

And then Jane was back, carrying a plastic tray in which lay syringes – fat, slim, long, squat. Needles, swabs, IV tubing, tape. All the ingredients.

'Here we are,' she said, and the tray chattered on the bedside locker as she set it down.

'What do you want me to do?' Kathy asked. Her knees were like knuckles cracking as she squatted beside Maya's chair. She touched her arm. The atmosphere in the room changed. Like turning on a light, or turning one off.

Maya hesitated. The world and the room were still. She was suddenly in a vacuum of time and energy. All she knew was her breathing and the sharp of the drugs in the syringes. Brightly coloured, like cordial syrup, or liqueurs.

'Would you wait outside until I'm done?' she heard herself saying. 'Then you can come back.'

'Are you sure?'

She nodded. She didn't speak because she wasn't at all sure – about this, about anything – and if she was to speak, she might find herself saying, I've changed my mind. I don't want chemo. I don't want cancer. I'm going home. She might, and so she nodded. She touched her head, just to make sure. Jane hadn't said anything about the scarf. Odd, but maybe she was so used to people looking like this, it hadn't occurred to her to comment.

Maya watched her prepare the drugs. Laying them out, like a dentist lining up instruments on the tray before you. Close enough that you can see the glint of the metal, the shine. But you are bibbed, reclined, reflected in the yellow light that illuminates the soft and cautious parts of you and you cannot do anything except watch the mouthwash tablet hiss and sizzle as it dissolves in a tumbler of water.

First, the IV that would go into a vein. It was a butterfly – a fine needle, with two plastic wings that Jane would grip as she slid the needle under Maya's skin and into an engorged vein. A length of tubing dangled from the end of the butterfly needle. It was through this that the drugs and fluids would be injected.

Second, Normal Saline to squirt into the tubing to ensure the vein remained patent.

Third, Maxolon, to prevent nausea and vomiting, although Maya and Jane both knew it wouldn't work.

Fourth, the chemo drugs themselves. Cyclophosphamide, Adriamycin, names like constellations or diseases themselves.

Fifth, more Normal Saline (although was anything normal, any more?), to be pushed into the tubing between each of the drugs. They were not allowed to mix in the tubing even though they would traverse Maya's bloodstream as a pack (hungry, salivating).

Sixth, a cottonwool ball, to be pressed where the needle pierced Maya's skin. The butterfly would be pulled out, dropped into the tray of discarded syringes and da dah, it was done.

Just like that. Six easy steps.

'Let's begin,' said Jane quietly.

Maya gave up her hand. Jane slipped a tourniquet around the plump of her forearm and they watched as the veins on the back of her hand filled. She felt sweat spring out on her forehead, her upper lip, her palms.

Jane tore open an alcohol swab and wiped the back of Maya's hand. She held the butterfly between her practised fingers, its pale wings together.

'Okay?'

'Yep.' Maya looked out the window. Roses, sweet william, mown grass, clouds like December lambs, blue that filled up the sky.

And the needle went in.

'Will you take me home for a rest, please? I feel like I've been run over.'

'You do look pretty ghastly,' said Kathy.

She had tried hard to be positive. She told herself it wasn't going to affect her. She wouldn't feel sick, wouldn't vomit, wouldn't be so weak she couldn't walk unless she leaned, like the Queen Mother, on a stick, or the arm of a lady-in-waiting, she wouldn't need to sleep fifteen hours straight, after her treatment.

But she did. She did.

She thought death might be a better option.

'How are you, Charlie?'

'Hi, Kathy. Good. Where's Mum?'

'She's on the couch. She had her first chemo today.'

'Oh yeah, that's right.'

'Did you have a good time at Jacob's?'

'Yep.'

'You might need to be quiet this afternoon, Charlie.'

'Why?'

'I think Mum's asleep. She's pretty exhausted.'

'I'm not asleep.' Maya's voice was small, struggling out from the lounge to the front door.

Charlie ran into the lounge. Maya lay on the couch, in teeshirt and shorts, covered by a cotton throw. Her scarf lay on the floor, a swirling rockpool beside her.

'Guess what we did –'

He stopped still, his mouth a tight circle in his face.

'Hi, buddy,' Maya managed.

'Wow. You were right, Mum.' He didn't move.

'What, chap?'

'The chemo stuff. It *does* make your hair come out.'

'Do you know, I've never eaten so well.'

'What's that?' Maya looked up from the magazine she was reading. Or trying to. She had read the same paragraph four times now, but the words still didn't make any sense. When will I get my brain back? she wondered.

'I've never eaten so well. Since you've been sick. I don't know how many lasagnes and quiches there are in the freezer. And your biscuit tins are absolutely bulging.'

'That's nice.'

'People are kind, aren't they?'

Maya watched Kathy nibble around the edges of an afghan, spinning it around its walnut-topped centre.

'They want to help,' she continued. 'But what can you do, except offer food?'

'I suppose.'

'It's like that joke about the three wise men and how different it would have been if they'd been women attending the birth of baby Jesus.'

'Eh?'

'You know. If it had been women there, they would have followed a map to get there, moved the animals out, swept and disinfected the stable, not to mention actually arriving in time to help with the delivery. And they would have brought nappies for

Jesus and haemorrhoid cream and makeup for poor old Mary, and stocked the freezer with lasagnes and muffins.'

Maya let the words flow over her like a breeze. 'Yeah,' she said when she realised Kathy had finished.

'You're not listening, are you?'

'Not really.' Maya smiled. She was safe here with Kathy.

'Mum. There's someone at the front door. Do you want me to see who it is?'

'Ssh.'

'But they're knocking.'

'We're pretending we're not here.' Whispering.

'Why?'

'I'm too tired to see anyone.'

'Why don't you put up a sign? On the door. Like they had when you were in hospital. Patient resting. Do not disturb, or something.'

'You're smarter than the average bear, aren't you, Charlie?'

Maya waited five minutes, watching the long skinny hand on the kitchen clock creep around. She opened the front door and peered out. The street was empty; her visitor had gone. On the doorstep was a chocolate cake, two fat layers sandwiched with fresh cream. Chocolate sprinkles were confetti on its thick foamy top. She bent down, collected it up and took it into the kitchen.

Fresh cream. It would have to be eaten today. Maya swallowed, pushing down the bitter saliva that filled her mouth. I hope Kathy will be hungry when she gets home from work, she thought.

'I think it's a record,' Maya said.

'What, Mum?'

'No one has knocked on the door today. Call the *Guinness Book of Records* people.'

'Do you feel better?'

'I do, actually, chap. And thank you for asking.'

'Hey, Mum,' Charlie said after a moment.

'Yeah?'

'Do you want me to bring the sign in?'

'Pardon?'

'The sign I made. I stuck it on the door.'

What a boy. Maya nodded, afraid that if she tried to speak, she would cry instead.

'Wow. We've had a good score,' she heard from the front door. 'Chocolate muffins. And a pie thing. Cool, eh?'

He carried them in and presented them to Maya. 'This is excellent,' he said.

'What do you mean?'

'Well, with my sign idea, you get to rest, *and* people still bring us stuff. Awesome, eh?'

'Very awesome,' Maya said.

'What's Charlie's favourite colour?'

'Eh?'

'Charlie's favourite colour? It's green, isn't it?'

'I think it's black, actually. But who knows?' Maya picked up her glass of water. Ice clinked against the sides of the glass. She watched the cubes get smaller and smaller until they disappeared, swallowed up by the water. 'It might be purple for all I know.'

Kathy pulled off her gardening gloves. She sat up on her knees and stretched, her hands in the small of her back. 'That doesn't sound very good.'

'What?'

'You sound a bit grumpy.'

'It's nothing really.'

'Are you sure? You know that I'm your official counsellor as well as your nurse. Sister-in-law and best friend too, by the way.' She shielded her eyes from the sun with her hands, then sat down next to Maya, who was stretched out in her garden lounger.

'And official gardener.' There was silence between them, companionable, easy. 'The petunias look good, don't they?' Their flowers, like heralding yellow trumpets, poked out from Maya's garden ornaments.

'Don't forget to pull off the dead heads,' said Kathy and she took the glass out of Maya's hand and swallowed greedily. 'That's better,' she said. 'You'll get more flowers that way.'

'Are you trying to keep my mind off things?' Maya took the glass back and held it between her hands.

'What do you mean?'

'Deadheading petunias. It's hardly high on my list of things to do right now.'

'I know, sweet thing, but life carries on, doesn't it?'

'Ain't that the truth,' said Maya, and she squeezed her hands tight around the glass. 'So why do you want to know Charlie's favourite colour?'

'It's just something I might be organising for his birthday.' Silence again. A soft breeze danced around them. Maya took off her wide straw hat and rubbed her bare head.

'Aah,' she said. 'That feels nice. Fresh air.'

'Is that how the oxygen gets to your brain?' said Kathy. 'I've often wondered.'

'I'm not sure about your bedside manner,' said Maya. 'It's no wonder you work in theatre. With all your patients unconscious, you don't have to be nice to them, do you?' She fanned her face with her hat. Sweat cooled and tingled on her forehead.

'Very funny. You're looking better, by the way.'

'Thank you. I feel like shit.'

'Yeah, but you look better.'

'Oh well, that's all right then.'

'You know what I mean.'

Maya looked over at Kathy. 'I'm not sure I do,' she said. She pulled blades of grass out of the ground and fashioned them into a tiny posy. 'It's a funny thing,' she said after a while, staring at the grass between her fingers.

'What?'

'Have you ever noticed that after you mow your lawns the grass doesn't grow straight across when it comes back? Look.' She brought the fingerful of blades up to Kathy's face. 'The grass is all pointed. You'd expect it to look chopped across, wouldn't you? It's as if it's defied man's attempt to tame it and it's grown exactly as nature intended.'

'God,' said Kathy, sitting back in her chair. 'That's a bit heavy, isn't it?'

'Probably,' said Maya, and she dropped the grass into the palm of her hand, then threw her hand up in the air. The blades floated momentarily, caught on tiny thermals and gusts of air, then fell back down and landed on the lawn, swallowed up by the green.

'Is everything okay with you and Charlie?'

'Of course it is,' said Maya.

'Hmm.'

Wait.

Wait.

'He's just – I don't know.'

Wait.

'Distant. Like he's pulling away from me.'

Wait.

'I suppose he is. I mean, it's probably too much for him to handle right now, isn't it?'

Wait.

'So I should just give him some time. And space.'

Wait.

'And let him know I love him. Always will.'

Wait.

Wait.

'You're good at this counselling thing, aren't you?'

'It's one of my specialities,' said Kathy, smiling.

Maya swallowed the last of her drink. 'You know what?' she said. 'What?'

'I think I'll go for a swim.'

'Really? Do you think you're up to it?'

'There's only one way to find out, isn't there?' And she got up from her lounger (slowly, carefully, like someone decades older) and went to find Charlie.

He was in the lounge, battling creatures from a distant galaxy.

'Hands up who wants to go for a swim.'

'Really?' said Charlie. A blue and yellow Lego alien was suspended between his fingers, awaiting its doom. 'Awesome.'

'Right, then. Go and get your togs on.'

Maya pulled her swimsuit from her drawer. It fitted in her hand. Black and shiny, with mesh around the neck. Hello, old friend, she wanted to say. She ran her hands over the smooth fabric instead and dropped it on her bed while she undressed.

'Are you all right?' a voice called from the other side of the door.

Maya sobbed once, twice, her chest tight and aching from the spasms of grief. She screwed a tissue to her face.

'I'll be out in a minute,' she said. Her voice was forced through a funnel.

'Are you sure you're okay?'

'Yes,' she gasped but her throat was constricting, strangling her with its giveaway fingers. Kathy pushed the door open. Maya covered her face with her hands.

'Oh, honey,' Kathy said and her arms were around Maya, protecting her from robbers, the bogeyman, the dark.

'I can't go.'

'It's okay,' Kathy whispered. She began to rock Maya in her arms, back and forward, back and forward like a baby, and she stroked her smooth head and whispered shh shh over the top of her. Eventually Kathy's rhythm and the futility of crying overcame her and she became calm and silent.

'All right?' Kathy said.

She nodded. She shivered, suddenly cold in her swimsuit.

'What was it?'

'It seems silly now,' said Maya, gasping as she breathed, her chest still full with the effects of her crying.

'What?'

'Look.' She shrugged Kathy away. She stood up in front of her, her thin legs trembling, her arms straight at her sides. 'Look,' she said again. She pointed to her chest, thumbs and index fingers like boyish guns.

'Oh,' said Kathy. Maya's swimsuit clung to her, shadowing the outline of her, colouring her in. Except, the left side of her was a plane, a black cliff. 'I see,' she said. 'I guess stuffing tissues down your front is out of the question.'

Maya laughed, in spite of it all. Because of it all.

'No one's going to see once you're in the water, are they?'

'No, I suppose not.'

'Well, let's get you in the water then.' And she was up and gone, breezing out of Maya's bedroom like nighttime. All Maya could do was follow.

She clutched her towel to her. Her hand gripped the bumpy fabric as she sat on the long concrete step. No one was watching her. No one took any notice. She made her fingers prise themselves from the towel and dropped it on the concrete. She brought her arms up across her chest, folding them casually, as though she might be waiting in a queue. Still no one noticed.

She snapped her bathing cap down over her ears.

'Why do you need to bother with that?' Kathy had asked.

'It's part of the package. The ritual. It's what I do.'

'Oh,' said Kathy, but Maya could see she didn't get it.

Her bathing cap was wrinkled, oversized now on her head. It looked a bit obscene, she had thought as she checked herself in the mirror at home. Oh well.

'Right then.' She tiptoed to the edge of the pool, slipped under the water and stayed there for a moment, allowing the warm of the water to surround her before she came up for air.

Charlie was down the other end. Maya could see him tumbling and spinning. His hair was slick and dark against his head.

Just a few lengths, Maya thought. To get back into it. Maybe just a couple. She backed up against the end of the pool and looked over at Kathy, sitting on the concrete step. She was like Mother, watching, watching that her children didn't drown.

She pushed off, her legs sending her out into the water. Right arm left arm breathe, right arm left arm breathe. This was swimming. Feet kicking up a frilly skirt.

Right arm left –

Her wound, a tight band of scar tissue, pulled away from her chest wall and sent a sear of pain through her. She stopped, stood up gasping, coughing, holding herself in with her thin arms. She shook her head. This had worked in the past, scattering fragments of pain away.

She set off again.

Right arm left arm –

There it was. Like a branding iron, she imagined, or a stab with a knife. Blow out the pain, she told herself. Like being in labour. Carry on through it.

Right arm left arm breathe, right arm left arm breathe. The pool was hundreds of metres long. The wall kept moving, sliding away just as she neared it. Twenty-five metres was the longest swim.

And then her fingertips touched the blue concrete and she brought her other arm over and slapped the wall with her hand. Her legs tingled, her chest heaved. She was exhausted. She had done it.

Her breath came hard in her throat but she slowed it down, talking to herself, cajoling the voice inside her. The pulse that stormed in her ears and neck slowed too. She was sure she could swim back.

Don't overdo it, one step at a time, walk before you run. I could be Rachael Allen, she thought, and her face, pinched and tight from the unaccustomed effort of twenty-five metres of freestyle, slid into a smile.

She flipped onto her back and kicked off, letting her hands sway at her sides. Her feet were pointed, kicking softly, hardly disturbing the water. Maya felt as if she was gliding – she was a leaf being carried downstream on a gentle summer current. Warm water washed over her face, her ears, blocking out the noises of the day. It was all around her.

I want to stay here forever.

'I'm sick of playing Scrabble.' Kathy flicked the green tile holder with her finger and her seven letters scattered across the table.

'Well, I guess that's that, then,' said Maya.

'Sorry.'

'No, it's okay.'

'You always win anyway. You're too good at this game.'

'It's just my predilection for words. Letters, you know, arranging them.'

'Drink?'

'Sure.'

They sat opposite each other, the Scrabble board and a bottle of Millton's Reserve Chardonnay between them.

'It's probably not good for me,' said Maya as she brought the glass to her lips.

'Probably not.'

'But what the hell.'

'Indeed.'

The wine was glossy, glistening in the crystal glass.

'Twenty-six letters,' said Maya.

'Eh?'

'Twenty-six letters in the alphabet. And look at all the combinations. All the words you can make.'

'Fascinating.'

'I'm being serious, smart-arse. Don't you think it's amazing?'

'Yeah, I suppose. I don't know. I've never really thought about it.' Kathy picked up a handful of tiles and shook them as though they were dice. She let them fall, one blank, a couple face-down, some with their letters facing up. 'That didn't make anything,' she said. 'B-r-e-g-m. Bregm.'

Maya took a sip of her wine. 'Bregm,' she said authoritatively. 'The ancient art of tying rope around logs and rolling them downhill. Originated in Scotland. Bregm.'

'Really?'

Maya laughed. 'No, you idiot. But it could be a word. Don't you think that's interesting?'

'Yeah, I suppose so.'

The conversation fell between them like fine net.

Kathy drained her glass and poured another. 'So,' she said, 'you're falling behind.' She nodded at Maya's glass.

'We can't have that,' said Maya, and she emptied her glass in one swallow. 'Fill 'er up, bartender.'

'Sure thing, pilgrim.'

They said nothing. The silence was companionable, that between friends who do not need to stuff it full of sounds.

'Is Charlie at Jacob's?' Kathy said eventually.

Maya nodded.

'So,' Kathy said again.

Maya filled her mouth with wine. She let it sit there for a moment. She closed her eyes, tried to identify the flavours, the characteristics of it. All she could taste was wine.

'Do you miss him?'

Maya swallowed. Her mouth was still full of alcohol fumes. She wondered if this was how fire-eaters felt. 'Pardon?'

'Philip. Your husband. My brother.'

'I know who you mean,' Maya said quietly. The fumes were evaporating on her tongue, leaving it dry.

'You never talk about him, that's all.'

'Neither do you.'

'So, do you?'

Tears suddenly appeared in Maya's eyes. Salty, stinging tears. 'Shit,' she said, and she wiped them away. 'Where did they come from?'

Kathy said nothing. She spun her wine glass around, around. The wine sloshed dangerously inside.

'I thought I'd cried my quota of tears for Philip.'

'Is there one? A quota?'

'I don't know. It's just something to say, I guess.'

'Words.'

'Yeah.'

'Ha.'

'Ha to you too.'

'So what about him do you miss the most?'

134

Maya opened her mouth, then paused. The most? How could she quantify her feelings? Her loss?

'The companionship, I think,' she said eventually. 'You know, not having anyone to discuss the news with. Or a good TV programme. Something Charlie did at school, or if he said something funny. That kind of thing. The grief has gone. It's a partner I miss now.'

Kathy nodded. 'I know what you mean.' Maya thought she looked misty. She was starting to blur.

'What about you?'

'I miss not having a big brother. Of course it's a different relationship when you're adults, but he was still the big brother and I was the little sister and I knew he would always be there if I needed him. Big brothers are supposed to look after you.' She took a swallow of wine. 'Bastard,' she said, staring into her glass.

'So are husbands.' Maya gulped at her drink. 'He turned out to be completely unreliable, didn't he?'

'Completely.'

Maya filled their glasses. The bottle was unsteady as she set it down on the table. It took a moment to find its footing. 'You know, when he first died, I used to sleep with one of his sweatshirts next to me. So I'd have the smell of him with me. Weird, eh?'

'Probably, but who cares? Whatever it takes, Mrs Wimple.'

Maya could suddenly recall the smell of those clothes. She used to lie in bed on her side and drape her arm across the place where Philip should have been. Her arm was limp on the duvet. She held one of his shirts or his jerseys to her. The wool scratched her skin and she smelled him in the shapeless garment, which the next morning she folded and put away again, and she felt a sting in her chest as she pushed the drawer shut.

She'd waited for it to get better. She held her breath sometimes and pressed her fingers against her wrist, feeling her pulse. Her lungs were crushed, her throat screaming to her to take a breath but she was intoxicated with the power of her slowing heartbeat. Philip, Philip, she said inside herself in time to her slowing pulse. Philip, and she was sure she could see him. Sure that she could. But now

135

she was empty and she had to breathe, and as she did, the movement scared him away and he was gone.

The Scrabble tiles on the table were magnified through her tears, which formed a shimmery see-through wall in front of her eyes. She refused to blink. She would wait until the weight of them spilled them down her face.

The tiles were blurred, convex, elongated. She tried to add up the points value of the ones that were face up. She couldn't think what forty-six plus seven was. Bugger. It seemed important, but she wasn't sure why.

'What's the funniest thing you remember about Philip?

Kathy's unexpected words made her blink and the wall of tears became a waterfall but then it was gone and she wiped her hot cheeks and how tight the skin felt and this was what the colour red felt like, surely.

'Jesus, Kathy.'

'What?'

She shook her head. 'Nothing. You go first.'

'Okay.' Kathy piled up a stack of Scrabble tiles into a tower. It leaned to the side. Maybe it was drunk too, Maya thought. 'When we were, I don't know, fourteen and sixteen, Philip had this group of friends around. It was Sunday afternoon or something. They were all trying to outdo one another, like boys do, and Philip said he'd get one of his mates to light his fart.'

'What?' The tower of Scrabble tiles crashed onto the table.

'They decided to light his fart.'

'What? Can you do that?'

'Shit, Mrs Wimple, you've had a sheltered life, haven't you?'

Maya picked up four tiles. S-T-P-A. Past, spat, taps. 'Yes, I think I have, actually. So what happened?' She leaned in closer.

'Well, he stripped down to his jocks and bent over. You know, so his arse was sticking out. Someone had some matches.' Kathy began to laugh. Maya joined in, trying to picture Philip, a gawky teenager, in his underpants, about to set fire to a fart. 'So he's yelling out – light the match, light it, and everyone's falling about laughing.' Maya could hardly make out what

Kathy was saying, through her own laughter.

'And?'

'One of the guys crouches down beside him, match poised by Philip's arse. He lights the match and holds it there. Philip lets one rip, a really big one, and it catches fire as it shoots out of his bum and this streak of flame shoots down the length of his friend's arm!'

They were both laughing like horses. Gasping, shrieking, slapping the edge of the table, rocking their chairs back. They were crying with the hilarity of the story.

Suddenly Kathy stopped laughing. She was motionless. Maya wiped her eyes, gasped once, twice and also became still.

'Do you know,' said Kathy. 'His friend had all the hairs on his arm singed off.'

'I don't think I can beat that story,' Maya said a long time later. Her chest ached. Her wound hurt. It had been a long time since she had laughed like that.

The outpatients door opened automatically. She had no choice. She had to go in. The crowds parted, pointed her to the day ward. Maya was carried there every third Monday and into the same brown La-Z-Boy chair, where she waited, palms sweating, belly aching, for her chemo.

'Your white count's a bit lower,' said Jane from behind her folder. Maya's life was getting thicker. The tops of the pages poked out. 'Still, you're doing really well.' She smiled widely. Maya thought she looked relieved. Maybe I remind everyone of their own mortality, she thought as she waited for Jane to get her tray ready. A nurse, a hospital employee. Other people get sick. Patients. Not hospital staff.

But I'm getting better. I'm sure of it. She closed her eyes and visualised the cells in her body receiving the chemo. She visualised the cancer cells shrivelling up like bacon left too long under the grill. She visualised her lymphatic system sparkling clean like a motel bathroom, sweeping away the remains of the charred and blackened cancer.

She opened her eyes. 'I can't do it,' she said to Kathy.

'Oh, honey, you've come this far. You can.' She smiled like a cheerleader.

'No, you idiot,' Maya laughed. 'I can't do this visualisation thing. It just doesn't work.'

'Eh?'

'I was trying to visualise the chemo working.'

'Oh, thank God for that. I thought I was going to have to be a counsellor again.'

'I'm sorry to disappoint you. If you'd like the practice . . .'

'No thank you,' said Kathy. 'So what if you can't visualise? It's your body that's got the cancer, not your brain. Let your body deal with it. Leave your brain for other things.'

'Do you know that's very good advice?' said Maya.

Kathy stood up as Jane approached. 'Do you want me to go?' she asked. Maya went to speak, then paused. 'You can stay if you like,' she said. 'You can see what I have to put up with.'

'I hope you don't mean me personally,' said Jane. She placed the tray on the locker beside Maya's chair. The syringes glinted.

'I've heard she pulls the wings off flies on her days off,' Maya said to Kathy, blank faced.

'I've heard that too,' Kathy replied.

Maya felt her mouth fill with saliva. It was metallic, like touching your tongue on the end of a magnet. Like the taste of blood.

'Bowl,' she whispered.

'Not long to go,' said Jane and she slowly injected the last drug into the needle in Maya's hand.

'I don't think I'm ready to go home just yet.' The drawsheet was hot on the back of her head.

'Do you want to have a bit of a sleep?' said Kathy.

'Yes please.' Suddenly her eyes filled with tears. They overflowed and ran down her cheeks and soaked into her shirt, making two mirrored patches in the fabric.

Kathy passed her a tissue. 'Careful,' said Maya. 'Don't forget that my tears are contaminated.'

She *was* contaminated: a threat to anyone who might come in contact with her. Flush the toilet three times for twenty-four hours after each chemo session. Doublebag any vomit, tissues containing phlegm, saliva, tears. It was funny how the very drugs that were injected into her body to cure her were toxic to the people around her.

Avoid anyone with the flu, a cold, anyone who might blow their nose or cough. Stay away from large crowds, animals, extremes of temperature. Isolate.

'I'll go and pick Charlie up from Rachael's,' said Kathy. 'You sleep as long as you need to.'

Maya closed her eyes. She was too tired to say thank you, too tired to smile even. All she wanted to do was sleep and wake up when she was better.

The touch of Kathy's fingers was featherlets on her skin. She wanted to rub at the spot, to erase the tickle, but she resisted the impulse.

She wasn't even sure why. Maybe she was just too tired.

Now she felt another touch on her face. Her eyes flickered open, then shut again. She was in bed at home, under her Holly Hobbie continental quilt. Her throat hurt from coughing. There was a glass of lemonade on the table beside her bed. She watched the bubbles bounce at the bottom of the glass, once, twice, then float up to the surface where they popped, in a tiny droplet explosion.

Her mother came in and sat next to her. Oh Maya, it's no fun being sick, she said, and she brushed Maya's hair off her hot cheek, tucked it behind her ear. Would you like anything? she asked. Maya shook her head. She closed her eyes and sank into her pillow. She could smell her mother there: powdery, floral, even the sharp bite of her hairspray.

She liked being sick. It meant her mother stayed with her. She

139

wriggled close to her in bed. She brushed Maya's hair. She taught her to crochet, and they made brightly coloured squares that somehow her mother crocheted together with thick black wool. It became a blanket that sat at the end of her mother's bed.

She taught her to knit on those sick days. Here, love, and she wound the wool around the needles, through here, and Maya passed the stitch from one metal needle to the other. Around through and over. Around through and over. Soon she was knitting. Peggy squares of leftover wool in fawn, red, aqua, sewn together this time into a blanket that Maya kept on the end of her bed.

She read to her: *Millie Molly Mandy, What Katy Did, Heidi.*

I think you'll be ready to go to school tomorrow, her mother would say. Maya would be resting on the couch by now, still with her pillow behind her head, her mother's crocheted blanket over her legs. But I want to stay home with you, she wanted to say. Just you and me.

I don't feel very well again, she whispered. Maybe another day in bed, her mother said, would be good for you. Would you like me to teach you how to do cross-stitch?

'I'm going round to Jacob's,' said Charlie.

'Isn't it his turn to play here? You've been around there heaps these holidays.'

'It's okay. His mother doesn't mind.'

What about this mother, Maya thought, as she watched Charlie get smaller and smaller and then disappear completely in the shimmer of that hot Gisborne summer.

'You've got to eat something.'

Maya shook her head.

'Sandwiches?'

Too dry.

'Milkshake?'

Milk produced phlegm that stuck in her throat.

'Watermelon?'

Acidic and burning against the ulcers that ripped at her mouth.

'If you were Charlie,' said Kathy in an even voice, 'I'd say that you get nothing and I'd leave you to sulk.'

Leave me then, thought Maya.

If she didn't move, she was okay. Well, as long as her movements were slow, it was as though her stomach was giving her brain enough time to catch up.

It was cool in the shade. Maya looked over her garden. If you ignored the weeds, it was okay. They filled in the gaps anyway.

Charlie was in the far corner of the garden: the jungle, he'd named it years ago. It was dark and cool there, and he could chase tigers and battle monsters among the trees and wide shrubs that protected him from being seen.

'Are you okay, chap?'

'Yeah.'

'What are you doing?'

'I'm building an ant hotel. Out of mud.'

'Cool.'

'Hope so.'

'Do you need any help?' (Hoping hoping he didn't, because then she'd have to move.)

'No thanks.'

'Okay then. Sing out if you do, won't you?'

'La la la.'

'Ha ha bonk.'

'What, Mum?'

'Ha ha bonk.'

'What's that?'

'Me laughing my head off.'

Charlie stood up and stepped out of the jungle. He rolled his eyes, then a moment later he grinned. He couldn't help himself, Maya knew. It was a smile as wide as the Pacific, sparkling, wondrous. It was all around her, Charlie's smile, keeping her warm and keeping her safe.

Her garden blazed. Her roses, thorny sticks just six months ago, sagged with the weight of their flowers. Sexy Rexy, Tess, Matawhero Magic, First Love, Peace. Dublin Bay stretched along the back fence. Its blooms were like red Christmas lights. She imagined their perfume, made strong and heavy by the heat of the day. Her lavender bushes, which once bordered the path to the front door in two tidy rows, now swayed waist high, and bees danced drunkenly from flower to fragrant flower.

Everywhere there were daisy bushes: yellow, white, pink, frilled, pompoms, singles like children's drawings. Sweet williams like tiny carnations hugging the dry soil. Poached egg flowers, quaint yet quirky, spilling out onto the paths. And pansies following the sun.

Sparrows splashed in her concrete birdbath, the bowl of which was a swirl of china mosaic. A white angel cast spells over a corner of the garden. The sun glinted on the shoulder of a copper statue – a lady gardener with sticky-out hair, a rake in her cylinder fingers. It had been Kathy's birthday present last year, left standing on Maya's front door with a birthday card stuck between the prongs of the upturned rake. I'll get you the man gardener next year, she'd said.

She pulled herself up from her chair and went to the back door for her secateurs, which stood points down in a basket. Their handles were thick with dried soil. They fitted so well in her hand. She made her way back to her garden. Have to tread carefully, she thought. A fall could be serious. And suddenly thinking, am I thirty-seven or eighty-seven?

She could hear Charlie on the trampoline, around the corner by the side of the house. There was the dull thwang of his feet (or knees or bottom) contacting with the mat and then a whoop, a shriek. She pictured him flying up to meet the sky, legs and arms outstretched like a starfish, his straight yellow hair startled on his head. And then falling back down, deciding in less than a second how to position his body, which parts of it should contact the mat.

142

Somehow the idea of Charlie there, challenging his body with every leap, every bounce, forced Maya to stand straighter, move with more purpose. She cut branches off her fairy rose, their stems red and fleshy, bursting with summer strength. She laid them on the lawn. Careful that the thorns don't scratch. Even a tiny cut could turn. Delay her treatment.

A stand of Christmas lilies nodded by the garage. Snip snip and they were hers – heady, pungent, their white petals speckled with crimson, stamens like candied orange. Maya placed them on the roses, a thorny bed.

Now white daisies with yellow centres. Primitive flowers, part of every child's artwork. An armful of them. And lavender and having to compete with the bees for them, their legs thick with pollen. Snip snip, the long stalks, each supporting a single furry head, fell into her hand, snip again, and she dropped them (by the score) onto the pile of flowers on her lawn.

Finally going to the front verge and reaching up into the magnolia and cutting off end branches. The leaves were thick and shiny, sumptuous.

There.

She sat on the back step. She wiped her hand across her top lip. Her hand nudged the planter box Charlie had given her. Now it was a rainbow, blue violas, pink begonias – neat flowers, their two perfect petals tied together with a yellow tuft, white nicotiana.

Charlie. He-e-y, yay, yeah, in time to the bounce of the trampoline. Beautiful, perfect boy.

She went inside and got a big glass vase. She usually arranged her flowers on the bench, but today she would take the vase outside and pattern them on the lawn, where they waited for her.

It was all about layers and symmetry. Keeping it even. She started with the magnolia branches. They splayed out from the vase, a fleshy base. Then the fairy roses, tall but bending over at their tops, unable to stand the weight of themselves. Lilies, one here, one here, one here (groups of three are easy on the eye). They were slender trumpets. Maya separated the daisies into single stems and poked them between the magnolia leaves, behind the lilies and in front of them, high above the roses and at their base. And the lavender, filling in the gaps. Filling it out.

She would put her arrangement on the coffee table in the lounge. She would fill the vase with water once it was in place. She went to lift it up but her arms couldn't manage. Today, it was too heavy. Shit. She tried again. Still couldn't do it. She struggled to her feet and went to get Charlie. He was a good helper. Hadn't he said he'd look after her?

'How are you doing, buddy?' Maya's breath came in short, shallow bursts.

'Okay.' Bounce, bounce, touching the blue. Not even knowing he was doing it.

'Could you do a job for me?'

'In a minute.'

'I need you to take some flowers inside.'

'Okay.'

'Could you do it now?'

'Yep, in a minute.' Bounce, bounce, but he turned away and Maya could only watch his back. And she saw him go higher and his hair flew out further and his arms reached out wider.

Maya turned around. She walked around to the back door and inside to where it was cool in the kitchen. She didn't look back at the vase of flowers, which stood in the middle of the lawn like a debutante abandoned by her partner in the middle of a song.

Twelve

'I hate having my birthday in the holidays.'

'Why is that, buddy?'

'I bet half my friends will be away.' Charlie sat opposite Maya at the table. He pushed grains of sugar from around his breakfast bowl into a pile in the corner of his placemat. 'They might have forgotten me,' he said quietly.

'Oh, Charlie. How could anyone forget you? You're very important to your friends. You know that.'

He shrugged. He poked his finger in the middle of the sugar mountain. It collapsed and a crystal avalanche skated across the table in front of him.

Quick. Think of something. Kiss it better. Wipe it clean. 'You can remember all your friends from last year, can't you?'

'Yeah, I guess.'

'So they'll all remember you. That makes sense, doesn't it?'

'I suppose.'

'Well, then.' She sounded triumphant, as though she had solved one of life's puzzles. Maybe she had. 'Do you want to have a sleepover for your birthday?' She didn't really want to – all those boys, all that mess – but Charlie was turning nine. It was a rite of passage.

'Can I, Mum? You're not too, you know –' He paused, looked up.

145

Maya thought it was as if he was searching in his brain, looking for the right word.

'I'm fine,' she said. 'I'll make sure I'm not too – you know.' She smiled, a twinkling grin. 'Now, let's make out your guest list before I realise what a bad idea this is and change my mind.'

Seven friends. Charlie had put Jacob, of course, first on the list. The names were like rings on a tree trunk, she thought, depending on the length and depth of the friendship. A new ring would grow by his next birthday.

'Okay,' she said, turning over a sheet on her notepad. 'Next Saturday? I'll have recovered from Monday's treatment hopefully and that's only three days after your actual birthday. Is that okay?'

'Yeah. I've been thinking what we could do. We could go to the movies and then play spacies afterwards. What about tea at Pizza Hut? Maybe we could go swimming at the beach. We could have a bonfire and everything. And McDonald's for breakfast on Sunday.'

Maya held up her hands like a traffic policeman. 'Hey, hey,' she said. 'Wait on. You can't fit everything into one sleepover. Let's just choose one or two activities.'

'Oh, Mum.'

'One or two.'

'Oh, but – '

'Or we could have no sleepover.'

'What about three things?'

'Charlie.'

'All right.'

She picked up her pen. She drew a line of daisies along the top of the page while she waited for Charlie to decide. She linked them with filled-in stalks.

'Okay Mum, this is what I want to do.'

And she began to write.

She turned over another page on her notepad.

Cake
Icing sugar (check pantry)
Coconut
Pizzas – square (deli)
Cheerios
Tom sauce (check fridge)
Rice bubbles
Kremelta
Mallowpuffs x 2
Icecream – vanilla
Pink wafers
Watermelon
Pineapple
Balloons
Pass the Parcel treats x 8
Lollies for party bags
Pencils for party bags
Erasers for party bags
Party bags

It all looks so overwhelming, but I can manage as long as I have lists, Maya thought. I'm sure I can.

'Right. Things to do.' Her pen paused over a new page. Charlie had long since got bored with the mechanics of party planning. She could hear the familiar stretch and twang of the mat of the trampoline. I hope he's wearing a hat. And sunscreen, she thought. Did motherhood ever stop? Would there ever be a day that she didn't think about him? Wonder about him? Worry whether he was warm enough, had enough to eat?

She remembered when Charlie was just five. He'd been at school three weeks, maybe four. She had walked him to school as usual, his soft hand upstretched to find hers. The day had begun unseasonably cool – an autumnal blast in February. She slipped a sweatshirt over his teeshirt. It was too big, a size six (but he'd grow into it). She rolled the sleeves up until his wrists were fat fleecy cuffs.

She'd hung his backpack on his hook in the corridor outside the classroom. There was a picture of a yacht above his peg. It was his peg, his hook, for the year. Pictures were easier for the littlies, Charlie's teacher had told Maya. Not all the children could recognise their names yet.

She had ambled home, the leisurely walk of the unemployed. She'd go back to work once Charlie was settled at school. She was looking forward to it. She'd be a good role model for him. They'd be independent.

It had turned into a scorching Gisborne day. Tar melted on the roads, sliding into the gutters like runny licorice. The horizon shimmered at the end of every street. God, men had it lucky on days like these, she'd thought. Being allowed to go around with no shirt on. Her bra felt sticky across her back as she walked back to school in time for the three o'clock bell. Her teeshirt clung damply to her.

She slipped into the classroom and waited at the back. Twenty-something shining five-year-olds sat on the mat, listening to a story. She scanned the faces for Charlie. And then she saw him, sitting up straight, arms folded. His cheeks were two scarlet splashes. His eyes watered. There he was, still in his sweatshirt.

'Buddy,' she'd said in the corridor, as she pulled his arms out of the thick sleeves. 'Why did you keep your sweatshirt on all day? You must be nearly cooked.'

He looked up at her, with his big eyes and flashes of red on his face. 'Oh Mum, I didn't know I was allowed to take it off.'

There's so much to teach him – how will I manage it all? she thought. And if I – you know (and she couldn't even think the word), will I have to leave him lists? How to deal with high-school bullies, girls, buying a car, choosing a flat, getting his own lunch . . .

Charlie, Charlie, I can't leave you.

If I die, you'll be alone, and that would surely be worse than dying.

But everyone has to die sometime. Everyone. And life goes on.

There's a hole, initially, where the person was, but eventually it fills up, the sides attracted to each other, uncomfortable with the sharpness of an edge, and the coldness of it.

And then you can't see where the hole (the person) was.

Am I right, Philip?

I could touch you if I wanted to.

What I want to know is this. In heaven, or space, or wherever you are, do you grow older or stay the age at which you died? So, Philip, will you still be just-turned-thirty, and will I be thirty-nine or forty-nine, or however old I happen to be when I die?

Is there music? Gardens? Laughter, parties, birthday cakes and candles to blow out, or do you celebrate deathdays instead?

Is there room for one more?

Will we find each other? Will you recognise me?

What if Charlie came too? Then we'd be a family again, and how good that would be. We'd be complete.

Maya dropped her pen on the pad. It made a feeble scrawl down the page. She was suddenly tired and lowered her head on the table. Her body refused to move. I might stay here forever, she thought. Her brain floated inside her head. It may have become disconnected from the rest of her. It bobbed about, bounced against the inner layer of her skull. I'll do the rest tomorrow, and as soon as I've got the energy I'll get up and take myself to bed. That's what I'll do.

'Is that Maya?'

'Yes it is.'

'It's Wendy Mallard here. Harvey's mother.'

'Hi. How are you?'

'I'm good, thank you. I'm ringing about the invitation you sent for Charlie's birthday.'

'Charlie's really looking forward to having Harvey stay over.'

'I'm sorry, but Harvey won't be able to come. I thought it might be too much for you. I've heard that you're not well, and, well, Harvey has a lot on these holidays and I thought it would be – you know . . .'

'Oh.'

'I thought that was the best thing to do.'

'I don't know what to say.'
'I'm sorry.'
'Me too.'

Why do birthdays so often turn out to be a source of misery and humiliation for kids? Maya placed the receiver back on the phone, carefully, precisely, because she didn't think she could trust herself if she didn't move with caution.

Where do you think I would get the money to put on a birthday party for you, Maya? It doesn't grow on trees, you know. But I'm turning twelve, she wanted to say. This was an important birthday, in which to celebrate childhood and anticipate adolescence. She had one foot in the territory of girlhood, the other pointed towards becoming a woman. She remained silent, sulking because she didn't know what else to do. Maybe she could annoy Gran into letting her have a party.

But Gran was more resilient or maybe Maya just got bored with sulking. Sorry, she mumbled the next day. They stood at the sink. Gran passed the washed dishes to Maya and she wiped them dry with a Souvenir of Rotorua teatowel. A slim Maori girl with a moko and thick hair that tumbled over her bare breasts smiled as the grass of her skirt dried Gran's everyday dinner set.

That's all right, said Gran.

So can I – ?

I'm not changing my mind.

And now she remembered an earlier birthday. Had she been turning seven? Seven or eight, she thought. She was at the table, sitting opposite her mother. The table was covered with cake-decorating books from the library. None of these is just right for my little girl, her mother was saying, and when she smiled Maya thought she might burst. We're going to have to put our thinking caps on. She picked up an imaginary hat (or cap) and placed it on her head. Maya could almost see it among her glorious silver curls.

She straightened her imaginary thinking cap. Well, she said. This will help.

Got it, her mother said after the shortest time, and she packed up all the library books into a pile. We don't need these, honey. Leave it to me.

Anticipation bubbled up inside Maya's belly. This would be the best birthday ever. She was sure of it.

As her friends arrived for the party her mother stood at the front door calling out Hooray, here's another party guest, and clapping her hands. Into the lounge, dear, she said, until they were all there. Maya's very best friends.

They played Pin the Tail on the Donkey and Pass the Parcel, in which each of the guests got a paper doll and a lollipop. Maya, the birthday girl, got to open the last layer and there was a set of clothes for her Sindy doll. A pink evening gown in shimmering tulle, which became silver and gold when you turned it in the light. A tiny pink stole and long white gloves that would reach to Sindy's elbows when she was going out.

Thank you, Maya began, but her mother brushed the words away like sandflies. Come on, girls, into the dining room. It's cake time.

They stood around the table, scrubbed clean, waiting. They heard Happy Birthday begin from the kitchen and they joined in and then they were singing for Maya and she looked at all of them and their eyes sparkled and their smiles were wide and they were all singing for her.

Her mother came in carrying her birthday cake on an oven tray. Her face was golden and flickering from the candles. She smiled as she sang. And the cake. Maya had never seen anything like it. She could never have imagined it.

It was a mountain, bursting up from the tray. Blue-green, like the sea on a rainy day, and white snow covered its peak. A tiny mountaineer doll stood on the summit, holding a flag that said Happy Birthday in her mother's tidiest miniature writing.

Oh, said Maya. Where was the castle cake, the butterfly with jubes edging its wings? Even a plain square cake with a plastic Happy Birthday stuck in the middle and silver balls around the edge. But a mountain? All she'd wanted was a pretty cake. Her friends looked at one another. One of them sniggered. Blow out the candles, dear, Maya's mother said. They lined the side of the mountain, lighting the path that the mountaineer, with her yellow hair and pink mouth, had taken. Her friends clapped and cheered as the candles were snuffed out. Maya smiled politely.

Just wait, her mother said, and she disappeared into the kitchen again. When she came back she was holding a tray of glass bottles, the kind that tomato sauce came in, and a glass shaker with a shiny metal lid. She placed the tray on the table and clapped her hands together. We're going to turn this mountain into a volcano, she said. The girls exchanged glances again. What was she talking about? Each of these bottles has flavoured syrup in it, Maya's mother said, pushing away the girls' uncertainty and Maya's disappointment. Look, here's chocolate, strawberry. This one's passionfruit. It's lava, girls. She picked up the glass shaker and held it out like she was a Tupperware Lady. This has coconut in it. It's snow. Now, turn this mountain into a work of art. Nobody moved. Maya wanted to crawl behind the couch.

Well, then, I'll start. Her mother picked up a bottle and turned it up over the mountain top. Chocolate lava poured down the snow, engulfing the happy mountaineer.

A hand reached out for passionfruit sauce. It mixed this flavour with the chocolate and sauce ran down in thick brown and yellow speckled gloops to the mountain's vegetation.

There's one for each of you and they all took a bottle or a shaker and soon the mountain sagged with sweet, sticky lava. Coconut snow clung to the syrup.

This was the best cake ever, Maya said later, once everyone had gone home and they sat on the couch together, just the two of them. The house sighed with sudden quiet. I'll never forget this birthday. She snuggled in to her mother. She should have known to trust her. She would never disappoint her. She snuggled in tighter. They were warm and safe and full and happy.

'No one wants to come to my party.'

'That's not true, love.'

'Yes it is. Look at the names you've crossed off.'

'There was only one of your friends who couldn't come. Look at all the names that are still there.'

'I bet they'll phone up and cancel, too.'

'Oh, buddy.'

'It's all your fault.'

Nothing.

'It's because you're sick. Your stupid cancer. No one wants to come around any more. It's all your stupid fault, Mum.'

'I hate to ask, but why is there a vase of flowers out on the back lawn?' Kathy dropped a handful of snow peas into the wok that sizzled and spat with the dinner's fresh vegetables. She flipped them with a flat spoon.

'Modern art. Self-expression. Weight.'

Steam from the wok smothered Kathy's face for a moment, before the extractor fan sucked it up and sent it outside. 'Pardon?'

'Well, if truth be told, I did the arrangement out there, and when I had finished it, it was too heavy for me to carry inside.'

Kathy stopped stirring. 'You should have said, Mrs Wimple.'

'Yeah, I know, but . . .' Maya shrugged her shoulders and fingered the towel she held in her hand. 'I quite like it out there now, anyway.'

'You know what? So do I.'

'Would you mind keeping an eye on Charlie? I'd love to go for a quick swim.' Maya rolled the towel into a cylinder, wrapping her goggles and bathing cap in the middle. Bits of them poked out like sandwich filling. 'The dinner looks lovely but I don't really feel much like eating. I've kind of lost my appetite lately.'

'I was going to go out after I'd made you this incredibly healthy and delicious dinner. Into town. You know, have a bit of a life.' Kathy looked away.

'Oh.'

'And you really have to eat stir-fries straight away. But go and have your swim. Don't worry about me.'

'Are you sure?'

'Not really, but go.'

The conversation sat on Maya's tongue like medicine as she swam. She was stronger now but she still tired easily. How strange it was to have a body capable enough, yet one that was like a wind-up toy. She wound down so quickly these days.

Backstroke. She watched her arms swing through the air. The water that fell from their fingertips dropped back into the pool and was swallowed up by the mass. But at each stroke there was more. Water washed over her face. She spat out at each breath. I was going to go out. Stroke, stroke, feet kicking all the time. Go and have your swim. Stroke, stroke. Go. No matter how many lengths she did – and today she pushed on past the point that she knew was enough – no matter how much water she bathed her mouth with, she still couldn't get the taste out.

Kathy placed a cup of tea on the table beside Maya's chair. 'Cats' piss,' she said.

'Just how I like it. Thanks.' It was smooth and hot. Two rogue tea leaves clung to the side of the cup. 'Aah,' she said as she felt it slide down her throat. It soothed the lining of her stomach, angry and raw from the chemotherapy.

'I'm off to work,' said Kathy. She picked up her keys from the bench. 'You remember work, don't you?' Her face remained almost completely impassive but the corners of her mouth gave her away with a slight twitch.

'It's a hazy memory,' Maya said. 'You'll have to tell me about it sometime.'

'Will you be okay? I feel bad going back and leaving you here.'

'I'll be fine,' Maya said brightly. 'I've got Charlie to keep an eye on me.'

'If you're sure?' She stopped at the doorway. 'Is this what it's like being a mother?'

'Being a mother is much harder than looking after me. But thank you for the sentiment.'

'What's on your agenda today?'

'Oh, you know. Lie around, read a magazine. Sit in the garden.'

'Don't overdo it, Mrs Wimple, will you?'

'We might go to the beach later. If it's not too hot.'

'Take it easy, then.'

'Hey, before you go, I'm sorry about the other day.'

Kathy shrugged. 'Don't worry.'

'No, really. I'm sorry to have burdened you with all this.'

'Don't be silly.'

'Well, I just wanted to tell you. Now you'd better get going before you get the sack.'

'I'll leave the door open,' Kathy called from the front door. 'Let some breeze through.'

And she was gone, but there was something unresolved about not hearing the front door shut, Maya thought, so she got up from her chair and went down the hall. She stood there, looking out onto the quiet street. The garden across the road blazed with Californian poppies. Even from where she stood she could see their papery petals wave slowly in the hot morning air. A cat leapt out from the orange and ran across the street to Maya's hedge, stopped suddenly, then ran back. She shook her head and smiled.

She turned back to the lounge, stood there in the hall for a moment, then pushed the front door shut.

Her tea was just warm now. Still refreshing, still a delicious ritual. She looked into the cup. This was the way to best enjoy it: delicately flavoured, no milk, pale like ginger ale. Cats' piss indeed.

She set the cup down on the table, folded her hands on her lap and closed her eyes.

'Mum, Mum, guess what I've been doing.'

Maya opened her eyes and wiped the corner of her mouth

with the back of her hand.

'What, buddy?'

'I've been playing with the new cat that lives across the road. It came over and I built a fort out of little branches and stuff and it was jumping in it and chasing the sticks and everything. Come and have a look.'

She followed him outside, where the black cat she had seen earlier was lying on the lawn, sleek and low, its bottom wiggling, as it prepared to attack a ribbon that Charlie had tied onto a branch in his fort.

'Isn't it cute?' Charlie said.

Maya sat on the step. Red and white nemesias spilled over the sides of the planter box.

She watched the cat, but now she was seeing another one, a grey striped cat called Cash. Its belly was white and soft.

We love cats, she could hear her mother saying, but especially Cash. He's our special one.

Cash would wait at the corner for Maya to come home from school. How did he know? she wondered. How long did he sit there, waiting for her? As soon as he saw her round the corner he ran up, slipping through her ankles, his tail tickling the backs of her knees. He miaowed and purred all the way home, as though he was telling her about his day.

I see your friend found you, her mother said as Maya and Cash tripped over each other to get inside.

He ate stewing steak, which Maya's mother bought from the butcher and cut into tiny cubes. She parcelled up the meat into plastic bags and froze it. Look, two weeks' worth from that cut. Won't Cash love this? Or fish from which Maya had to pull the tiny bones and scales. Fish bones could get stuck in his throat, darling. We wouldn't want that to happen. But cats eat fish in the wild, Maya thought, and no one takes the bones out for them. Still, we love Cash, she reminded herself, as she separated the flesh and placed another bone, as thin as a needle, into the pile on the bench.

He lapped water from his bowl with his delicate tongue. Maya sometimes pretended to be a cat but she couldn't get her tongue to curl up the way Cash's did.

Every night Cash followed Maya's mother to bed.

Sometimes Maya crept into her mother's bed during the night because she was lonely or cold or frightened by dreams that breathed on the back of her neck. Sometimes she stood at her mother's door, on her way back from the toilet, just to watch her sleeping (and her face was soft and smooth as she slept). And always there was Cash, folded into a small bundle, no distinguishable parts of him visible, lying in the wedge behind her mother's knees, or tight against her belly.

How lucky he was. To be allowed to sleep on Maya's mother's bed every night. Not gently coaxed back to another bed after a sleepy cuddle, shh, it's all right, you're safe now. But claiming that space whenever he chose.

When she was feeling really brave she would go right up to her mother's bed, listen to her soft breathing and stroke Cash's fur. He would make a small cat noise but he never moved. The tingle of his cool fur remained on Maya's hand long after she went back to bed.

After her mother's things were boxed up and given away (to poor folk who need them more than us, Gran said), there was only Maya and her belongings to move to Gran's. And Cash.

I'm not having that thing in my house, Gran said. Look at him. Cats are dirty animals. Look at how he licks himself – even there – and you let his nose touch you. It's disgusting. I won't have him.

Go and get a cardboard box from the shed, Maya. And the Sellotape.

And because Maya's mother had died only days earlier and now she was living in Gran's house (which smelled of a strange mixture of lavender and cabbage), and the bed that she now slept in and was so high off the ground that she made herself not turn over in her sleep in case she fell out – because of all of that, Maya did as she was told. She stood still and watched as Gran pushed Cash, spitting and scratching, into the box and she stood still and watched as the lid was taped shut.

He won't be able to breathe, she said in a quiet voice.

That's not your worry, Gran said. Now, in the car.

157

She could hear Cash in his box, in the boot, miaowing as they drove. North, past Te Karaka, past Matawai and into the gorge where the rock face lurched up on one side of the road, and fell away, down steep, steep banks to the Waioeka River on the other.

Gran pulled over and parked her big noisy car in a patch of gravel off the road. Dust flew up all around them as they got out. Maya could taste it.

The boot lid opened up like a wide mouth and Gran leaned in for Cash in the cardboard box. *Griffin's Best Biscuits* was stamped on four sides of the box. *This way up.*

Follow me, Gran said.

She scrambled down the bank, the box wide in her arms. Maya was right there, behind her, watching the back of Gran's short-sleeved cardy flap from side to side. They skidded to a stop at the bottom, among the rocks and craggy plants; lupins and golden-tipped gorse, and there was the Waioeka, roaring past them, in front of them, all around them it seemed.

Gran stepped forward, balancing on the smooth rocks like a tightrope walker. Forward, forward, and now she stood in the water. Her feet disappeared, her thick ankles. The hem of her summer dress swirled on the surface.

Maya stayed back, pressing herself against the bank. She could not take her eyes off Gran's dress and the flowers floating there.

Then she saw Gran lean back, then lunge herself forward, thrusting her arms out and Maya saw the cardboard box and *Griffin's Best Biscuits* and the Sellotape that went around and around the box and glinted and twinkled in the sunlight, fly up into the sky, up, out, out, and down in a perfect arc and then splash into the water.

The box landed upside down. *This way up* was upside down. *Griffin's Best Biscuits* was upside down. Cash was surely upside down.

Gran turned back and wiped her hands down the front of her dress (and Maya was sure they would leave red streaks down the fabric). 'Well, that's that, then,' she said and she began to climb back up the bank.

'Are you okay, Mum? Mum?'

Maya shivered and wrapped her arms around her legs. 'I'm fine, buddy.'

'Then how come you're crying?'

'Let's go to the beach.'

Charlie squinted up at her. His small face looked like an old man's, the skin across his forehead furrowed. A stick hung uselessly from his hand. The cat from over the road padded across the lawn and lay on the hot soil of Maya's vege garden. A cherry tomato dropped off the vine as the cat wriggled against it. The tiny ripe fruit rolled along the ground. The cat watched it for a moment, then yawned its wide, sharp-toothed yawn and went to sleep.

'Well?' she said.

'Yeah, I guess. Only if you're feeling okay. We won't if you don't feel well enough to go. I mean, you're sick and everything and . . .' Charlie's voice flickered like a candle trying to stay alight. He shrugged and looked down at his feet.

Suddenly, Maya was drenched with anger, overflowing with it. Her body was shaking. She was afraid of what she might do, how her body might behave, so she pressed her lips hard together.

Why did everything, *everything*, have to be measured in relation to her cancer? Why could they not be an ordinary mother and son having an ordinary near-the-end-of-the-holidays conversation about what they should do?

Why should Charlie have to carry the weight of this disease? Be affected by it, whether it be through Maya's increasingly irrational moods or her physical deterioration?

He never knew whether she would be tender or harsh, loving or silencing, physical or distant. It must be so confusing for him, she thought. But she couldn't help it. She tried to be even, deliberate, calm, but the somatic and mental demons won out every time and she had to give in to them. She had to.

It seemed that her heritage was being thrust upon him. Would Charlie, in time, be required to relive the fear, the anger, the

159

uncertainty, the loneliness and the despair that she had felt when her own mother became sick? And died.

Was this disease going to thrust a cyclic inevitability on them? How could she let that happen? How could she allow him to wander, as she had, bumping into walls and finding himself (herself) in dark corners?

Treading water.

Her hands shook at her sides. She slapped them against her legs and jumped up. Sparks of electricity leapt through her – from her toes, up her legs, across her torso, zap zap at her chest, over her shoulders, down her arms to her screaming fingers and through her head at the same time. If she opened her mouth, she was sure she would exhale lightning.

Fight it, fight it, a voice (God, her mother, Charlie, herself) said. This anger, edged in deathly fatigue, swirled about her like sea foam.

Charlie was still looking down at his feet, curling and uncurling his toes. His toenails needed cutting, Maya noticed. I can't do everything, she thought. I can't do it all. It's too fucking hard. And her next thought –

But who else is there? There's no one else in the whole wide world for him. No one. We're it.

She brought her hands up to her mouth as if to prevent this thought (uncensored, unprepared for) leaking out from her lips and becoming real.

'Mum?' Charlie's voice was tentative like the rustle of tissue paper. 'Are you okay? Can I get you . . .'

There it was again. She was the needy one, the one who required tending, and a boy who was about to turn nine, was burdened with her. With it all.

It was all so confusing. She shook her head, rubbed her hands over her cheeks.

'Oh, Charlie,' she said. 'I'm sorry.'

He stood there, as still as the copper gardening lady who smiled endlessly, benignly as she watched over the garden.

'Look, you have to stop worrying about me.' She gathered him to her and his body was tight and resistant against her. She smoothed her hands down his head. His hair was silk in her fingers. Aah, the feel of his hair. Clean, like washing on the line. Now he relaxed and hugged her back. 'It's my job to do the worrying,' she said. 'You just be the kid, okay?' These were the words she knew she had to say. Straight from The Mothers' Handbook. She didn't believe them, but she sounded so convincing she almost had herself fooled. Almost.

Fuck it all, she thought.

'Okay,' said Charlie.

What was he talking about? That's right. He would be the kid again.

'Are we still going to the beach?'

Maya wanted to stay home, crawl under the sheets in her bed and close her eyes to everything. She wanted darkness, silence. She did not want the midsummer dazzle of the beach.

'Are we?' he said. He pulled a daisy from the lawn and held it out to her. Its petals were as soft as a butterfly kiss as she held it between her fingers.

'All right.' Concession. Giving in. Giving up. Smiling weakly. 'Go and get your things.'

And then he was at the front door, baggy swim shorts on, his towel rolled up under his arm.

'Have you got your flippers?'

'Oh, I forgot.'

Come on, Charlie.

'Have you got sunscreen?'

'Oh, I forgot.'

Jesus.

'Have you got your hat?'

'Oh, Mu-um.'

See, I still have to do everything. Think of everything. Even if you say you'll look after me, Charlie, you can't, can you? You're a boy. You just can't.

'In the car,' she said, and she shivered. That was what Gran had said. Her past was all around her. It would never leave her alone.

161

'Which beach?' she said, trying to drown out Gran's voice.

'I'm right here, Mum. You don't have to shout at me.'

'All right,' she snapped. Charlie flinched, as though it had been her hand she had raised to him, not just her voice. Maybe that was just as bad.

As she clipped in her seatbelt Maya's forearm grazed her scar. It was hard, flat, and it still tingled like pins and needles when she touched it.

'Haven't you got your seatbelt done up yet?' She glared at Charlie in the rearview mirror and slammed the car into reverse. This power over him gave her a perverse sense of pleasure. It tasted bitter in her mouth all the same.

'I'm not ready,' he said, and she could see him trying to find where the clip fitted.

'You'll just have to hurry up in future.'

Stop it. Just stop it, she thought. But there it was again, that thrill that ran through her.

'Are we going to Waikanae?' a hesitant voice asked.

'I suppose.'

The silence in the car pushed against the doors, the windows. It filled up all the available space.

'Why are you sitting in the back?' Maya said when they stopped at the traffic lights. She turned around to Charlie and smiled at him.

He looked out the window. 'I dunno.'

By the time they got to the beach Maya's mood had eased. It smouldered still in her belly, but she was sure that an ice-cream and some time by the water would smother it.

'Stay between the flags,' she called to Charlie's back as he ran down to the water. He skipped over the tiny waves lolling at the edge, and once the water was up to his knees he dived under, surfacing a moment later, grinning and signalling to her. Maya raised her arm back to him. It would all be okay now.

Thirteen

This cancer was like a silent monster, an undersea creature, a taniwha maybe. It could hold its breath for weeks, months, years (it had), and when it came up through the surface you hardly noticed the swell it made.

It may have looked around for a few moments, its dark and liquid eyes swivelling, while it sucked on the fresh air, fed from it. And then it may have sunk down again, flicked its terrible tail, closed its eyes and waited until it was time to breathe again.

Her hand itched to pick up her book. This was the first time she'd felt like reading, or had the concentration to, since – when? Since it all started. And that felt like years ago. It's funny how everyday life travels so slowly and normally, and then when something catastrophic happens, days and weeks scurry past, Maya thought. It was as if they were trying to get through it as quickly as possible.

But instead of reading she watched Charlie in the surf. She shuddered involuntarily, as though her body was ridding itself of the anger that still surrounded her. Like an aura, she thought. What colour would it be? Grey, probably. Or brown like the baked farmland on the Makarori hills. Or black.

She rubbed her hands up and down her legs. Grains of sand

bruised her skin. They were specks of rocks and shells that had rattled against one another here for a million years and had shed layer and layer of themselves until Maya could sift their remains between her fingers. The sensation of the sand on her legs made her feel alive. Her calves tingled, sizzled.

She looked back out to Charlie. The sun shimmered directly above him, a dazzling marker. She shielded it from her eyes with her hands. Sand dropped off her fingers. It was gritty rain. There he was, jumping up out of the water, his body wriggling and sleek like a dolphin. Bodysurfing in on thick waves, up to the shore, and coming to rest on the wet sand. Lying on his back and letting the force of the water tumble him along.

He was born for the sea, she thought. He was so secure, so strong out there.

There was something about standing on the edge of the land, about being in constant danger of floating out on the receding tide, or being swept away, caught in the arms of a riptide, that made you strong. It anchored you to the land. You knew how big it all was when you could see the straight line that was the end of the world.

'Mum, Mum, you should come in. It's awesome.' Charlie collapsed beside her, falling dramatically onto his back, his arms flung wide. Water beaded his skin. A crust of sand stuck to his back and shoulders, like a shell.

'You look like you're having fun.' She wanted him to go back in the water so she could watch him but at a distance. She didn't want him right here, panting, dripping seawater and sand onto her.

'Come on.'

She had no choice. 'All right then.' She stood up and undid the sarong knotted at her waist. She followed Charlie into the water, her arms crossed. Her head was bare.

'Watch this,' Charlie called, and he dived under. Maya saw him in front of her, this fish boy, swirling, his feet kicking like a scaly tail. The water tumbled about her, blue, now grey and black with a silver fringe. She looked around for the flash of yellow that was his hair (but dark, surely, underwater), for his torso that through the water looked like china. Where was he? Snapping her head from side to side, searching, staring. Charlie. The sea frothed still. She went to call out his name, but her voice was snatched from inside her mouth by the wind stirring up the surface of water.

'Da daah,' she heard behind her. She spun around and there he was, emerging from the sea as if it was giving birth to him, as if he really might be a sea creature.

'Jesus Christ,' she said. There was no relief, no compassion, or if there was, it was hidden many layers beneath the anger and fear that now overwhelmed her. Or maybe it *was* relief, calling itself by another name. 'Don't ever do that. Out. Now.'

'But Mum . . .'

'Now.'

She waded back through the surf, her legs trembling. Charlie was behind her, following in her wake. Once she found the safety of her towel she let her breath come in gasps. Charlie sat down next to her, his legs bent up, arms wrapped around them. She pressed her hands to her head. Absurdly, the words of one of his school songs came into her head.

One day a taniwha
Went swimming in the moana,
It whispered in my taringa,
Oh won't you come with me,
There's such a lot to see,
Underneath the deep blue sea.

What was the next verse? She hummed the tune. Maybe she'd remember that way.

Chemo day. Again. Every third Monday came around so quickly. Everything related to that day. There was the build-up – the Saturday and Sunday before, when Maya was physically feeling stronger but hammered by the prospect of her imminent treatment. Then the Monday itself. And then the effects of it, which left her so weak for the next forty-eight hours she was unable even to sit up. There was nausea when she opened her eyes and when she kept them closed. When she lay on her side or on her back. When she went to sleep.

When she woke up again. And vomiting that racked her body until she cried.

Shh, Maya, it won't last long. Look how brave you are. She could feel her mother place a damp flannel on her forehead. She leaned into it as she vomited. And now she was running the flannel across the back of Maya's neck. It made her shiver. Her mother smelled of violets.

Tummy bugs are the worst things. Shh, sweet. She replaced Maya's sickie bowl as soon as she had used it, even if she had only spat up the saliva that built up in her mouth. She changed the linen twice a day and the fresh sheets were as cool and smooth as ice-cream against her cheek. Her mother flicked the folded sheets open and they snapped like a cowboy's whip as they separated themselves. She never complained, even though she had already been diagnosed with her own disease.

It won't last long. You'll be better tomorrow, my love. You'll see. There was ginger ale in a glass on Maya's bedside table, and when she couldn't do anything else she watched the bubbles pull themselves off the bottom of the glass and float to the top, where they were suspended for a moment before exploding silently, an army's worth of tiny liquid gingery bombs.

You'll be better tomorrow. Maya repeated these words as she lay in bed, afraid to sleep (in case she wasn't) but too exhausted to stay awake. This was like having a tummy bug every day, and no amount of ginger ale or damp flannels would make her better.

Her mother just might have, Maya thought as she finally gave in.

Then there were several days of respite, of relative normality before it was chemo day again.

And it *was* chemo day again.

Maya closed her eyes but the sun pounded through her eyelids still and she had to roll onto her side with her hand over her face to block out the burn of the day.

'Rise and shine.'

'Go away, Kathy. I'm on strike today.'

'I don't think so. You've got an appointment with a very fine bag of IV fluids, I think.'

'Go away.'

'Come on, Maya. You don't want to be late and have to rush around at the last minute. That'll just make things worse.'

'Oh, will it? And who died and made you the oncology expert all of a sudden?'

'I'm just trying to help.'

'Well, don't.'

'Maya.'

'For God's sake, Kathy. I just want to stay in bed.'

'Well, for your information, I just want to get on with my life and not have to be your nursemaid and Charlie's surrogate mother. If you must know.'

'Fuck off somewhere else, then. Leave us alone. We don't need you, you know.'

'All right then,' said Kathy. She turned with a flourish more extravagant than was necessary and stalked out of Maya's room.

A host of sparrows chatted outside. You can shut the fuck up, too, Maya thought.

'Jesus, Charlie, will you hurry up and get organised.'

He placed a piece of Lego onto the World's Tallest Tower of Blue Lego Bricks. He said he was going to be in the *Guinness Book of World Records*. 'I'm just –'

'I am so sick of hearing I'm just. Just do it, will you? I'm taking a taxi to hospital today and I need to drop you at Jacob's first, so we need to get on with it.'

'All right. I'm just –'

'Charlie!' The tower swayed as Maya slammed her hand onto the table. Charlie protected it with his hands to hold it steady. It was almost as tall as he was.

'Why can't Kathy take us? She always takes us.'

'Not today she can't.'

'Why can't you drive us then?'

'I might be feeling too tired to drive afterwards, buddy. It wouldn't be very safe to drive like that, would it?' She was already

167

feeling too tired. Too tired to drive, to talk, to argue, to think.

'I don't think this chemo stuff is a very good idea if it makes you so yucky. You felt okay before you started having it, didn't you?'

That was the truth of it. Right there. She *had* felt okay before her course of chemo. Perfectly fine. Perfectly fit. Just the owner of a breast lump that wasn't really doing anyone any harm, sitting there, minding its own business (yet all the while its telescopic octopus arms were caressing her, feeling out the softest places to hide within her). That was all.

'Yeah, I did. Rachael would say the cure is worse than the complaint. But it's working. It's making me better.'

'But you look stink, Mum.'

The blood fled from her face. She felt it – the chill that was her cheeks blanching. Her fingers found the edge of the table and gripped it.

'Thank you very much,' she said quietly and she turned to the phone to call a taxi.

The La-Z-Boy chair – her La-Z-Boy chair with its stiff off-white drawsheet tucked under its arms – looked like the scariest place to be and yet the safest place to be. Maya closed her eyes against the stinging tears as she sat back, pulling up a rough blue cuddly blanket to her chin. She began to shiver.

'Are you not well?' said Jane. Always poised, perfect. Even her shoes were immaculate. 'I'd better check your temp.'

'It hasn't been a very good day, so far. That's all. I'm fine.' She smiled weakly. Her teeth felt too big for her mouth.

'Best to check, though.' She slipped a thermometer into Maya's mouth. It tasted of alcohol. It jabbed into the soft tissue under her tongue. Maya began to cry.

'Lots of patients get down like this towards the end of their treatment,' said Jane. 'It's like the end is in sight, but you can't imagine it yet.'

Maya nodded. She wiped at her nose with a tissue. There was an ulcer, like a coldsore, on her nostril. It leaked serum and blood onto the wad of paper in her hand.

'See, I'm falling apart.'

'Not true,' said Jane as she read the thermometer, turning it between her fingers to see the mercury line. 'Afebrile. And your bloods look good. You're doing well, Maya.'

Am I?

Am I?

And how would you know anyway? A lab results form and a normal temp are not the indicators of my state of being, she thought.

'You'll be having radiotherapy, won't you? Then we'll have this cancer beaten. Now, let's get started.'

Maya waited for the cold sweat to overtake her. There it was. It was surely a physiological response, coming on within minutes of the first drug being injected.

And the exhaustion that threw her against the chair and was like anaesthetic in its intensity.

And the vomiting. More severe now, long-lasting.

Let's hope it's all worth it.

Let's.

I'm so tired. Maya lay there, staring at the pattern on the wallpaper. She followed a faint squiggly line, one in a wall full of muted scribbles, around, around, up, left, down, with her eyes until it disappeared into another line that was like worm tracks in front of her. What an awful first thought of the day. But there it was, thought, and so a reality. She couldn't take it back.

I'm so sick of myself. There. Another one. She wanted to prick those thoughts with a pin and they would disappear – poof – and it would be as if they had never existed.

It was Saturday. School had started again. A new year. Charlie, who was probably downstairs eating cereal and watching cartoons, should have been getting ready for cricket. He should have been laying out his bat, with his name printed on it as neatly as he had been able to manage, and his red ball with the white stitching, by the front door. What else? Drink bottle, muesli bar, apple, floppy sunhat and Gameboy.

I don't think cricket would be a good idea, Maya had said when he'd brought the notice home from school, his eyes bright with anticipation. I'm not sure that I'll be up to it. You know – every Saturday. Getting you to the matches.

I'll make it up to you though.

Whatever, Charlie had said, and he turned his shoulder away and scratched at the edge of the dining-room table until flakes of varnish scattered across his thin legs.

I'm sorry, Maya thought. She was always saying sorry, subsuming herself, apologising for being late, being absent, keeping people waiting, troubling them (doctors, lab technicians, nurses).

I'm sorry my veins are so bad, she said to Jane on one of those Mondays. Her mouth was bitter tasting, her tongue coated. Jane tapped along the length of Maya's forearm with the tip of her finger. She flicked at Maya's veins as if to bully them into life.

Even her veins were tired, refusing to cooperate. I'll have to get one of the house surgeons, Jane had said.

But that's no use, Maya wanted to say. You're better at finding a vein than any first-year house surgeon with coat pockets bulging with copies of the Oxford Handbook and the tails of stethoscopes. They just rush in with their sweaty palms and jab the needle in and in, distracted by the beepers that go off in their pockets, and by theatre lists and outpatient clinics and discharge notes that have to be written. They jab and jab, using the principles of anatomy, this is where the cephalic vein should be, not understanding that Maya was not a page from the textbook, or a teaching specimen (a cadaver that they named Doris or Bob or Frank and spent Tuesday afternoons cutting up and poking into and sewing up again for a year during Anatomy).

She was none of these things and she was sorry that her veins had backed themselves up against the walls of her, standing as flat and thin as they could, but there it was and they were refusing to step forward. I'm sorry for being a nuisance, she said. The house surgeon had jabbed and jabbed and Maya wondered when it would be over and tears fell down her face and onto the paper sheet that was under her arm, keeping the field sterile. Now it was splashed with her tears and she sat there staring at the spot and wondered if tears were sterile, and as hard as she tried to remember, she could not.

But it was Saturday morning and Charlie couldn't play cricket because of her. Because of this disease that was making her feel like shit. No, that was wrong, she thought. It wasn't the disease that was to blame; it was the treatment – the drugs, the needles, the mouth ulcers, the vomiting, the nausea that lay in her belly, rolling over from time to time, stretching its putrid limbs, making itself comfortable.

I'll make up to you, Charlie. I promise. She closed her eyes, as though keeping them open would allow the promise to leak out. But as she did, her old friend nausea suddenly sat up and so did Maya and she made it to the toilet just in time to retch bubbly saliva and bile into the bowl. Her knees pressed into the cold tiles and she stayed there, trembling, crying, gripping the edges of the toilet. She watched the slippery bile float on the surface. It was like an oil slick, making use of the water for its home but remaining separate from it. She spat out saliva and it hit the green scum, disturbing it and breaking it in two.

Outside, Charlie was drawing alien attackers on the concrete with coloured chalk.

Maya was back in bed now. The curtains were closed; her room was cool and grey. She was on her side, her hands pressing against the wound across her chest. Pushing against the nerve endings there, squashing them flat. Her throat hurt. Now she cried silently. Everything hurt a little less that way.

Fourteen

'You have to start radiotherapy, Maya. Five weeks, one treatment every day. But of course we don't have the facilities to do that here, so we're going to have to send you down to Palmerston North.'

Maya stared at a spot on the floor, a ragged stain that might have been from a spilled cup of coffee. She traced around the edges of it with her eyes until the mark became blurred and wavy and she had to blink the image away.

Palmerston North. It might as well have been San Salvador.

She'd known, of course, that this would happen – having to undergo radiotherapy, and having to go out of town for it, but she'd hoped it would be one of those things that if you didn't think about it, it might not happen. She was sure that trick would work. She'd fought off a host of problems and possibilities using that method.

Where would she stay? What would Charlie do? Five weeks was such a long time, especially for a kid. Would he come with her, and if so, how would she look after him? She knew that radiotherapy caused devastating fatigue. She wouldn't be in any condition to care for him or keep him safe. But he if stayed in Gisborne who would look after him then? Why was this all so hard? God, where was Philip when you needed him? Or his parents, or hers? Why did death hold the balance every single fucking time?

'Well, then,' she said. 'We'd better get things organised.' She knew, of course that she had no control in the planning of this treatment. She would be handed a letter, a card, an invitation to attend the radiotherapy department at Palmerston North Hospital. She would have no say in when. She was slipping further away from herself. For the first time she was really scared.

The oncologist, Dr Goodman, lived in Palmerston North and travelled up to Gisborne once a month to see the cancer patients there. He handed her a brochure: *Welcome to Palmerston North. Your home away from home.* There was a photo of a turn-of-the-century villa framed in wisteria. Maya could almost hear the bees buzzing. Jaunty yellow daffodils edged the path from the picket fence to the front door.

'This is where our patients stay,' Dr Goodman said. 'Everything is there for you: your own room, private bathroom, staff on hand to help should you need it.' He smiled at her. 'Most patients find it is a very pleasant environment.'

'Good. Sounds better than a Caribbean cruise.' She sounded so feeble, she knew.

'Here's the number of our coordinator. She'll give you all the details. I'll see you in balmy Palmy, then.'

He held out his hand and Maya slipped hers inside it. He stood up and opened his arm, indicating the door.

I'm being dismissed, she thought. And she allowed herself to be. She no longer had the energy to do otherwise.

Charlie couldn't keep still. He jumped around the lounge, out to the front door, back again. He stood by as Maya tied balloons to the letterbox. Blue and orange, this week's favourite colours. When the first car arrived, he ran out and pulled open its doors.

'Jacob!' They bounded inside, these two best friends, Jacob's present unnoticed on the back seat of the car. Then out through the back door like two small easterly blasts, and onto the trampoline.

'Good luck,' Rachael said from behind the steering wheel.

Maya bent over to look in through the passenger window, her

arms crossed. She saw herself as *her* mother; this was how *she* stood, how *she* carried herself. 'We'll be fine,' she said. It was her mother's voice that came out of her mouth. Rachael didn't seem to notice.

'Hope you all manage to get some sleep.'

'Thanks.'

'You'll be okay?'

'Absolutely. Don't worry about a thing.'

'Okay, then. See you tomorrow.'

And Rachael was off. Maya stood on the footpath, one hand on her hip, the other waving. She suddenly felt very alone.

'Are you sure you don't mind staying?' Maya stood at the bench, tipping popcorn into a big plastic bowl.

'Of course I don't. I said I'd help.' Kathy took a chocolate crackle from a plate and peeled off its paper case. 'Yum.' She rearranged the others on the plate to fill in the space.

'You're not supposed to eat the party food.'

'Oh, you're no fun.'

'Are you absolutely sure you're okay to stay and help out?'

'I said, didn't I?'

'Yes, but –'

'But nothing. I love kids' parties anyway. Fairy bread. Yum.'

'We could have kids' food for your next birthday.'

Kathy took the bowl of popcorn and placed it on the table, a rage of colours and tastes. 'You're on, Mrs Wimple.'

Soon the house filled up with boys, each outdoing the others in noise and energy. They were commandos, super heroes, alien attackers. The trampoline became neutral territory. Home base.

'Didn't you have a two-people-on-the-trampoline-only rule?'

Maya followed Kathy's gaze. A flurry of arms and legs wrestled on the trampoline. 'Once upon a time I did. But you want to try getting them to stick to that today? We'll have a party game when the first argument breaks out,' she said.

The afternoon fled by. They played Spin the Bottle, sitting in a circle, each child with his gift in front of him. Whoever the bottle pointed to, Charlie opened that boy's present.

'It's not like the Spin the Bottle I remember,' said Kathy.

'Cool. Awesome. Wicked.'

These were very good presents.

'Okay.' Maya clapped her hands together. 'Who's ready for the cake?'

Small arms shot into the air. A circle of voices chorused me, me.

'Right then. Everybody around the table. Charlie, I need the birthday boy standing here.' She manoeuvred him by his thin shoulders to the head of the table. The ideal photographic position. 'Now, everybody shush while I get the cake.'

She lit the candles on the cake, which stood on the bench in the kitchen. They made a line of small flames. Nine. She shook her head. How did that happen? How did Charlie suddenly get to be turning nine?

She went to pick up the cake, a blue-green volcano, snow-capped, standing on an oven tray, exactly like the one she remembered from years before. But her hands couldn't manage it. Her arms couldn't lift the tray.

'Shit,' she muttered. She tried again. Nope. 'Kathy, can you carry this for me, please?' She had no choice. She couldn't carry the cake; she was no longer strong enough.

The realisation caused a pain in her chest. A physical ache, like when you swallow a mouthful of fresh white bread without chewing it properly, and then another one, and they jam up against each other in your gullet, unable to move. Heartburn.

A burning heart.

How could she let Kathy take over the most important part of Charlie's birthday? The presentation of the cake, an offering, a ceremonial gifting. It was her job, as the mother, the carer, the nurturer, it was she who had a physical, physiological connection to this child. It was she who should present him with the cake.

She couldn't do it.

175

Kathy picked up the tray as easily as if it were a piece of card. She smiled the smile of the bearer of very good news. She began to sing. 'Happy birthday to you . . .'

No, Maya thought. No.

And then she picked up the camera (because there was nothing else she could do) and followed Kathy into the dining room.

She pushed away the feelings that were building in her throat: jealousy, resentment, helplessness, fear. They were such ugly words.

'This is what you do, guys.' And now she was her own mother again, but instead of billowy hair like foam, Maya's head was yellow and pink paisley, fabric as soft as the sea. 'There's a bottle for each of you. And this one's coconut. For the snow.'

She looked down at her hands, holding the tray of squeezy bottles full of sauces: maple, chocolate, strawberry, passionfruit with seeds like tadpoles. They were her mother's hands. The veins that ran the length of her forearms, the spots that were starting to form on the backs of her hands, the shape of her fingers, even the peep of white moons at the base of her thumbnails.

Maya scooped ice-cream into the bowls lined up on the bench. It curled around itself inside the spoon. She sprinkled hundreds and thousands on each one.

I'll ask Rachael when she comes to get Jacob in the morning, Maya thought as the tiny sugary grains landed on the ice-cream. The colours bled into the white. It'll just be for when I'm in Palmerston. I'm sure it will be okay. I'll be able to pay her back. Look how well the two of them get on. (Thinking – almost like brothers – and then hurrying that thought out of her head.) It might even give Rachael a break. I mean, the two of them being best friends, they'd be easier to take care of than just Jacob on his own. Charlie would keep him company.

Maya was convinced. She was sure Rachael would see it the same way. She didn't want to burden Kathy with Charlie any more. She was talking about moving back to her own place anyway. It was clear that she had had enough of looking after the two of them.

Charlie loved Kathy. Theirs was a special friendship. A mixture, a marbelling of aunt and nephew, adult and child, teacher and student, wise friend and novice. But Maya didn't want Kathy to look after him when she went away. It would be too easy to hand him over. Too easy to give him away.

If she did, would she ever get him back? Of course she knew she would. Intellectually, common sense and trust told her this. But a small emotional place inside her knocked with its fine fingers (like a pixie, an imp), saying you'll lose him. His spirit. His soul.

Give him away for five weeks and you've lost him forever.

I'll be like Scarlett and think about it tomorrow, she thought. 'Come and get some pudding,' she called, and almost before she got the words out, the party boys materialised in front of her. They clambered over one another like puppies (with paws and ears they were sure to grow into), grabbing the bowls of ice-cream. It was as if they were starving. 'I'm sure you guys had a whole heap of party food just a little while ago,' Maya said.

They were so noisy, so physical around her. Her ears buzzed. Her body ached.

'You look terrible, old thing,' said Kathy. She piled dirty plates onto the bench. 'Go to bed. I'll deal with these boys.'

She didn't argue. She lay in bed, drifting uneasily between sleep and wakefulness, hearing the boys lined up on the lounge floor, in their sleeping bags and best pyjamas, laughing, telling jokes, shushing each other. She heard Kathy go in. This is your last warning, boys. I'll phone up the mother of whoever makes the next sound, and that person will go home. And then there was silence. Just when she thought she would get up and check, because it was surely too quiet, she closed her eyes again, just to rest them for a moment.

Laughter again. These boys had an endless supply. Like Willie Wonka's everlasting gobstoppers.

Maya turned onto her side. 8:11. Late summer slipped into her room. It was hot and as yellow as butter. Only three more hours and Charlie's party would be over. She should get up and make breakfast. He had wanted fresh fruit, cut up and laid out on big plates like in a restaurant, and muffins, blueberry in one basket and chocolate in another. Maya had spent ages cutting up melons: mushy orange ones, clear green ones with skin like worm tracks, and juicy pink watermelon with black seeds. She'd sliced pineapple into thin rounds and cut the stems off fat hairy strawberries. With every piece of fruit she cut, her nausea became more intense. It's Charlie's birthday, she said to herself. He's what matters. I'll be fine.

It was all in the fridge, perfectly arranged on white plates she had unearthed from the bottom of the china cabinet. They'd needed washing before she used them. I'll keep them out from now on, she'd thought.

All she had to do was go downstairs and put the things on the table. Pour juice into glasses. That was all. She closed her eyes, just to rest them for a moment.

They were outside playing statues when Maya eventually went downstairs, knotting her scarf behind her head as she went through the kitchen. The day was hard at work. The remains of breakfast littered the table. A single sliver of pineapple, one watermelon triangle, a single strawberry. Why did no one want to eat the last piece of anything on the plate? Maya wondered. It was always the case. Maiden aunts, Gran used to call them – the last biscuit or piece of cake left. What was wrong with being a maiden aunt, then?

Maya had had no aunts to test this idea on. But Charlie, of course, did. Not that Kathy was ever thought of as a maiden aunt. Not even an aunt, really. If she asked him, she was certain Charlie would describe Kathy as a cool grown-up friend, or maybe a kind of mother figure that didn't nag, or tell him to pick up his clothes. (Exactly the kind of person a nine-year-old boy would love to go and live with.)

A muffin sat on the edge of the table, one bite taken out of it. She picked it up and put it on a plate next to a slice of musk melon. Somehow that was better. She followed the noise outside.

The concrete was too hot under her feet so she stepped onto the lawn to where the boys were dancing and jumping around in time to the music. All except Charlie, who moved slowly, deliberately. It seemed he had worked out he'd have less chance of being 'out' if he kept his movements to a minimum. The boys who flung themselves around wildly weren't able to stop so easily when Kathy turned off the music.

'You're out.'

'You're out.'

The game continued. Boys peeled off as they were caught moving when they were supposed to be statues, or because they got bored with the game.

Soon there were only Charlie and Jacob left.

'Come on, guys. Let's call it a draw,' said Kathy as she pressed Play on the cassette recorder again and again. When the music stopped they were completely motionless, and when it started up again they moved like small astronauts on a moon walk.

They began to glare at each other, make faces to distract the other. Maya could see the game had turned. It was more than playing now. I'll have to put a stop to this, she thought. They're going to end up fighting. She went to get up from the garden seat under the kowhai and just as she moved she saw one of the two lurch forward, his fists balled. The other boy lunged as well and now they were on the ground, rolling over and over as if they might be tumbling down a hill, but they were jumbled together – arms, knees, elbows, fists.

And now there was the tearing of fabric. And there was blood. Both boys became still, lying on the grass, panting.

'You've ripped my shirt,' Charlie said. 'I got this for my birthday.'

'Well, I'm bleeding. You made me bleed.'

They stood up, straightening their torn and stained clothes. Jacob had a bleeding nose. His face was smeared with red. It dripped onto his good shirt.

No one else moved. No one said a word.

'Man, my mother's going to spew when she sees my shirt. This is my only good one. Look, it's all dirty. I wear this shirt to church.'

'Sorry, Jacob.'

He shrugged. 'I've never had a bleeding nose before.'

'I'm so sorry, Rachael. I don't know what happened. I don't even know who started it. And neither of them is saying.' She held out Jacob's party bag.

Rachael took it as though it might be a used airsick bag. 'These things happen,' she said in a strained voice. 'Come on, Jacob. Now what do you say to Charlie's mum?'

'Thank you for having me,' he said automatically.

'And?'

'And . . .' Jacob looked up at his mother. He frowned.

'I'm sorry for what happened,' Rachael hissed.

'But –'

'I'm sorry for what happened,' she repeated, more quietly, through her teeth.

'I'm sorry for what happened,' Jacob said. He looked at his feet. Maya watched him flex his toes in his sandals. Up down up down.

'That's –' Maya began, but Rachael was gone, the party bag swinging in her hand. Jacob ran after her. They got into Rachael's car and drove away. Neither of them looked back. Not even once.

Maya shut the door. 'Fuck,' she said. 'Fuck, fuck, fuck.'

Maya squinted in front of her mirror. Her mouth was an O. The mascara wand was suspended halfway between her face and the mirror, where her other face was registering something like shock.

Her eyelashes were falling out. Like pickets of a tumbledown fence. One or two stood defiantly, and look, here was another one. The rest had succumbed.

Maybe it wasn't shock that had overtaken her face.
Maybe it was grief.

Sleep. Sleep. It was what her body wanted. What it needed to restore itself. But Maya's legs were twitchy, aching. Floosey legs, Philip had called it when she'd been troubled by the same jumpy legs during her pregnancy. She rubbed the outsides of her thighs, her knees. Keep them still, she told herself. Keep them still.

Her mother held one hand on top of Maya's hair, as if to anchor it to her head, while she brushed.

Hush little baby, don't say a word, as she ran the brush through her fine hair. It shone like a film star's, like the photo of Miss New Zealand that she had seen in her mother's *Woman's Weekly*.

Maya caught the perfume on her mother's wrist, stroke, stroke. She closed her eyes. We could stay here, me sitting at my mother's dressing table, her standing behind me, both of us looking into the mirror, her, me, brush, brush, our eyes meeting in the glass, for ever and ever.

She heard her own breath. It woke her up. She sat up, her heart thumping in her ears. Her face was wet. She looked at her hands, trembling in front of her like an old woman's.

Everything in her room seemed normal. The clock, the pile of books on her bedside table with their bookmarks sticking out like flat tongues, her dressing gown asleep at the end of her bed, a scarf stretched out on her dresser. It all looked the same.

She went to run her hands through her hair, but as they touched the bare skin of her scalp she pulled them away as if she had been burned on the stove.

And if that diamond ring don't shine.

She was sure she heard it. Her mother singing, and there was the smell of her. Maya slid out of bed, shivering in spite of the night's warmth. There was still the smouldering of an ache in her legs. Her feet took her from room to room. Mother, she wanted to whisper at each doorway, Mother, but as she did she knew the song would be caught on the outgoing tide and float away out to sea.

Heat radiated off her head.

Daddy's gonna buy you a horse and cart.

Running now, and her cotton pyjamas had worked themselves out of their buttons, and the top tucked itself under her arms. It flapped behind her like a cape.

The scar that ran across her chest was a silver ribbon, gathered, pleated to fit her.

Gasping, crying, she had to hold on to the bathroom door as she made sense of it all.

She was becoming two separate people.

One side was a woman, thirty-seven and a half, slim enough. The other was shapeless as a boy.

One side of her was a mother, in charge, making decisions (having to); the other was a little girl having her hair brushed by her own mother.

One side of her was managing, muddling through, thank you.

One side of her was married, a bride, a wife, hi darling at the end of the day. The other had sprinkled a handful of soil over the shiny lid of her husband's coffin. She thought she would never forget the sound it made.

She sat on the edge of the bath and brought her fingers to the inside of her wrist. Practised nurse's fingers. She was alive. But what was happening at each heartbeat? Was the cancer pulsing through her, to her bones, her lungs, her brain? Was that what the dreams were about?

Would she get weaker?

Maya, fill up my glass, there's a dear. Charlie, get me a drink, would you, chap?

Maya dear, heat up some soup for your dinner. Charlie, you'll have to have sandwiches or something for tea; I don't have the energy.

Maya, I've arranged for you to go and live with Gran. Charlie, what will happen to you?

And what would happen to *her*? Bedbound, coughing up blood into a wad of tissues, forgetting her son's name, or the way to the toilet?

Would she suffer pathological fractures, where there was no injury involved, but a bone, maybe a radius or a femur, shattered like the bone of a roast that's been left in the oven too long? Would she need increasing amounts of pain relief so that the shelf by her bed would become a jostle of bottles and pills? No, that had been her mother's shelf.

She didn't want any of the loss of dignity her mother had had, which seemed to be inevitable. She didn't want Charlie (yes, that was his name) to see her suffer, to suffer himself. She wasn't brave, no matter how hard she tried to be. It was just too hard. She was afraid. She was selfish.

If only the outcome, whatever it was, was certain.

The big kowhai swayed outside, its arms swishing elegantly in time to the breeze. It made shadows on Maya's bedroom wall, on her ceiling.

She was sleeping with her curtains open. It was something she did occasionally and she would wake up in the morning enveloped by the hot Gisborne sun. It was a more intense sun there, more warming, quiet, motionless. Even though it was the same sun everywhere, it was a different sensation there, on the East Coast. Sultry.

Where else have I felt sun like that on me? she thought. Napier, Wellington maybe. Auckland, when she was little and her mother had taken her for a few days in the school holidays. They'd caught the Farmers bus from Queen Street and had morning tea in the cafeteria, on the top floor of that most elegant and enticing of department stores.

She'd lain on the crowded beaches of Bali, trying to avoid the watch sellers and hair plaiters when she and Kathy had taken a ten-day holiday after passing their final nursing exams. There was no doubt that it was hot there, and sunny, Maya thought, but it still wasn't like Gisborne.

And what about Las Vegas, where she and Philip spent their honeymoon? It was hot there, so hot that outside you couldn't take a deep breath or you thought your lungs might burn. It was hot, all right, Maya thought. Hot and heavy, she heard Philip whisper in a fake American accent as his honeymoon hands found her.

A tear slid out of one of Maya's eyes, and now the other one. The kowhai's shadows shivered around her. She could still feel the sound of the sea, so solid, so certain in her head.

Everything she had to deal with was piling up around her. On the floor either side of her bed, in the doorway blocking her path, on the bed itself, so she was pinned under her summer sheet, barely able to breathe. It was all dumped there randomly, her cancer and all the baggage that came with it (chemotherapy, surgery, nausea, anorexia, hair loss, dry mouth, ulcers, fatigue, fatigue, never mind mortality), Charlie, Kathy, Rachael, work (or lack of it now that she was a Sickness Beneficiary), her mother, Gran, Philip. All of it. The sum of her life strewn around her.

More tears escaped her, staining her pillowcase.

Fatigue, fatigue, her mother, Philip.

Never mind mortality.

She looked out the window and there, between and behind the branches of the kowhai were stars. Hundreds of them. Thousands probably. Someone had told her once that every star was the soul of someone who had died. It had comforted her at the time, to know she could look up (heavenward) and there was her beautiful mother, always, twinkling and smiling, looking out for her from her vantage point in space.

But as they now slid behind the kowhai's branches, behind a cloud, then popped out like peek-a-boo babies, how could Maya tell which stars were hers? And once she'd located them, what would happen when the Earth spun and the sky rotated and her stars found themselves in the Northern Hemisphere, or over Argentina or Ghana, looking down over unknown landscapes, searching,

searching for Maya and not finding her among the millions of exotic faces?

Surely the sky would one day fill up with stars. There was a never-ending supply of dead souls, so surely there would eventually be celestial congestion and nighttime would be as bright as day, or brighter, and the stars (the souls) would find themselves shoulder to shoulder up there, and there would be no way Maya could identify those that were her special stars. Surely.

Even though she knew it wasn't true, it was comforting to think that a star might be a scrap of visible evidence of her husband or her mother. And Gran, even though she wished that she were an exploding star, shrinking, devolving into a black hole at the edge of space.

Was that what a falling star was?

Maya turned her head and looked outside again. The pillow was cool under her cheek as she moved. I've never seen a falling star, she thought. Isn't it good luck to see one?

Perhaps that was what this was all about. Luck. There might be a certain percentage of people who were designated as good luck people and they were the ones who won Lotto (some of them even won twice), they were the ones who could always find a parking space in town, they had good hair and teeth and they never got burgled.

Then there were the bad luck people. Like me, Maya thought. Whose lives were dominated by death and separation, loss, longing. Misery, illness.

She sat up suddenly. Her wound stretched and pulled as she did so but she ignored it. She stared straight ahead, her vision blurring, jumbling all the things on the top of her dresser. This is one hell of a pity party, she thought. She could almost hear herself say the words.

It can't be all bad. It just can't be.

She got out of bed, slid slippers on and went to go downstairs. Instead, she found herself in Charlie's room. His duvet trailed off the end of his bed along the floor, like a veil. He was sprawled over his bed, arms and legs at odd angles, as though he had to take up as much room as possible. He wore shiny boxers with pictures of basketballs on them. His hair was smooth around his head. He breathed without making a sound. Honey Bear lay beside him, using his upper arm as a pillow.

Maya picked up the duvet and placed it over her boy. He opened his eyes, stared at nothing, then his eyes closed again.

It's not all bad, she realised as she stood there, watching Charlie sleep.

I could stay here forever, she thought. She never tired of the sight of him. He was perfect when he was asleep. If they'd argued during the day, or she had had to punish him for something he'd said or done (or not said or done), seeing him there, asleep, unravelled any anger she felt. Was it Mother Nature's way of ensuring forgiveness, harmony?

Now Maya was walking through the kitchen and unlocking the back door. She slipped outside where the world was still, silent, enclosed within the confines of the tall brown fence. She followed the edge of the garden. Why do we have our flower gardens on the edges? We construct beautiful and careful floral frames around a plain, green, mown-every-second-Saturday portrait. Surely it should be the other way round? she thought. Imagine it. A strip of grass bordering her property, with shrubs and annuals bursting out from the middle. Penstemons, bushy camellias with polished leaves, nigella, lavender, soft lambs' ears, snapdragons that she had pulled off and given to Charlie a thousand times. Put your fingers here, chap, and look – the dragon's mouth opens. They could see its throat, yellow with pollen, and Charlie had roared in his most terrifying three-year-old voice.

That's what I'll do, Maya thought. Tomorrow. I'll dig up the lawn, shift the plants, get some annuals (what's flowering this time of year? For a moment she couldn't remember), re-place the lawn around her new garden. Easy peasy.

It was hard to make out the individual plants in the dark. The flowers had all gone to bed, faces tucked into the foliage like sleeping birds. Her fingers ran over the plants, caressing the shrubs and taller annuals; the sunflowers' prickly leaves, cosmos like filigree netting. The sensation was on her fingers still, after she pulled away. She rubbed her hands together and the feeling scattered onto the cool ground.

She lay down on the grass, not at all surprised to find herself there. It was dry and brittle under her. Her nightie brushed her knees, she placed her arms on her belly, then by her side, then under her head, fingers laced together. Her wound hurt like that, but she knew that if she waited the muscles would relax and soften, stretching themselves to accommodate her, and of course they did.

She looked up at the sky, at the stars she had seen from her bedroom window. They were the same stars but they somehow seemed more distant, less significant there, when she could see the universe in its entirety. The souls were remote there, way out of reach.

There were no sounds out there, on the lawn. No wind in the trees, no traffic, no cats fighting, no burglar alarms. Maybe the world had stopped.

Maybe this was what being dead was like, staring at nighttime in utter silence. And suddenly finding it seemed an attractive idea. No chemo, no vomiting, finding a vein and watching it collapse as the needle pierced its weakened walls, no pain, no questions (why, what if, when).

Just watching.

She closed her eyes and found she was still watching. She was aware of her breathing, she felt a pulse in her neck, one behind her knee. She could feel her breath in her mouth. It was warm, slightly sour and metallic from the chemotherapy. She let her eyes relax, sag back into their sockets. This was the moment before sleep, she knew. A breeze, as slight as a sigh slipped over her.

Maya opened her eyes and pressed her fingers against her head. Just in case, she thought. Just in case what? Just in case I'm dead. Or disconnected. Just to be sure I am not.

Her scalp was completely hairless. She had got used to it quickly, and for most of the time she forgot she was bald. Like when, in the eighties, she had had those tight spiral perms that turned her normally smooth, slightly wavy hair into a jumbled frizz. It was only if she caught her reflection in the mirror or in a shop window that she was aware of the transformation. It was the new Maya.

And now, when her bald head attracted stares, she wanted to challenge the curious. What? Defiant, petulant, until she realised she was something of an oddity, a freak-show exhibit. The Hairless Wonder. Hey, she thought, I could be the Titless Hairless Wonder. Double the Spectacle for the Same Price. People would pay to see that. It wasn't every day you could get to see A Woman, Afflicted by Disease, Mutilated and Disfigured. Roll up. Roll up.

No, Maya thought. Maybe I could wait until I have secondaries somewhere. Spine, perhaps. Or liver. Then they could stare at my yellow skin and eyes as well as my bald head, and at the wound on my lopsided, cutaway chest. Now that would be a freak show.

She turned onto her side. The grass was still warm. She brought her knees up to her belly and rested her head on the palm of one hand. At the tip of one of the kowhai's branches was the moon, silvery blue, fat-bellied. She shivered. She hadn't noticed it until now. It dominated the sky, dwarfed the stars (the souls) around it, balanced on just a puff of air above the tree.

Suddenly her body ached. It was as though she had lain there for hours, days even. It might have been hours; she couldn't tell. She struggled to her knees and then stood up, appalled at what an effort it was.

Isn't everything these days? she thought as she went inside, leaning against the back door and locking it. Isn't fucking everything?

The phone had never frightened her before. Not like this. Come on, she told herself. She wiped a line of sweat from her top lip.

'Right,' she said. She sounded certain. That was good. The receiver was cool in her hand. She pressed the numbers carefully, slowly, as though Rachael would know her intent. Her caution.

'Hello.'

'Hi, Rachael, it's Maya here.'

'Yes?'

Shit.

'How are you?'

'Fine.'

'Jacob?'

'Fine.'

Shit, shit.

'Good. That's good.'

'Was there something you wanted?'

The air was sucked out of her as though she had been punched in the belly. She held on to the benchtop with one trembling hand. Her mouth opened and closed.

'Oh.'

'I'm a bit busy, Maya. Did you want something in particular?'

She breathed again. Filled her lungs to overflowing. Held the air in, closing off her throat. She exhaled.

'Not really. Just wanted to say hello. That's all.'

'That's nice. But like I said, I'm busy.'

'Oh. Okay, then.'

'Thanks for calling.'

She stood there, leaning against the bench, holding the receiver, staring at it but not seeing it.

What would she do with Charlie now?

They were lying on the trampoline. It was like floating on the sea, Maya thought, as Charlie sat up, and she felt herself bobbing on the surface.

'I can see a dragon. There, look. It's got a dog on its head.'

'Where, buddy?'

'Right there.' He pointed up at the sky. It was so big today. It surely wasn't real.

'Where?'

'There, Mum. It's right there.' His finger stamped a small hole in the blue. 'I'm pointing right at it.'

'Oh. Okay.'

'You can't see it, can you?'

'Of course I can.'

'You two have a great life, don't you?'

Maya hoisted herself up onto her elbows. Her hat tipped off her head.

'Hi, Kathy. Come and join us. We're looking for cloud animals.' She ran her hand over her scalp. There was no stubble now, and no individual hairs that sprouted like wavy flagbearers.

'Do you know how hard I've been working all day? Look at these fingers: worked to the bone.' Kathy kicked off her sandals and climbed up onto the trampoline.

'Hard day at the office?' Maya found her hat and jammed it back on her head.

'Not really. I was on the eye list so I spent all day doing eyeballs.'

'Gross,' said Charlie. 'What was the worst thing you saw?'

'I knew this would happen when he turned nine,' said Kathy, turning away from Charlie with exaggerated deliberateness.

'He's turned into a real boy, hasn't he?'

'You make him sound like Pinocchio.'

'Hey, Charlie,' said Kathy, and she turned back to him. She held his chin between her thumb and forefinger. 'Tell me a lie and I'll see if your nose grows.'

'Oh, Kathy.' He wriggled out of her grip and lay down between the two women.

They lay on the trampoline and the clouds languished above them, folding themselves in on one another. A sparrow hopped across the concrete by the back step. Maya closed her eyes. Clouds floated in front of her, orange and black. She could feel her body sinking into that soft, warm territory of sleep. It was a good place to go.

'Oh, Maya, guess what.' Kathy sat upright and the trampoline billowed. Maya was spat back into the glare of the afternoon.

'What?' There was an edge to her voice. She didn't hide it; she couldn't be bothered.

'I'm going to a theatre nurses' conference. In Christchurch. Six days away. Great, eh?'

Maya nodded. This would be good for Kathy. Getting away, having some fun.

'Just think about it,' she continued. 'All that fabulous restaurant food, flash lunches during the conference, all the wine I can drink.'

'Sky TV in your hotel room.'

'Exactly.'

'What's the conference?'

'The Role of the Theatre Nurse in the 21st Century. Something like that.'

'Well, I hope the food's good, that's all I can say. When is it?'

'It's the week after next. Weird timing, eh? You'd think they'd have it in the next school holidays so it wouldn't be such a hassle for all the mothers. But maybe they thought they deserved six days away from their kids in the middle of the term.'

'I know that feeling,' said Maya, and she patted Charlie on his head.

'Thanks, Mum.'

'Charlie, you're developing a wonderfully authentic sarcastic tone,' said Kathy. 'Have you been practising?'

'I've just been watching you,' he said.

'Touché,' said Kathy, and she clutched her fist to her chest and fell back dramatically onto the mat of the trampoline.

A cold wave passed through Maya's body. It began at the top of her head and ran down the length of her, gaining momentum as it consumed all the parts of her.

'When did you say the conference was?' The clouds continued their slow dance above them.

'The week after next. Why?'

Somewhere down the street someone was mowing their lawns.

'It's nothing. That's when I start radiotherapy, that's all.' There it was. Her last hope, extinguished.

'Maya, oh shit.'

Charlie sat up. 'Kathy, did you say a swear word?'

'Sorry, Charlie. You can smack my hand. There. Did you need me to look after him while you're in Palmerston North? I thought Rachael would do it.'

'No, look, it'll be okay. Don't worry.'

'I'm really sorry.'

'Don't worry about it, I said. We'll work something out. Won't we, Charlie?'

'We'll manage, eh, Mum.'

'We always do, chap.'

Kathy handed Maya a glass of wine. She flopped down in the couch opposite Maya's chair. 'All right?'

'Mmm.' She sipped the wine. It was thick and soft, like butter on her tongue.

'Are you sure?'

'Yeah. Just tired, you know. Although I'm getting sick of saying that. I'll have to stop it. Tell myself something else. A mantra. I did have one. Now, what was it? I must be losing my memory. Or my mind. Do you think they are the same thing? How was work?' She took tiny sips as she spoke, punctuating her words with small silences as she raised the glass to her lips. She noticed that her hand trembled.

'You're babbling, Mrs Wimple.'

'Charming.' Sip.

'You are. Is there something bothering you?'

Maya shook her head and shivered as the breeze fingered her bare skull. Sip. Sip.

'Or, as you would say to Charlie, tell me your biggest worry.'

'Don't have one.' Her hands were becoming heavy, as though they had weights suspended at wrist and elbow. She lowered her glass onto the table beside her. It landed heavily and she watched the wine slop redly from side to side against the glass. She counted the small waves. Her eyes were thick, her head was struggling to

192

stay open. No, it was the other way around. She leaned her foggy head against the back of the chair.

'Are you pissy-eyed?'

Maya nodded and grinned. She felt wilful, mischievous. She put her hand up over her mouth. To show too many teeth was vulgar. That's what Gran used to say. Maybe she didn't, but it sounded like something she might.

'I'm not sure if that's a good idea. I'll get you a glass of water and then you'd better go to bed.'

Maya slapped her hand down on the arm of the chair. 'Do you know what? I'm fucking sick of going to bed. I'm fucking sick of being sick.' She folded her arms, jamming her fists into her armpits. Kathy made soothing noises as she placed a glass of water on the coffee table, in front of the wine. Maya peered through the water and stared at the wineglass, oddly distorted, concave sides if you looked from this angle, convex from this. The wine was darker, magnified through the water. Certainly stronger. She reached past the water with her weighed-down hand. Sip. Sip.

'I'm fucking sick of it all, actually. I can't do this any more.'

'Oh, Maya, I know. But I think you should get some sleep.'

'Do you think? Am I going to wake up in the morning better? Cured? Is that what will happen?' Sip.

'That's not what I meant.'

'Well, what did you mean?' Maya felt her face grow tight, the skin stretched across her hot cheeks. Her legs were disconnected from the rest of her.

'I don't want to get into this, Maya. You're pissed and you're talking crap. Go to bed.'

'Well, that's fucking lovely.' She stood up and walked (staggered) to the door. She held on to the doorframe and turned around, dramatically, she thought. 'You know what?' she said. 'I don't really need you as a friend. And right now, having you as a sister-in-law is more than I can handle.'

When Kathy moved out, Charlie went around the garden picking what flowers he could find. Pansies, poor man's orchids, nemesias like miniature snapdragons. They peeped out from between the weeds. And dandelions, tiny lawn daisies, buttercups. He held them out, his arm stiff and awkward. 'Here you are,' he said. 'These are for you.'

'Thank you, Charlie. You be good, eh?' She bent down and held him to her. A yellow dandelion, its teeth spiky yet soft, fell from his hand. It skated down Kathy's back and landed on the path. As she stood up it was crushed under her foot.

Maya turned away from the window. She sat down in her chair. The fabric felt hot and sticky under her. Her feet burned. Her mouth was dry. She closed her eyes.

Fifteen

'*I*'ve got a present for you, Mum.'

Maya stared at the cup of hot water on the table in front of her. She had become a hot-water drinker. Coffee was too bitter, ditto tea. Milo left a film in her mouth. Herbal teas were too fruity, too leafy, too floral.

'Oh, buddy, what for?'

'I dunno. It's just something I found, and I thought you'd like it.'

His arms were behind his back. His eyes shone. His legs jiggled, one, then the other.

Maybe this was something he had to do, Maya thought. Maybe it was a need – part of Charlie's grieving, accepting, dealing with Maya's illness.

She hadn't really considered Charlie so far, she realised. There had been a straight line from Maya to her cancer, from the cancer back to Maya. Like an equals sign with an arrow at each end. Maya cancer cancer Maya. Charlie had not been part of the equation. But of course he was. He was there in every decision, every question, every step, every breath. And she knew that how she dealt with him (and it) would shape him. It was as simple as that.

Maya watched transparent spires of steam drift up from her cup. If she had been included in her own mother's disease . . . If she had been spoken to as someone who wanted to understand, instead of

195

a child that had to be hushed (your mother's resting) . . . If she had been accepted when she went to live with Gran (after, after) . . .

But Gran was dealing with the death of her daughter. And how distressing that must have been, Maya thought as her gaze fell on Charlie, expectant in front of her. She had never considered Gran's pain. Gran had watched her daughter shrivel like an apple left out on the windowsill. She had buried her. She had distributed her belongings: given most of them away, even the wooden letter-holder that Maya had made at school for Christmas (the last Christmas, as it turned out). She had burned *Mother* into the front with the tip of a poker-work iron, and the *e* and the *r* were squashed together, jammed up against the edge of the wood. Maya hadn't allowed for all the letters, hadn't left enough room, hadn't planned sufficiently, Gran said as she threw it in the box of things for the Red Cross.

That's my trouble, then. *Maya doesn't plan sufficiently.* Well, in this instance I will, she thought.

A tear slipped out of Maya's eye. She hurried it away with the back of her hand. 'You're so sweet to me.'

Charlie jammed his hands into his pockets. 'That's okay, Mum,' he said, and he stared down at the table.

He stood there for hours, it seemed. Maya was suddenly uncomfortable. Should she ask for her present? It might seem rude, but Charlie looked unsure of what to do. He looked nervous.

'Well,' Maya said eventually (sounding like Mr Gaskin). She shivered.

'Are you ready?' Charlie ran his tongue over his lips.

'I think so.'

'Okay then.' He brought his hands around in front of him and held one hand out, his fingers curled over his palm, holding the object there.

Maya watched him, his hand.

She held her breath. He had her, she realised.

He opened his fingers one by one, as though he might be counting. He was perfectly still.

On the soft of his palm lay a baby bird. Blades of grass were

196

carelessly woven across its pink body. Its head flopped against its quiet chest. Its eyes, transparent and bulging, were empty. Its wings were damp, fused to its puckered sides.

'Cool, eh,' Charlie said, and he closed his fingers around it again.

Maya stared at it. It was obscene, this naked scrap that was a dead birdling. She could see its beak was open. Had it been anticipating a mouthful of food when it fell from its nest? Or was it calling out for its mother? she wondered.

Here you are, little things, she heard her mother call. She was standing on the back step, throwing old bread out onto the lawn. The bravest sparrows nibbled at it as soon as it settled on the grass. In the kitchen she had passed the slices and the dried crusts under the tap. Why are you doing that? Maya had asked. It's nicer for the birds, her mother had answered, if the bread is moist. Then it's soft enough so they can get it more easily. We like to be kind to the birds, don't we, dear?

Maya stared still. The baby sparrow's tongue was a tiny yellow grub in its throat.

'It's for you,' said Charlie. 'Do you like it?'

'Train tracks, Charlie.'

He shrugged. 'Whatever.'

They drove in silence. Charlie turned his body away and stared out the window. Shit shit shit. Maya knew this was going to be hard. It would be much easier to go to the dairy instead, get lollies and ice-cream, go home and ignore whatever demons were sitting on Charlie's shoulder. And hers. That would be much easier. But it would also be running away and the problem with running away, Maya thought, was that eventually you had to come home.

'Right then,' she said as she pulled up to her usual spot. She crossed her arms, holding her keys in her fist. She turned towards the railway line. Charlie was still in the car, his hands tight between his knees. His head dropped down to his chest.

'Shit,' Maya muttered. Then, 'Fuckity fuck.' She had heard that

197

in a movie once and had thought at the time what a useful expression it was. The right mix of hard consonants and the exhalant eff that makes *fuck* so satisfying. It had been funny at the time, but there, on the edge of the train tracks, with Charlie sulking in the car, it just seemed pathetic.

She sat down, bracing her legs against the downward slide of the gravelly bank. He couldn't stay in the car forever. Sooner or later he had to give in. Luckily he hasn't got all my genes, Maya thought. She used to be able to sulk for days when she was with Gran. Philip had been the opposite. He'd go somewhere quiet, think about what he was angry about, then come back and discuss it, try to solve the problem. Charlie, she knew, would do a bit of both: he'd sit there in the car, fuming, silent, then when that didn't achieve a result he'd come out, sit down next to Maya and begin to talk.

She picked up a handful of stones and passed them from one hand to the other. The image of that tiny dead bird filled her up. She looked down the railway track, two parallel lines that seemed as though they were convergent. Her eyes were playing tracks on her brain, pretending that the tracks would meet at a point somewhere further along. Suddenly she was thinking about Philip, imagining that he would appear at that apex, striding down the centre of the track like a gunslinger, an outlaw.

After he died, Maya often thought she saw him as she walked along the streets or drove through town. There he was, stepping into a shop doorway, or getting into a taxi, turning away, always not quite visible, not quite identifiable, but it was him, she was sure. She'd raise her hand, go to call out, and then she remembered.

And now she was certain that if she just kept looking down the railway line, there he would be. She was positive. Absolutely.

But he didn't appear and he didn't appear and Maya held her head in her hands, her careful, practised hands that had failed her again (failed to save Philip, failed to touch his pale and silent body in his coffin, just to be sure, failed to find her own breast lump, even though they were trained, experienced hands and they should have known better). She held on to her head because it was so heavy and so full and if she didn't, it might explode or simply roll off her shoulders and onto the railway and be knocked aside by a train.

She imagined that bird opening and closing its mouth, making no sound at all.

If she wasn't watching, Philip couldn't appear, she knew, and so she turned her head into the breeze that came down the tracks, and she looked and she waited and now her sight was blurring and she tried to blink away the haze but she couldn't keep up with the tears, with the pace and ferocity of them, and so she stopped trying and they soaked her face and her hands and the wind sealed them onto her skin and still Philip wasn't there and the more she searched for him, the more she knew it was no use looking.

A wound was opened.

Not the one across her chest – and why did she always refer to it as the wound? Because, she realised, ideas and people and sorrow whipping around her like an autumn leaf windswirl, if she did then she was seeing it as something she had acquired, instead of something (a breast, a body part, her womanness) she had lost.

This wound has been quiet for seven years, when it had been too painful and too dangerous to give in to it. Charlie had just been a baby and Maya had had to keep going, be strong, cope or look as though she was, and so that other cancer that was grief had grown, multiplied cell by cell, and now here it was, a fetid sore, and what could she do but open it up and let it drain.

She tipped her head back and her throat was an open channel and she breathed deeply so that every single cell in her lungs was bloated with oxygen. She held the breath there, closing off her throat, feeling the pressure in her chest and how good it was because it masked another pressure, which was not so much a lump in her throat as a hill the size of Mount Hikurangi squashed inside her. Eventually she let go; she allowed her throat to open and stale air spewed out of her mouth. As she did she made a noise, an instinctual animal cry. It was loud, strong, deep, and it flew down the length of the railway line just above the tracks. Maya could almost see it, like a cloud of bees or evening birds returning to the trees on the banks of the Waimata River, hovering and swooping as one.

When it had disappeared around the bend Maya did it again. And again.

A rabbit, the colour of the gravel, skipped across the tracks. It stopped halfway across (careful, little bunny), stood up on its furry hind legs, twitched its nose at Maya and hopped off into the scrubby shrubs on the other side.

Fuckity fuck, she thought. It sounded like a bunny's hop. Fuckity fuck, fuckity fuck, off to your warm burrow, and have parsley broth and carrots tips for tea. Hang up your little jacket and sleep under a leafy cover.

Fuckity fuck.

Charlie never hung up his jacket. Or made his bed. Or did anything except be a kid, and that was all you could ask of him really. But there he was, in her car, filled up to overflowing with confusion and fear and giving her dead birds for fuck's sake and how could she reach him, from there, from the crumbling edge of the train tracks, when she was drowning in it too?

She looked up at the sky, to the edges of it.

Philip. What would you do? The clouds were motionless. Of course if you hadn't gone and been so careless and died this would all be different. Thoughtless, really.

She began to sob. Her breath came in spasms but the tears flowed effortlessly down her face.

Surely, Philip, there was a moment, a split second, when you were lying there in A and E, surrounded by all those people who were doing their best, dammit, to save your fucking life, when you must have thought – that's it. I've had enough. When they were calling for more bloods, more X-rays, bag him nurse, we're going to have to intubate, more fluids, he's in V-tach, adrenaline, more of everything please, when you could see, couldn't you, just how hard they were trying. Was that the moment you thought fuck it, I'll just die, and that'll be the end of it? Is that how it was?

And it *was* the end of it. For you, Philip. But how selfish that was, and how selfish death is, really, because look at how hard it's been for us.

Everything around her disappeared. The shrubs, the grass, the stones, the train tracks. Maya was alone with just her body and its sensations. She continued to cry, and her body shuddered with heaving, racking sobs. Her shoulders ached. This is too hard, she screamed inside herself. Why did you have to die? Why did you let yourself die? Snot bubbled from her nose, down onto her lips. She wiped it away with the back of her hand.

I can't do this.

I just can't.

I just fucking can't.

And then –

I don't want to die too.

Now she was like an animal, rocking, crying, crying out, holding herself, throwing her head back.

I don't want to die. I don't want to die. I – I – I –

The car door slammed. She heard it and was jolted back to that spot on the slope of the railway tracks. Small feet scrambled to her. A small body found its way into her lap. Small arms circled her neck. Small tears splashed onto her.

Oh, Charlie.

Maya hugged him, held on to him in case one of them might disappear. She could feel him, his jutting bones, his soft face, his long legs, and yet he might have been a million miles away. Or an inch out of her reach. It was like one of those dreams she used to have when she was at Gran's. She was hovering at the ceiling of her room, in the corner, above the door. She reached down to touch the people playing in her room, having a tea party. Her mother and Gran, sipping sugar water from miniature china cups. She reached and reached, but they were tiny and she was huge, or was it the other way around? She bobbed about, like a balloon, or a paper sailboat, and no matter how hard she tried, she couldn't touch them.

Oh, Charlie.

She stroked his hair and together they rocked back and forward, back and forward, and they cried until they had each run out of tears and they said nothing.

'I'm bored.'

Wait. Say nothing.

'Mum. I'm bored.' The trampoline creaked with each leap. Charlie could now do somersaults. How quickly he learns, Maya thought. 'Did you hear me? I said –'

'Yes, I heard you. It's Sunday. You're supposed to be bored. It's in the rules.' She could see the baby bird stricken in mid-gasp.

'Mu-um.'

'I'm sorry.'

'Could I have a friend over to play?' Flip, bounce, Charlie's hair flung around him.

'Sure. Who would you like?'

'Could I ask Sam over?'

'He's that new boy, isn't he?'

'Yeah. I was going to invite him to my party, but . . .' He shrugged.

Maya hesitated. Her initial reaction was to say not today, Charlie. I'm too tired. It'd be too much work. But she felt guilty. She'd make the effort. 'Sure, buddy.'

Charlie jumped off the trampoline, landing like Spiderman beside Maya's chair. He was crouched, ready for action. 'Can I phone him now?'

'Go on. We'll just hang around here, though.'

'No problem. Thanks, Mum.'

She closed her eyes. The sun blasted her eyelids. There was orange in front of her. She could hear Charlie inside, awkward and gangly on the phone. 'Mum,' he called out. 'Sam's mum wants to talk to you.'

'Can you bring me the phone?'

She held the receiver against her ear for a moment before speaking. 'Hello,' she said in a voice that contained no trace of illness.

'This is Penny. I'm Sam's mum.'

'Hi.'

'I believe our boys are keen to get together.'

'Yes. Charlie would love to have Sam over to play.'

'Is that all right? I heard . . .'

There it was. Always. Behind every conversation, every inter-action, every movement, every thought.

'We're fine. If you drop Sam around, I'll have the jug on and we can have a coffee.'

'That sounds nice. See you soon.'

'Do you know where we are?'

'Oh yes. We've been past your house.'

Maya shivered, suddenly cold as though a cloud had passed in front of the sun. Is that what people did? Drove past the homes of the sick, the less fortunate? What would they expect to see if they slowed down and turned their heads? There's nowt so queer as folk, her mother used to say in a *Coronation Street* voice, and she'd shake her head. Maya smiled now at the memory of her mother's fluffy hair and how the soft smell of her perfume fell around her as she moved.

'It's lovely to hear them playing.' Maya slid a cup of dark coffee across the bench.

'They won't be too noisy for you, will they?' Penny spooned sugar into her cup and stirred it round and round, scraping the spoon against the edge of the cup. Round and round. Maya stared at the coffee forming a whirlpool, and the spoon gaining momentum, round and round, and the spoon followed the path of the thick liquid – or was it the other way round? She held her own coffee between two hands and pressed her palms against the sides of the cup so that the flesh there scorched a little.

'I appreciate your concern,' she said. (Careful careful.) 'But I really don't want to be mollycoddled. Sure, I'm not quite a hundred percent, but I'm managing just fine.' (Liar liar.) 'What I do want is to be treated normally and just to get on with things. Looking after Charlie. Having a life. You know.'

Round and round. Surely that damn sugar was dissolved by now.

'I'm sorry,' Penny said, staring into her cup. Round and round.

Take the fucking spoon out of the cup.

But Maya didn't want to get on with things. It was a lie. She wanted to take to her bed, as Gran sometimes used to say. I'm taking to my bed, and she'd shut the door and Maya was sure she could hear her crying. She'd come out a couple of hours later (and Maya would have done the dishes, folded the washing and watered Gran's African violets on the dining-room windowsill) with fresh makeup and a hanky tucked into the band of her wristwatch and things would carry on.

Maya wanted to take to her bed too, and cry for a couple of years, not a couple of hours. 'So,' she said brightly, 'what have you got planned for today?'

'What's your favourite colour?'
  'Blue.'
  'Same. What's your favourite food?'
  'McDonald's.'
  'Same. What's your favourite TV programme?'
  '*The Simpsons.*'
  'Same.'
The walls of their cave, blankets thrown over chairs in the lounge, trembled as the two boys stretched out. Maya could see two pairs of bare feet sticking out. She loved to hear kids' conversations. Their uncensored freedom was a quiet delight for her.
  'Have you got a girlfriend?'
  'Doubt it!'
  'Me neither. You've got a Gameboy, eh?'
  'Yeah.'
  'Same.'
  'My mum said that your mum's sick.'
  'Yeah, she is. So?'
  'My mum said she's got cancer.'
  'Yeah.'
  'And she might die.'
  'Doubt it!'

It took all Maya's strength not to rush into the lounge, pull away the flimsy cave roof and hold Charlie to her. Don't listen, buddy. Don't listen to anyone else. I'll look after you. We're a team, remember. You and me. We're partners. In spite of everything.

'Well, that's what my mum said.'

'What does she know?'

'I dunno.'

'Your mum's lying. My mum's not going to die. She's going to get better. She's better already.'

Go Charlie.

'Your dad's dead, isn't he?'

'Yeah. So?'

'So what will happen to you if your mum does die?'

Maya held her breath. Her eyes were dry, scratchy. She refused to blink. She leaned against the wall, hoping it would hold her.

'What do you mean?' Charlie's voice was small.

'If your mum dies, silly. You won't have anyone to look after you.' There was a sudden silence that engulfed the house. Maya thought it might swallow them all up. She coughed, and said in a stranger's sure voice, 'Okay, men, who wants to have an ice-cream in a cone?

They dropped Sam at home, waved him goodbye as they got back in the car and got fish and chips on the way down to Waikanae beach.

'They do taste better here,' said Maya.

'What?'

'Fish and chips. At the beach.' Food tasted good today. Maybe her body was getting used to the break between chemotherapy treatments. Maybe her brain was, too. 'Have we had this conversation before?'

Charlie stuffed salty chips into his mouth. 'I dunno.'

'It feels familiar. Maybe I'm having a déjà vu.'

'What's that?'

'It's where you get the feeling that you've already had this particular conversation or experience before, just as it's happening.

It's French. It means already seen.'

'Oh.'

'It's like not being surprised when something happens because you know, somewhere at the back of your brain, how it's going to turn out. Because you've already known the outcome, through a dream, or just knowing, or something.'

'Weird.'

'Of course, the other theory is that it's just electrical impulses travelling from one side of your brain to the other, and so your awareness of whatever it is is slightly out of synch.'

'I like the first explanation better.' Charlie picked crunchy golden batter off his piece of fish.

'Me too, buddy.'

The holiday park right by the beach was still half-full. Families from everywhere having a school-time holiday in a tent or a cabin, there in Gisborne. They were lucky to be living in a holiday destination. But you still wanted to go somewhere else. Dissatisfaction was the norm, and striving for its antithesis is what drives us, Maya thought. We live in a state of negativity, and seemingly lurch from one crisis to the next, and all the time trying to fill a half-empty glass. Or half-full.

A group of people were playing cricket further down the beach. They were probably a family. Three children, one in the field in the soft sand and one at each end of the batting crease. The wickets were pieces of driftwood, angling into odd contortions. The woman stood at the high-tide mark and the man was the bowler. He tossed the red ball from one hand to the other, flicking his wrist and working his fingers.

He looks so serious, Maya thought, as though this was a first-eleven game, not just beach cricket. They always played to win, husbands fathers men.

'He's a good bowler.'

Maya blinked, bringing herself back to the moment. To the beach, the fish and chips, Charlie. 'You're a good bowler, too.'

'Yeah, but I need someone to practise with. At home.'

'I could do that,' said Maya. 'You could bowl to me.'

'I spose.' He looked back over at the family and their cricket game. The fingers of one hand poised over the fish and chips. Suddenly his face collapsed like crumpled paper. He began to cry. Maya could almost feel them, those painful lumps of anguish that catch in your upper chest, pressing against the vital parts of you before letting go and rolling up your throat (against the natural force of gravity) and out of your open and aching mouth.

'Oh, buddy,' she said, and she brought him to her and held his small frame against her. Maybe the counter-pressure of her arms around him would squash his sorrow.

'It's not fair,' he gasped. There were short, sharp intakes of breath, each one landing on top of the last, making a staircase in his throat.

'I know.' Maya made soothing mothering noises, she stroked his hair. She rubbed his back, his fine arms. Was this the same boy who had held a dead bird in his hands and offered it to her? She looked out to sea. The sky had turned, was turning, as she watched. A wash of grey-yellow coated the pale blue late afternoon bloom. A single star stood watch over the crest of Young Nick's Head.

The sea foam was whiter at this time of the day. You could almost feel the sand calling, cooling down.

Eventually Charlie's sobs eased. He stayed there, his head against the flat of her breast. It ached (of course) with the weight of him, but Maya remained still, stroking her child, shushing his fears.

'Sam said that you're going to die.'

There. It had been said. She had waited for it, impatiently, because once it was spoken, it could then be (would be) dealt with. Over. While it was still a thought, it could spoil and fester. A synergy, greater than the sum of its parts.

Maya's response was carefully thought through. She had rehearsed it, committed it to memory. We're all going to die, actually. That's the truth of it. But I'm not going to die from this cancer. All the treatment I'm having is curing me, and your love for me and my love for you is curing me. I'm going to die when I'm very, very old, maybe a hundred and seven, surrounded by my friends and family.

'We don't listen to crap like that,' she said instead.

How could that be? Why had her carefully constructed diatribe been replaced with such a poorly articulated response?

Truth, truth, a small voice in the back of her head whispered.

'Everyone that gets cancer dies from it, don't they?'

'No, chap.' Another wave crashed onto the beach. It broke into ten million fragments and was dragged by some invisible magnetism back out to sea. 'It's only the really bad cancers that you can die from.'

'If you did die, what would happen to me?'

Charlie wasn't listening to her. He was following his own path of questioning, regardless of Maya's answers.

'But I won't, Charlie.'

'How do you know?'

'I'm not sure. I just feel it. I *believe* that I'm going to get better, that's all.'

'Dad died, didn't he?'

'Yes, he did, Charlie. But that was different. He had been in a car crash. His injuries were so bad that his body just couldn't fight them.' Maya felt as if she was that house surgeon, hesitantly handing over the most difficult of parcels of news. She thought she might even be using the same words. This might be another déjà vu, or maybe the memory of that A and E night was so firmly lodged in her brain that she was able to recall it verbatim. 'Anyway,' she said, staring out to sea, to the horizon that was always an arm's length away, no matter how close you sailed to it. 'I'd never leave you alone, buddy. Never.'

The weight of this was becoming too much to bear. They were getting close to territory that was too dangerous to explore. They were circling it, looking inwards, and that was enough, thought Maya. 'How would you manage once you'd run out of clean clothes, anyway?' Maya laughed. She was sure it was convincing. 'And besides, the only thing you know how to cook is Two Minute Noodles.'

'And sandwiches.'

'And sandwiches.'

'I know the number for Pizza Hut delivery, Mum.'

'Oh, well, that's different,' Maya said. 'In that case, you'd be just fine without me.' She gripped at her throat with one hand, still holding on to Charlie with the other. She made a dramatic choking, gurgling noise, then fell back onto the sand. After a moment she opened one eye. 'Well,' she said. 'You'd better get on with life. I'm dead.'

'Okay, then,' said Charlie. He loved going along with Maya's role-playing games, she knew. The heavy tone was gone from his voice. 'Just one thing, though. You'd better give me the pin number for your money card.'

'No problem.' Maya still lay on the warm sand. It tickled her neck. Charlie had wriggled next to her, his body tight against her, his head on her shoulder. 'I can tell you my pin number,' she said, 'but I'll have to kill you afterwards.'

Now it was Charlie's turn to clutch at his throat and pretend to die. He pulled himself up into a half-sitting position, then fell back, jerking his arms and legs, and groaning long and slow. It sounded like a castle door being opened, a cartoon sound, from *Scooby Doo*, or *Archie and Jughead*.

'Acting lessons for you, I think,' Maya said, once Charlie had had his last convulsion and was motionless beside her.

Sixteen

You never know what's going on in people's houses, Maya thought. She gripped a white plastic bowl between her hands, cold and trembling. She spat a gob of saliva in. It floated on a slimy layer of green bile. No one would know I'm in here, spewing my guts out.

It'll only last a few more hours, this vomiting. Her thoughts were random and unconnected. Neurons firing in all directions in her dehydrated brain.

One day a taniwha
Went swimming in the moana.
Charlie, Charlie, Charlie.
My beautiful boy.
Humming the next line of the song.
Needing to spit again, bubbly white saliva.
Oh won't you come with me,
There's such a lot to see,
Underneath the deep blue sea.
I'll be right by the time Charlie gets back from Sam's. Mouth filling up with bitter spit again.

There's another verse to that song, but I can't remember what it is. Damn. That's going to annoy me.

I should ask Charlie when he gets home. He'll know.

If I remember.

'Beach or train tracks, Charlie?'

'Beach. Can we get some pizza on the way or something?'

'Good idea.' Maya phoned up for the pizza, which she knew she wouldn't eat. These days it was easier not to eat at all. Some nights as she lay in bed, waiting for sleep, wondering if it would come, she thought about what she had eaten that day. There might have been some toast, maybe half a banana. Was that all? Did it matter?

'You can go in and get it,' Maya said as they pulled up outside the pizza shop. She handed him twenty dollars. 'And get some Coke too, if you want.'

'Cool. Are you sure?'

'Hurry up before I change my mind.'

He walked into the shop taller, more confident. A moment later he was back, carrying the pizza out in front of him, the bottle of Coke balanced on the lid of the box. He looked at Maya waiting in the car, and he raised his eyebrows and flicked back his head.

My boy.

'There's only one thing wrong with doing this,' Charlie said once they had got to the beach and were sitting on the sand, in their spot. What would we do if someone else was in our spot? Maya had asked Charlie once. I dunno, he'd said. Go home, I guess.

'What's that, buddy?'

A seagull dived into the shallows, bickered there for a moment, then flew off.

'You get sand in the pizza.'

'Yum. Crunchy.'

Charlie began to laugh. I'd forgotten how easy it is to make him laugh, Maya thought. I could forgive him anything.

His mouth was open wide, his head tipped back. A triangle of pizza with its pointy end eaten flapped in his hand.

'Are you okay?'

'Yeah, I guess.'

Maya unscrewed the cap off the Coke. It fizzed and a layer of brown foam frothed up the neck of the bottle. She took a mouthful. 'I'm sorry it's been so mucked up. With my chemo and everything.'

Charlie shrugged.

'I know it's been hard on you.'

He bit into his pizza.

'We didn't have our holiday away at Christmas, did we?'

'Doesn't matter,' said Charlie with his mouth full.

'Well, buddy,' and she wondered how she would say it. The words were all there, inside her mouth, filling up the space between her tongue and the roof of her mouth. Would they come out in the right order? 'It looks like I have to have some more treatment.'

'More chemo, do you mean?' He reached over for the Coke and lifted the bottle, heavy in his hands, to his mouth.

'No. This is called radiotherapy. It's like an X-ray, or a laser gun. They zap it at the parts of my body where the cancer is. And it kills it.'

'But I thought the chemo was supposed to do that.'

Black waves threw themselves onto the beach, each one further up than the last. Eventually they would be washed away. If it wasn't for the turn of the tide, the gradient of the beach. There was always a safety net.

'Yeah, I know. But this is like extra-zappy, super-strength stuff. Just to be sure.'

'Man,' Charlie said, and he took another mouthful of Coke. 'But you're going to get better, aren't you?' he said after a while.

'Absolutely.'

'Cause if you, you know –' (there it was again, that avoidance that signposted the very thing) '– what would happen to me?'

Maya drew him to her. He was so warm, so small. 'That's not going to happen. I promise I won't leave you alone. Okay?'

He nodded, inside the walls of her arms. She looked down at him and saw he was crying.

There was nothing more to say. They stayed there, on the sand, under the black sky, in front of the row of black trees, surrounded by the pulse of the black sea, until Charlie fell asleep, his head falling onto her lap. She watched him sleeping. His mouth made sucking noises, his lips pursed tight. He brought his knees up. He scratched his neck.

It was as if she had never looked at him before.

There was a mountain of Weet-Bix in his bowl.

'Have you got enough breakfast there, chap?'

'Well, I am nine.' He looked at Maya as though he was giving her new information.

'Yes . . .'

'So I have to have nine Weet-Bix.'

'Is that the rule?'

'Yeah.' (Don't you know anything?)

'So what will happen when you're twenty-four?'

'Twenty-four Weet-Bix.'

'Well, you won't be living at home, my friend. I won't be able to afford you.'

He shrugged and spooned cereal into his mouth. 'That's all right. I'll be a famous Gameboy designer by then. I won't need you.'

'Charming.' Maya laughed. She sounded so light-hearted, she thought.

She didn't think about it very often, she realised. But there was something about being in the garden, about the mindless activity of weeding, that freed up her mind. Allowed it to wander about, uncensored.

It was when she weeded around her roses that she was reminded most of Philip. They were still blooming, their heads heavy, drooping with their own weight. Their perfume was spicy yet sweet, hot and mysterious. I don't know why you bother with roses, he used to say. All those thorns. And the pruning. Having to spray them every five minutes. They're just not worth the effort. And yet it was Philip who presented Maya with the first bloom, halfway between

213

bud and fully opened, of each of her roses every summer.

Here you are, rosebud, he'd say, and he laid the flower on the pillow beside her head. He kissed her softly on her cheek.

What a way to wake up, she thought. She could smell the rose scent, feel his lips on her skin.

She sat back on her heels, pulled off her gardening gloves and ran her hand across her forehead. Maybe I'm not up to this, she thought. It's pretty physical work. I'm not sure if I'm ready.

A bloom of Aotearoa, as big as her fist, waved.

Here you are, rosebud.

Shh, Charlie, we have to listen to what the doctor is saying. Staring at Charlie's booties and thinking that if she had spent two minutes finding a matching pair, just one hundred and twenty seconds, then this late-night A and E conversation might gone in a different direction. Believing it.

And here was Kathy rushing into the visitors' room and sitting beside them and her face was quite grey, her lips blanched. Wanting Kathy to comfort her because she was her best friend and it was her husband who was dying (dead), but of course Kathy was enveloped in her own grief. It was her brother who was dying too.

Two Henderson women: one by birth, the other by choice. They were a million miles from each other, there in the visitors' room, the arms of their chairs just a hand's breadth apart.

Maya had practised her signature in the days before she and Philip got married. Trying on her new name for size.

M Henderson
Maya Henderson
Maya Gabrielle Henderson
M G Henderson
M Bridgeman-Henderson
Maya Bridgeman-Henderson
M Henderson
M Henderson

Making sure it fitted.

It had seemed important at the time.

But there in the visitors' room it had seemed so trivial and juvenile.

And there in the garden it seemed more so.

Chemo day. Again. Her last treatment. A red letter day.

'I'm sorry. I had to bring Charlie with me. I didn't have anywhere else he could go today. He'll be good. I'm sorry.' Knowing that she could have asked Rachael, or Sam's mother, Penny, but wanting to keep her treatment, and any problems that went with it, within the confines of family.

She sat in her La-Z-Boy chair. Charlie sprawled on the bed, drawing. Don't mess up the bed. We don't want to make any extra work.

They waited. Maya looked out the window. The garden shimmered. The roses couldn't have been more beautiful, she thought.

'We could do with the hospital gardener at home,' she said. Weeds were becoming the dominant feature of her garden. Most of her annuals had died through lack of watering, and the shrubs that should have been pruned in spring were leggy and tired. Maya looked at her watch and spun the strap around her wrist.

'Eh?' said Charlie. He kept on drawing, making shooting noises as the guns in his picture fired off laser bullets.

'Nothing, buddy.'

Maya looked at the sign above the hand basin. WASH YOUR HANDS, in red capitals. She counted the letters – thirteen. She made other words out of them: rash, shun, dour. How long had they been sitting there now?

She wiped her hands down the front of her shorts. Draw, drawn, shandy.

'Sorry I've kept you waiting,' said Jane. She smiled as she spoke, without seeming to move her lips. 'I've been talking to Mr Goodman. From Palmerston.' (As if she didn't know.) 'Your blood count's not looking so good today.'

Sand, snowy. Shorn away. Sounds raw. Maya couldn't help smiling. She wanted to laugh. 'He thinks we should postpone your treatment this week,' Jane said. 'He thinks we should wait a week. Your white count should come up by then.'

'Is that what he thinks, is it?'

The pen was still in Charlie's hand.

'I'm sorry, Maya.'

She slammed down the lever on the side of the chair and the footrest skidded away. She pulled herself up, giddy, staring.

'Well, that's fucking lovely.'

She heard Charlie gasp. The pen fell onto his paper.

'I've been sitting here all morning. With my son. And you swan along with your perfect fucking lipstick and tell me *he thinks* we should wait. That is *just* fucking charming.' She thrust out her arm. 'Come on, Charlie.' He gathered up his things and gripped her hand. 'Fucking charming,' she shouted to the nurse, the chair, the bed, the roses outside.

Charlie clipped in his seatbelt without saying a word. He stared straight ahead. His hands were clasped between his legs. There was a pink mark on his right knee where a scab (from falling off his bike, or tripping over, or grazing it on driftwood or the edge of a shell) had come away. The new flesh was shiny and smooth.

'Let's go home,' Maya said. She swore at the traffic lights, giving the finger to a bus full of startled black-haired tourists. A car pulled out in front of her. Maya sounded her horn and the driver waved and smiled. She turned around to Maya and brought her hand up to her mouth as if to apologise for not looking. 'Jesus!' Maya shouted, although the windows were closed and the woman could not have heard her. 'Can't you look? I've fucking got cancer, you know.'

The words bounced off the side windows, off the windscreen, the soft fabric of the roof. They spun around the interior of her car, spiralling around her and Charlie, scattering fragments that settled over their shoulders like nuclear fallout, invisible, tasteless.

Seventeen

*f*uck

Maya stared at it.

fuck

Four letters scratched into her stainless steel bench top. She wiped the dishcloth over the place, somehow thinking she could erase the word with a damp sponge.

fuck

It hadn't been there yesterday, she was sure of it. She would have noticed it (as she was noticing it now). She would deal with this calmly. She would be a responsible parent, attuned to the needs of her child. She would, she would.

'Charlie, can you come into the kitchen for a sec?'

Good. That was the right tone.

'Yeah?'

Somehow he just looked insolent. Scruffy, loutish.

'Do you know anything about this?' Her finger pointed to the word, to that particular arrangement of letters that might have added up to anything, but formed themselves into the most emphatic of swear words.

He shrugged.

'Are you sure? It can't have got there by accident, you know.'

Charlie shrugged again.

Do not do that. Do not shrug me away.

'Do you have any explanation of how it got there?'

It was engraved into the shiny bench, fine silver lines etched into the metal.

'I dunno.' He looked down at the floor, at his feet maybe, at his toes that he was curling under.

'Well, it wasn't me, and the graffiti fairies didn't come in the night, so I guess that just leaves you, Charlie.'

He raised his face to meet her eyes. 'It might have been Kathy.'

'Kathy doesn't live here any more, remember?' Suddenly Maya was overtaken with fury. She wanted to strike this lying, petulant child who was confronting her. She wanted to knock him off his smart-mouthed, smart-arse feet. She began to shake, as though her anger was a volcano and this was the first rumbling of it.

'What the hell's going on, Charlie? This isn't like you.' The words were carefully measured somehow, in spite of the anger that was threatening to spill out of her. She crossed her arms. Maybe that would help.

He shrugged. Again.

That was it.

'Don't you shrug your shoulders at me. I've had enough. Do you hear me?' Shouting now. 'I've had a fucking gutsful of your behaviour, Charlie. You'd better own up to this, or – or . . .'

Or what?

She was still. What could she do to him as punishment?

It was suddenly clear. What could she possibly do to him that was worse than what was already happening? What castigation could match the one he was playing out in his head?

Charlie looked up. His small chin trembled. His eyes were huge, dark puddles. At that moment her child was afraid of her.

Shit, shit, shit, she thought.

Fuck, really.

'Hey, buddy, you know how I promised we'd have a holiday and we never managed it? Before everything happened?'

It was the avoidance technique again. If she pretended every-thing was okay (that there was no dead bird decomposing on Charlie's bedroom windowsill, or a swear word carved into the kitchen bench – a word that, had Gran heard her say it, would have sent her rushing for the carbolic soap), then it would be, wouldn't it?

Wouldn't it?

'Did you?'

'Yeah. Well, guess what I think we'll do as a holiday?'

'What?'

'We're going to go away. We're going to have a few weeks in Palmerston North. We'll be bunking the middle of term.'

Charlie laid down the stones he was jiggling in his hand. Five grey pebbles in a straight line on the grass, parallel to the train tracks. Perfectly so.

'How does that sound?'

'Where's Palmerston North?'

'It's about halfway between Napier and Wellington. It's really nice. There's a park with an awesome playground. And a miniature train that you can have rides on.'

'A miniature train? That's for babies.'

'Well –'

'What else?'

'Um, let me see. I think there's a great swimming pool.'

'Is it close to the beach?'

'No, but –'

'What else?'

'I don't know, buddy. I have to be there, that's all, for my radio-therapy. Remember I told you about that?'

'So it's not a holiday, is it?'

'Well, we'll be away from home. Somewhere different. That's a holiday, isn't it?'

'And I'll miss school.'

'Yeah. That'll be an adventure, won't it? But I might arrange with school to have some work sent down'

Charlie picked up the stones. He laid them down again.

They were still in a straight line.

'I guess,' he said, and he pressed his fingers on the stones, as though they were piano keys.

'Oh, buddy.' She opened her arms to him but he sat there, his legs bent, resting his chin on his knees, fingering the stones.

She hurriedly crossed her arms.

She remembered a holiday, in school time. Just Maya and her mother. Let's go away, she'd said, even though by then she was gaunt, and the whites of her eyes were like yellow food colouring straight from the bottle.

They'd driven to Napier, stopping at Morere for a swim in the hot pools. Even now the smell of the bush reminded her of that holiday.

They stayed in a hotel on Marine Parade and her mother had stood at the desk, patiently explaining to the man that they'd come all this way, and that this was a very important holiday – he could see that, couldn't he? – so if he could change their room to one that overlooked the sea they'd be most grateful.

It didn't matter to Maya. She saw the sea every day from their lounge window, but we need to know it's still there, we need to be able to see it, no matter where we are, her mother explained later as she hung up their coats in the wardrobe in their hotel room.

It even had a balcony. Wait here, love, her mother said and she was gone, returning a few minutes later with two drinks, lemonade in a tall skinny glass with a straw for Maya, and a shandy for herself. They sat on their balcony sipping their drinks and watched the sun go down over the same sea that they had at home.

Maya was sure everything would be all right.

The next day they went to Marineland, where dolphins jumped and dived and clapped their sleek flippers to the whistles of their trainers. They went to the aquarium, and in the entranceway was a crocodile in a long skinny tank. It was almost the same length as the tank so it couldn't turn around. People had thrown money in. There were coins on its back.

They went to Lilliput, the miniature railway, and Maya watched a tiny train pulling freight cars and passenger carriages round and

220

round the model town. Traffic lights changed. A small crane lifted its carry of logs and lowered them into a truck, again and again. A tiny family stood on a street corner mother, father, two children, plastic arms upraised to another family in a car across the street. Maya imagined they were heading home after visiting their very good friends for the day.

Maya and her mother had fish and chips for tea on the beach across the road from their hotel. The sea was the same, the setting sun was the same. Her mother tucked the folds of her sunfrock under her legs. She ate nothing. I'll have something once we get back to the hotel, she said. Maya's lips puckered with salt from the chips.

They slept side by side in their twin beds. Maya was sure she could touch her mother if she reached out her arm to her. She never tried, though, just in case she was wrong.

And then toast and jam in the hotel restaurant in the morning. Cornflakes and tinned peaches that her mother spooned from a huge bowl on the serving table. While Maya drank her orange juice, her mother tore slices of dry toast into small pieces. There was a circle of crumbs around her plate, which she brushed into her hand and back onto her plate. The waitress poured thick dark coffee into her mother's cup, which she left untouched.

This trip away would be nothing like that, Maya thought. Or would it? Would Charlie retain individual images of their trip to Palmerston North, which would turn out to be pivotal memories? Would it be the things they did, the places they visited, or would it be her cough that woke him in the night, the smell of her, the dull of her skin?

'Okay,' he said. He looked up at her, his face half in profile. God, you look like Philip, she thought. Or how she imagined he looked. She couldn't quite recall him.

Or maybe he looked like her mother. She was as vivid as if she were standing beside them. You would have been so proud of Charlie. So proud of me. I wonder, do you know what's happening here, to us?

'I suppose I'll be quite important when we get back,' said

221

Charlie. 'Seeing I will have missed heaps of school. Man, Jacob will think that's awesome. I bet he wouldn't be allowed to miss school like that. To go away.' He placed a stone in front of him and laid the others around it, like petals, or spokes. 'Palmerston North will be cool,' he said. 'As long as we can go to McDonald's. And the movies. I'll be able to take my Gameboy, eh?'

It's funny how time goes more slowly when you're waiting for something in particular, Maya thought. Like Christmas, or a job interview. Or the day you have to go away to start radiotherapy. There must be some physics law to do with it. The Law of Anticipation. Time moves in inverse proportion to the importance of the upcoming event. The Law of Anticipation.

But then how come, when there was nothing to look forward to or wait for when she went to live with Gran, every day seemed to last a week?

Thick porridge that bubbled and plopped on the stove.

Ironing Gran's sheets, her teatowels.

Pulling tiny weeds from between the flowering plants in her garden. And thinking of her mother and how she had always had fresh flowers on the table. Camellias, roses, lilies, even primulas and forget-me-nots in a squat crystal vase.

She knew what day of the week it was by what Gran cooked for tea. On the table by five. In the oven, or boiling away on the stove even before she got home from school. She could smell it as she opened the front door.

It was as though she had lived three lifetimes at Gran's.

Her radiotherapy would start in six days.

It was all organised. The accommodation was booked (no, we don't have any special facilities for children, but your son is more than welcome, all the same). She had let the school know. The travel arrangements were made.

'We're going on the train, Charlie,' she'd said. The deck was carpeted with oranges. She didn't have the energy to pick them up. She didn't even have the energy to ask Charlie to do so.

'You mean *our* train?'

'Yeah. What do you think about that?'

Bees buzzed around them, across the deck, over the lavender, over the oranges softening on the deck.

'Cool.'

'There's a dining car on the train.' How quaint that sounded. Like something from another era.

'Cool.'

'So it'll be okay, then?' Holding her breath. Tentative.

'As long as I can take my Gameboy.'

There were no goodbyes. No farewells. No hugs, tearful or otherwise.

Maya closed the door and stood by the taxi while the driver put their cases in the boot. Slam. He shut the boot lid.

'Railway station, please,' she said. She tried not to cry.

'We're going to Palmerston North,' said Charlie from the back seat.

'Shh, buddy. He doesn't want to hear about that.'

The taxi pulled away from the house. Maya stared back at it, craning her head around until the muscles in her neck ached. Her house, her garden, her letterbox with its brass numbers got smaller and smaller.

They turned into another street. Her house was gone.

The train rocked her to sleep. She was cradled in its arms. She dreamed of her mother.

'Mum, Mum, I'm hungry.'

She felt tugging at her sleeve. She brushed it off, this annoyance.

'Mum.' But it wouldn't go away. She was unable to incorporate it into her dream. She opened her eyes. There was Charlie, kneeling on the seat next her, holding on to the headrest with one hand, the other gripping her sleeve. 'Can I get something to eat?'

'Sure, buddy,' she said automatically, and she reached down to her bag and pulled out her wallet, automatically. 'Just call me Mother Money Bags.'

'What?'

'Never mind.'

He took the ten dollars she held out to him and jumped off the seat into the aisle of the gently shuddering train. He turned back to her. 'Do you want anything?'

'You're very kind,' she said. 'I must have been really good in a past life, to deserve you.'

He stood there, the money stretched between his hands. 'Do you want anything?' he repeated.

Food. Her stomach lurched as if she was in an elevator. But she had to eat. She heard her mother's voice, felt her cool hand against her cheek. You have to eat, love.

'Maybe a muffin. And a cup of tea.' She wanted to close her eyes there in her seat and go back to sleep. Wait for Charlie to bring her food and drinks. But he was only nine. He couldn't manage by himself. It was too much to expect. 'Come on, chap. I'll give you a hand.' His face softened. She saw him relax. She hadn't even noticed how anxious he had been.

They bumped their way down to the dining car at the back of the train.

'Look at the view,' Maya said as they stood there in front of the window, which was the entire width of the train. Knee high to ceiling. Lumpy green hills sped past them. They watched skittery sheep running from the train, this snaking, lumbering beast that shattered through the quiet green of the country.

They carried the trays of food back down the aisle, holding them aloft like offerings. Charlie gripped Maya, who gripped a headrest as the train lunged one way, then the other. They fell into their seats. 'It's like being on a boat,' said Maya.

'Is it?'

'Yeah, it's funny – you expect to take a step or whatever, and you expect the ground to be right there. But it moves away from you.'

224

'Weird,' said Charlie, his mouth full of sausage roll. Flakes of pastry fell onto his lap. He dabbed at them with a finger.

'You okay, buddy?' She smoothed her hands down his head, immediately chiding herself for doing so. She had promised herself she would stop doing that. She was sure she had.

'Yeah. This is fun.'

'I bet no one in your class went on the train in the holidays.'

He looked up at her. 'Yeah,' he said, stretching the word in his mouth. She saw him puff his chest out. Just a bit. No one else would have noticed.

Every metre gets us a bit closer, thought Maya. They had been in the train for hours. How much longer would the journey take? She rested her head against the cold glass of the window and looked at herself in reflection.

Where were they? She couldn't identify their location by the scenery. Rural New Zealand was just rural New Zealand. Hills, cows, sheep resting in groups under trees, rows of dark pine trees that cut big green paddocks into smaller ones.

Occasionally a group of children ran up to the wire fence that separated them from the train tracks. They waved to the train, running along beside it, unable to keep up. Maya waved back.

Charlie lay on the floor across the aisle of the carriage. You have to get up straight away if someone comes along, she had said. His thumbs flicked over the Gameboy controls.

They had eaten until they were sick of food. (Charlie had. Maya had picked the blueberries out of a muffin and sucked the juice out of them.) They played I Spy. They had read all the signs in the carriage.

Stand clear of the doorway.

Emergency stop button.

For your comfort smoking is not permitted.

They had dozed, lulled by the rhythm around them but unable to sleep properly.

And now they waited.

Outside the fields were bumpy, loosely shaken out onto the flat of the land.

Maya looked at her reflection, at the scarf on her head. Black and white stripes. The edge of the scarf was a line of red. The end of summer, on the cusp of autumn, and she was wearing a scarf. Was she protecting those people around her, for whom a bald head (a woman's bald head, anyway) was surely an absurdity? Or a reminder of their own frailty?

She undid the knot and pulled the scarf off. She let it fall on the seat beside her, where it settled over her bag and the armrest of the seat like one of Gran's gauzy throws over her afternoon tea things set out on the table.

She rubbed vigorously at her head. That felt better.

She looked outside again. The scenery was changing. Right there. The green paddocks were folding themselves up, being pleated, squeezing into a narrow waist, right beside them and making way for a huge rocky cliff that had pushed itself there. It stretched up to the sky.

She turned and looked out the other window, across Charlie, across the seats on the other side of him. The farms and fields had gone from that side too. Again, a huge range had appeared, dressed with kahikatea, ponga, rewarewa, gorse.

'Charlie,' she said, 'come and have a look. We're in the gorge.' He scrambled up beside her and wriggled onto her legs. His arms found their way around her neck. His head rested against her shoulder.

'Cool,' he said.

'And look down there, chap.' She pointed across the aisle, her arm suspended, bouncing slightly as the train shuddered along its tracks. 'Look at the river.'

He craned his head. 'I can't see it,' and he got off her (and how his pointy knees and elbows jabbed into the weakened parts of her). He scooted across and pressed his face against the glass. He brought his hands up, palms on the window. 'Boy,' he said, without moving, 'it's so far down.'

Maya pulled herself out of her seat and went and sat next to him. She rested her hand on his back. It took up all the space between his shoulder blades. She could feel the warmth of him through his teeshirt.

'Hey, look down there, Mum,' and he pointed at the river, thirty metres below them. How was it that they could be suspended there, held somehow onto the skinny ribbon of railway, on the very side of this vast cliff? How was it that the wind, or the curve of the tracks or the hillside itself, didn't tip them over and tumble them over the craggy rocks into the river, splash? And they would be a child's Thomas train that just needed to be righted again, toot toot, and it would be on its way, around around, circling the track, breathing onto plastic trees, past the Fat Controller, there on the platform. Hey ho, and everything would be all right.

'Can you see them? Those dots in the river?'

'Where, buddy?' The wild plants that grew on the side of the train tracks blurred past them. Maya began to feel sick.

'Down there.' His finger stabbed the glass.

And there were dots in the river. Three of them. Kayakers. Being swept along by the rush of the Manawatu, paddling to keep up with themselves. 'Wow.' She had no energy to say anything else.

'Man, see over there. That's a road. Look how small the cars are, Mum. And the trucks. There's one now.'

Maya rubbed his back, wishing she had someone to rub hers. Someone to take over. Take charge. 'We're nearly in Palmerston, Charlie,' she said. 'We'd better get packed up.'

'See how the road is all twisty turny,' Charlie said. 'Man, it'd be cool to drive along that road.'

And if you were on that road, buddy, you'd look across the gorge at the train tracks and say how cool it would be, to be there, travelling on a train. We always want what we haven't got. The other side of the gorge is always greener.

She pressed the heels of her hands against her eyes. Sleep. Fresh air. Did people kill for these commodities? Maya thought she might.

'Right, that's the end of the gorge,' she said as the flat green paddocks again took the place of the rocky cliff face of a moment ago.

It had all changed so fast.

Eighteen

'Mrs Henderson?'

Maya spun around. 'Yes?' Who would know her, here, at the railway station in Palmerston North? And who would call her by her formal title? Funny, she never thought of herself as Mrs anything. Not any more.

'I'm Heather Woodley. From the Cancer Society. I'm here to meet you. I'll take you to The House. Help you get settled.'

Maya stood there in the midst of the chaos of the station. Taxis idling at the kerb, mothers running to their daughters, hugging them, crying, someone shouting into their cellphone, a loud-speaker announcement.

She was drowning. Her mouth opened – she could feel her jaw moving. It closed again. Her chest was still, void of air, unable to take any in. Unable to release any. Cancer Society.

Cancer cancer cancer.

She had become a Cancer Society recipient. In the instant of time after stepping off the train, when her foot connected with the grey of the platform, there.

'Are you all right? Mrs Henderson?'

It had happened.

'Mrs Henderson?'

Would she ever breathe again?

'I didn't expect anyone to be here,' she said. Her voice was lost somewhere at the back of her throat. Mixed up with a sob that threatened to find its way out of her mouth.

'It's all part of the service,' Heather Woodley said. She swung their bags into the boot. 'In you get,' she said, and they did, like compliant children, too tired and too confused to do anything else. 'Seatbelts on? Right.' She pulled away from the railway station. 'Would you like the radio on?'

'I don't mind,' said Maya. Heather Woodley squinted into the windscreen. She wore a black skirt screenprinted with a huge zebra head. Its ears were folded into the creases of the fabric. Her head whipped from side to side as she checked the road for traffic. She held the steering wheel with tight hands.

The service? What was the service? Was she somehow now compartmentalised into a category of some description? A Cancer Society Recipient.

'Was I referred?' Maya asked as they waited at the traffic lights.

'Pardon?'

'Was I referred? To you people? I didn't make contact.'

'I'm not sure about that side of it, Mrs Henderson. I much prefer dealing with people. You know.'

'Being of service.'

'Exactly.' She straightened herself up in the driver's seat and peered into the rearview mirror. 'How are you, young man?' Her voice suddenly turned into that of someone unused to children. It quavered, several notes higher than her earlier voice.

'Okay,' said Charlie. His thumbs danced over the Gameboy controls.

'Charlie!'

'I'm very well, thank you.' He rested his head against the window.

Oh, buddy, you must be tired too, Maya thought.

'So, where are we staying?' Charlie asked.

Heather Woodley laughed. 'You're in The House. All our patients stay there. You've got your own room, of course, and bathroom, and there's a lovely communal lounge. And dining room. There's

229

even a reading room. She looked up into the rearview mirror again. 'Do you like reading, Charlie?' Up and down, like waves.

'He's tired,' said Maya. 'We both are. We just need some sleep, eh, chap?'

'Whatever.'

'Here we are,' Heather Woodley said, and she swung the car into the gravel driveway. The House was white weatherboards and stained-glass windows, deep borders of standard lavender and buxus clipped into domes. Like cannonballs, Maya thought. Where were the daffodils from the picture Mr Goodman had shown her?

Of course, it was too late for daffodils, Maya knew that (in fact it was time to get this year's bulbs in) but the picture had had them. Hundreds of them, a solid line along the front of the photo. She could see it exactly. This wasn't right. They had been cheated. Duped.

First, Heather Woodley from the Cancer Society with her firm grip on the steering wheel and her voice, and now this.

Maya stood on the stony path with her bag over her shoulder, her wound healed but suddenly raw and aching, her belly tight, her head smooth and shiny (and even her pubic hair was gone; she was a little girl, an old woman, lost somewhere between the two). And she began to cry.

It smelled like the geriatric hospital Maya had worked in during her training. She had cared for the same four men, there. Between them, they had three legs and thirteen toes. One of them thought he was in an army hospital in France. Let me go, he wailed. The boys need me back with them. My feet are numb, Sister. It must be the snow. Every day was December 1917.

It even looked like the geriatric hospital, Maya thought. Armchairs jammed up against the walls, around three sides of the lounge. There was a TV on the other wall, and a piano.

'Oh, look,' said Heather Woodley, 'here are some of our guests.'

She strode across the room. Maya and Charlie followed. 'This is Mr Rainforth. He's from Masterton, aren't you, Mr Rainforth? And this is Miss Parr. She's a bit deaf and she's not feeling so well at the moment. And this is Mrs Edwards. Your knitting is coming along very nicely, dear. This is Mrs Henderson and her lovely son, Charlie.' Maya waited for her voice to go on its upward climb, and it did. 'They're from Gisborne. Isn't that nice?' She nodded her head up and down. Maya felt Charlie nudge in against her. She put her arm around him. He held on to her fingers.

'Well, then,' said Heather Woodley. 'I'm sure you'll all become the best of friends.' She paused.

'Could you show us our room?' Maya said. 'Charlie's a bit tired, you see.'

'Right. Off we go.'

They followed Heather Woodley down one corridor, along another until they came to their room.

'Here we are.'

Twin beds, covered with apple-green quilted bedspreads. Charlie flopped down one of the beds, lay on his back and continued his Gameboy battle. A nightstand stood between the beds. There was a vase on it, clear glass, and the water in it caught the sun that came in the window. The vase was overflowing with rosebuds, creamy pink, their petals tight against one another.

Someone had put flowers in their room.

'Now, normally you have to provide your own food. We've got all the facilities for cooking in the kitchen, so there's no problem there. We provide tea and coffee, and Milo for the littlies.' And up went Heather Woodley's voice. 'And jam and Marmite.' And down it came again. 'We put together something of an emergency survival package for you, though. Just to start with. Most people don't want to have to think about bringing groceries with them, so we start you off with Weet-Bix, rice risotto, tinned spaghetti, biscuits, bread. That kind of thing. There's a shelf in the kitchen with your name on it. You'll find your groceries there. And whatever else you buy, you keep there. Just name your fridge things. Before they go in. Everyone's very good about respecting other people's food.'

She went on and on, giving them information, smiling, pulling at her top, on and on. Maya stared at the flowers.

'Thank you,' said Maya once Heather Woodley had stopped talking. 'We might just have some toast. And then we'll go to bed. We're both quite tired.'

'Right,' said Heather Woodley. 'Let me know if you need anything. I'll be along in the morning to take you to your treatment. 9:20. See you then.'

She breezed out, with the zebra twitching at her knees.

'Right,' Maya echoed. And then they were alone.

It felt like an adventure. A holiday. Once the cooked cabbage smell had permeated their noses enough that they couldn't smell it any more. (No one probably even cooked cabbage there. It was just how places like these were.) Once they'd unpacked their bags and eaten their toast with honey, on their beds. Tomorrow we'll eat in the dining room, Maya had said. But for tonight, we'll just keep to ourselves.

'Bedtime,' she announced once they'd washed their dishes and put them away. Hospital Property was stamped on the bottom of the plates. 'You're being so good, buddy,' she whispered as she tucked the sheet around Charlie's shoulders. 'Thank you.'

'That's okay, Mum. But we'll do something cool tomorrow, won't we?'

'We'll see, chap.' She kissed his forehead. His skin was damp with a fine film of summer sweat. She turned the sheet down to his chest. There, tucked against his belly, was Honey Bear.

She touched the bear's ear. The fur was worn where Charlie had held the ear between his thumb and forefinger. She kissed Charlie again and slipped into her own bed. She was sure that if she reached her arm out she could touch her beautiful boy.

Home seemed a long way away. She wanted to phone Kathy or Rachael, to hear a voice she knew, to smell salt air, to hear the roar of the sea, to taste the relentless heat.

But they'd both made it clear, in their own way, how things were to be. And Maya knew that she couldn't risk it, making contact, opening up a channel that Charlie might inadvertently slip through.

She hadn't cried when Gran died. She hadn't even felt that surprised. Not that it had been expected. A heart attack on the street outside Farmers. She would have been horrified to have seen herself sprawled on the footpath like that, petticoat showing, handbag fallen open and its private contents strewn all around, saliva dribbling from the corner of her mouth. No one in town that day seemed to know about CPR, so by the time the doctor arrived it was too late.

But she never cried.

Why had she suddenly thought about that?

'Are you sad, Mum?' Charlie crawled next to her, on the one couch in the lounge, resting his head on her legs. Honey Bear tickled her arm. One of the other guests sat three chairs away. Maya couldn't remember his name.

'I'm not sure, buddy.'

'It's only *Shortland Street*. It's not real. It's just TV. They make it all up. Honest.'

She kissed the top of his head.

'Do I have to come with you?'

Please don't argue, buddy. Not today. When she woke up, she was lying in the same position as when she went to sleep. She thought she had had a dream in the night but she couldn't remember what it had been about.

'It won't take long.' Her voice was heavy and sluggish.

'You always say that.'

'No, really. The radiotherapy only takes a few minutes. By the time you get your book open on the right page I'll be finished.'

'Yeah?'

'Absolutely.'

'So does that mean we've come all this way just for you to have your radio thingy for a couple of minutes?'

'Funny, eh? Every day for five weeks. 9:30. That'll be us. With weekends off.'

'Okay, so we'll have the rest of the day to do things. Have a holiday.'

'We'll see.'

Liar.

Liar, liar, pants on fire.

Why did motherhood have to be so full of saying things you didn't mean, saying things you knew weren't true?

'Here's that lady again,' said Charlie.

In she breezed, Heather Woodley, in a long green singlet top, green leggings and green suede boots, the tops turned over like fuzzy collars.

'Morning,' she sang. 'Ready?'

'Ready,' said Maya. 'Ready, Charlie?'

'Ready,' he answered, and stood up stiffly, saluting.

They followed Heather Woodley down the corridor, through the empty lounge, the chairs up against the walls like shy schoolgirls, and out into the day. Warm, still, quiet.

'Wait a minute,' said Charlie, and he ran back inside. Maya and Heather Woodley stood by the car, with nothing to say to each other. They smiled, the closed-lip smile of strangers aware of the awkwardness of the situation.

And then he was back, Honey Bear tucked firmly under his arm. 'I'm ready,' he said, and they got into the car.

A bear was just the right companion on a day like this, Maya thought.

She had had one when she was little. He was the colour of brown paper. Her mother had let her choose him in her last kindy holidays. There had been morning tea in town, a tomato sandwich fiery with pepper, a butterfly cake and a small bottle of Fanta. Her mother had sat opposite, drinking Cona coffee, dabbing at her beautiful lips between mouthfuls.

They went to a toyshop after morning tea. The owner addressed Maya's mother by name as if she was a frequent shopper there. Any toy you like, dear, she said, and Maya walked round and round the shop, looking up at the shelves stacked neatly with dolls, wooden trucks, hobby horses and soft toys.

This one, Maya had said and she pointed up at a plain brown bear with a flat smiling face and eyes the colour of curry around its black glassy pupils.

Really? Look, here's a lovely fluffy dog. Hasn't it got nice floppy ears? Or what about this doll? You can give her a bottle and then change her nappy.

No, it was the dun-coloured bear Maya wanted. Her mother took it off the shelf and handed it to her. It fitted perfectly against her as she hugged it. It was warm and soft. It even smelled right.

What a fine fellow, the shopkeeper said as Maya gave him the bear for wrapping. And so she named him Fine Fullah, because at nearly five she couldn't quite say fellow like the shopkeeper had.

Fine Fullah went to school with her every day, waiting quietly in Maya's stiff snap-shut school case until she took him out at playtime and lunchtime. He looked after her Marmite sandwiches and bottle of orange cordial.

He even went on the holiday to Napier, choosing to stay on the front seat of the car, keeping watch with his round bear eyes.

But she couldn't find him after she went to live with Gran. He'll be around somewhere, Gran said, but she never helped Maya look for him.

The car hummed and trembled slightly as Heather Woodley drove Maya and Charlie to the hospital.

The waiting room was hushed, sombre. It feels like church, Maya thought. And I guess a lot of praying goes on here. Charlie sat in a padded vinyl chair. Honey Bear sat on his knee, facing out into the room.

'I'm Maya Henderson.' Why was she whispering?

The woman at the desk drew a line through Maya's name in her appointment diary. 'Good,' she said. She wasn't speaking to Maya, or herself. It was just noise.

Of all the treatment so far, this felt the strangest. Here she was, dislocated from her home and her friends, white-gowned, lying on a cold tray and staring at a machine that might have been part of a science fiction movie. The technician manoeuvred it over the parts of her that had been marked with an indelible pen. X really does mark the spot, Maya had said.

There was no sound to this therapy except the hum of the machine, no taste, no sensation, no visible clues that this was doing anything except scaring the crap out of her.

The technician stood behind his clear safety wall. 'Here we go,' he said. Ready, aim, fire, Maya said to herself. Nothing seemed to happen. But the cancerous parts of her were surely being bombarded with radiation that would make them shrivel and die. And then she would be better.

Five minutes was the longest time.

And all she could do was lie there and trust that the dose and the distance and the area had been measured correctly, and that this was the best thing she could be doing under the circumstances, and that the cancer cells would give up their fight and somehow be vaporised out of her and she would live happily ever after. That was all she could do.

The technician emerged from behind the screen (his bunker, Maya thought). 'All done,' he said, and he swung the machine against the wall. Out of harm's way. 'Now you know the drill, don't you?' Was this military talk coincidental? 'No soap, no lotions, no perfume, no sunlight. On the treated areas, that is.'

Yes, yes.

'Drink plenty. Plain foods. You'll feel terrible for the rest of the day, though.'

Thanks.

'That'll improve as the course goes on. You need to get as much rest as your body demands. Okay? You don't have anything you need to worry about at the moment, do you? You've got to focus on yourself.'

Nothing to worry about. Nothing to focus on.

Just the nine-year-old in the waiting room, clutching his stuffed bear. I'm sure he can amuse himself while I help myself to after-noon naps, early nights.

No wucking forries.

Philip. She could hear him, with his voice that always had a laugh just behind it, threatening to bubble over the top of his words. She could smell him – cedar, sandalwood, vanilla, the suggestion of these aromas that always lingered on his clothes and his pillow. She could feel his presence around her for weeks after he died – his spirit, his soul, or maybe it was desire and impossible hope, yet it wasn't him that she cried for, or asked God or someone, to give back to her. It was her mother.

Philip's death, so sudden and brutal, resurrected every speck of grief that she had hidden for all those years. And because too much of it would kill you, Maya could only cry for, ache for, sit silently in the dark for one person at a time.

'Same time tomorrow then?' The technician guided her by the elbow back to the tiny cubicle where her clothes waited, folded neatly.

Same Bat time, same Bat channel.

'Boy, that was quick,' said Charlie.

'What did I tell you? Piece of cake.' Maya reached for Charlie's hand. She thought she might not make it to the door without it.

It was true. She was so tired she thought she might die from it. Her body would not move. Her lungs struggled to breathe. Was it worth the effort? Her arms were weighted onto the bed. Her head had moulded itself into her pillow. It sunk into the soft of it, was

237

cocooned by the fabric of the Hospital Property pillowcase.

If there was a fire, she would let herself burn.

If there was an earthquake, she would allow herself to be crushed by the ceiling and the roof tiles rather than have to move from this position.

If Charlie was abducted, electrocuted, hit by a car on the road outside, she would let it happen.

Just so long as she didn't have to stay awake.

'What have you been doing, buddy?' Maya tied her dressing gown around her. Her waist was hot and sticky.

'I dunno. Playing Gameboy mostly.'

'What time is it?'

'Three o'clock. Or a bit after. Can we have some lunch?'

'Oh, chap.' She sat down at the dining table and held her head in her hands. 'You haven't had any lunch.'

She felt as if she was being pulled, stretched into a thin thread. She threatened to snap in two at any moment. Charlie held one end of her, the hospital the other. They each shouted 'Go,' and ran in opposite directions.

She wanted to go back to sleep.

'Marmite sandwich okay?' she said, and she moved to the kitchen and took bread from the bag on their shelf and began to butter it. 'You could have done this, you know,' she said.

'I didn't think about it. Sorry.'

There it was. Thinking. Always having to do all the thinking. Still. Now. Even though. She blinked slowly, aware that her eyelids were sluggish. Her shoulders ached. Belly, hips, knees.

Maybe she had secondaries. Maybe the cancer had spread already, invading her bones, drilling holes like tiny speleologists, pinhead-sized mining lamps strapped to their cancerous foreheads. Maybe it was too late for radiotherapy. For any treatment. Many she should go home, to her house in Gisborne, draw the curtains, lie in bed and wait to die.

Or maybe this was just day one of her radiotherapy and her body

238

was reacting to it all, and so was her brain, and she should listen to what they both were saying, body and brain, and she should go back to bed and sleep until her body and brain told her it was time to wake up.

'How would you feel if I had another sleep? Let me have all of today off and tomorrow I'll feel better. I promise.'

I promise.

There she was, lying to him again.

One day slid into the next into the next into the next.

Maya wasn't sure whether she bathed, or ate, or dressed.

She wasn't sure if Charlie bathed, or ate, or dressed.

It didn't seem to matter.

But every morning that week Heather Woodley arrived in her white hospital car, and her pink smile, and drove them to Maya's appointment. She waited in the car (You know your way by now, don't you? Don't need me tagging along.) and drove them back to the house afterwards.

Heather Woodley got into the habit of making Charlie a cold Milo when they got back. But she didn't dissolve the Milo first. All she needed was a tablespoon or so of boiling water. But she spooned the powder on top of the cold milk, and stirred it around, and it stayed on the surface, like a swell of seaweed that butted itself against the wharf. It just wouldn't dissolve.

That wasn't how you made cold Milo. It wasn't how Charlie had it.

Nineteen

It was surprisingly relaxing, Maya thought. She lay perfectly still on the table. Well, it was a trolley, really. A tray. A millimetre this way or that and it would be the clean bits of her that would be irradiated. What was it they had called it in the Gulf War?

Friendly fire.

Five weeks of radiotherapy. Today was Thursday, so not counting today, she had twenty-one treatments to go. A hundred and five minutes. It wasn't much, was it? A hundred and five minutes and then she could go home.

Until then, she just wanted to sleep, hide, protect herself from everyone and everything. She wanted to withdraw, go under the covers, under cover, under water, in utero, in visible.

A steady stream of air passed over her face. It was cool. It tickled her forehead, her lips. She could not (was not allowed to) move her hand to touch the place.

Her head lay in a padded trough. Keeping it still. Her body was strapped in situ. She could be a death row prisoner, about to be injected.

The second hand of the clock opposite her swept agonisingly slowly. Why was it called a second hand? Surely it was a third hand. How much longer? The machine buzzed. You had to strain to hear it, really. But as long as it emitted its metallic hum it was also emitting radiation.

If you were to undergo a whole-body X-ray – that is, all of you imaged at once – the radiation would kill you, she thought.

If you were to get on a plane without travel insurance, the chances of you being killed would be no greater than had you signed up to something that very morning.

If you were to be practising your bowling in the nets on a Saturday afternoon you would be unlikely to be hit between the shoulder blades with a cricket wicket, hurled by some idiot pretending it was a javelin. If that were to happen, however, it would be unbelievably bad luck, especially if you were to be killed as a result of a haemo-pneumothorax.

It would be somewhat more unlucky than developing cancer in your thirties, but certainly a quicker way to go (and far more sensational).

She could hear Charlie in the waiting room talking to someone waiting for their turn at the machine, or maybe he was having a conversation with Honey Bear.

Charlie.

What really lay ahead for him?

Had she updated her will since Philip died?

Where would Charlie go? Like a chattel, a belonging, something to be parcelled up and sent somewhere. (This worry about him was like a round, a never-ending song, she thought.)

I should be grateful there is no Gran for him to go to.

Reading again and again the warning printed across the metal shield of the wringer as she fed the heavy, dripping sheets through – *Keep fingers clear of the rollers.* Polishing the silver tea service that never got used, not being allowed friends to play, not being allowed to go anywhere else to play, never being hugged even.

Yes, grateful there was no Gran for Charlie.

Kathy? His aunt, his closest remaining relative. He should automatically go to her. Here we go again, Maya thought as she lay there, looking up at the ceiling tiles. There were sixty-four of them. Kathy was sick of looking after her and Charlie, wasn't she? And, more important, she didn't know which way Charlie liked his sandwiches cut.

When you relinquish control (over yourself), your choices are so few.

Maybe today I won't be so tired, she thought. Maybe today we can have a holiday.

There was a knock at the door. A gentle tapping, almost apologetic.

'Maya?' The woman's voice had the quaver of old age, of sagging, the muscles of the face, the skin on the upper arms, the mechanisms of the throat.

Gran, Maya thought in her fuzz of half sleep. It's Gran. I'd better get up. I'll be in trouble if she catches me still in bed. You're lazy, girl, she'd said the first Saturday after Maya had gone to live with her. She had stayed in bed because it wasn't a school day and it was so soon after – you know, and she didn't want to have to face a whole day with Gran and she wasn't even sure what the rules of the place were. She would soon learn. You're lazy. Get out of bed. There's plenty for you to do.

She felt her feet touch the floor. She felt herself reach for her dressing gown. She rubbed her eyes and went to pull her fingers through her hair, because she wanted to (had to) be presentable on her first Saturday at Gran's. But her hand ran over the smooth bland surface of her skull. She wasn't at Gran's. That's right, this was Palmerston North.

Maya rubbed at her face again. Wake up, she told herself.

Knock, knock, again. 'Are you there?'

She opened her door and the knitting lady stood there, hands clasped over her belly. Maya exhaled, not even aware that she had been holding her breath.

'I'm sorry to bother you, dear, but there's a phone call for you.'

A phone call. Here. Who would be calling her? She shivered as a chill slid down the length of her. These were the bad-news calls. The late-night ones. I think you should come straight away. The ringing that woke you in an instant and had you out of bed and reaching for the receiver in one reflexive movement was the scariest sound she could imagine. It intimated tragedy, pain, and until you picked up the phone (and stopped the noise of it), the anticipation and the possibilities were a bigger, blacker, louder monster than the truth that waited behind it.

'Dear? Are you all right?'

'Yes, I'm sorry.' Maya shut her bedroom door, locking in her irrational half-woken thoughts. She followed the knitting lady into the kitchen. The receiver rested on the bench, attached by a spiral cord to the wall-mounted phone.

'Here you are.'

The knitting lady stood there, with her short straight hair that was obviously growing back after chemo. It seemed incongruous on such a woman. She should have soft silver waves curled around her face, but here she was with coarse spiky hair streaked grey and mustard.

Maya was aware that she was still standing behind her. Nosy old biddy. But no, maybe she was concerned that this *was* going to be a bad-news phone call and thought she should be on hand, in case she were needed.

'Hello?'

'Mrs Wimple? This is the Department of Child Truancy and Home Desertion. We've had a report.'

'Kathy.' She grinned. How good it felt across her face.

'Thought I'd give you a call and see how you were doing. Make sure you're behaving.'

'Thank you. There's no chance of doing anything else around here. It's not exactly Times Square.'

'But then you're not exactly a New York rocker at the moment, are you?'

Maya smiled. The conversation between them was easy, relaxed. Things would be all right. She reached over for a chair and pulled it close to the phone. The knitting lady made a drinking-a-cup-of-tea motion with her hand, thumb and forefinger pinched, little finger extended. Maya nodded.

'How are things? How's Charlie?'

'He's good. Bored.'

'What's he up to?'

'Right now? Watching TV, I think. Or playing on his Gameboy. Like I said, there's not much to do around here when you're nine.'

'And how are you doing?'

'Okay.'

'Honest?'

'Yeah.'

'I don't believe you.'

'You know me too well, Kathy. I'm okay, just tired. You wouldn't believe how much this stuff knocks you around.'

The knitting lady placed a cup of tea on the bench beside her. Thank you, Maya mouthed. She disappeared.

'Thank you for phoning,' Maya continued. She paused. The phone crackled. 'I feel really bad about – you know.'

'Me too. I'm sorry.'

'I think our emotions got the better of us.'

'So,' said Kathy. It didn't take much; a few words, enough, and not too many.

'How's Gizzy?'

'Hot.'

'Ha.'

'What about Palmerston?'

'I dunno, really. I haven't thought much about the weather. I've been too busy sleeping.'

'Oh, Maya, it sounds like you're having a really hard time.'

'It won't last forever.' Maya sipped her tea. It had sugar in it. Milk, too. Oh, well. She smiled.

From Gisborne to Palmerston North, through the hundreds of kilometres of phone lines, highway, train tracks, there was silence.

Maya watched the steam curl around her cup.

'Are you still there?' she heard.

'Yeah.' She was suddenly overcome with exhaustion. She leaned the side of her head against the wall. 'Just a bit wiped out. Sorry.'

'I'll let you go then. I wanted to tell you, before you go, that I saw Rachael the other day.'

'Oh?'

'She's going to send something down for you. Muffins or something. She knows she overreacted about Charlie's party and everything.'

'This is the day for coming clean, then.' She paused. 'You guys don't think I'm going to die, do you?'

'Of course not.'

'Just that all this clearing the air makes me nervous.'

Kathy laughed. Maya could hear the tinkling of ice against a glass. 'Is there someone who could take Charlie off your hands for a while and let you have some time out?'

'Not really,' Maya said. 'Everyone around here's either too old or too sick.'

'And which category do you fall into?'

'You know what I mean. Anyway, I couldn't let Charlie go off with anyone else.'

'Why not? They're hardly serial killers where you are. He'd be okay.'

'I don't know.'

'I'm sure there's someone who would look after him for a bit. Even just so that you could have a decent sleep. Don't you think?'

'I can't give him away.'

'It's not giving him away. It's about giving him some responsibility, if nothing else.'

'What do you mean?' Maya asked in a quiet voice.

'Well, he needs to do things on his own. With other people. And that's not because you're sick. It's because he needs it.'

Silence.

'Are you okay, Mrs Wimple?'

'Yeah. The truth hurts a bit, that's all.'

'Sorry.'

'That's okay.'

'Are you sure?'

'Yeah.'

'Really?'

'We've already had this conversation, Kathy.'

'Okay, then.'

'I'll see you.'

'Sure you're okay?'

'Kathy!'

'Just think about it, won't you.'

Maya placed the receiver in its cradle. The cord wound around itself. Her tea was pale, muddy. It had gone cold. She would tip it out as soon as she got up.

She'd think about what Kathy said. About Charlie. After she'd had a rest.

It's funny that they've both come around, Maya thought as she lay in bed. The curtains were pulled, but slivers of mid-afternoon still showed at the edges of the window. Maybe just being away from each other helps us get things into perspective.

I'm trying, she thought.

The knitting lady, Mrs Edwards, was taking Charlie to the park across the road from The House. Call me Dulcie, she'd said. You'll just have him for an hour, won't you? Yes, dear. Trust us.

I'm trying, Maya thought. Her body slipped under the top layer of her consciousness. She was warm, light.

I'm trying.

'Let me have this morning to recover, and then we'll do something. All right?'

It was Saturday. The end of week one. The fatigue was as strong as ever. There had been no getting used to it, allowing her body to adjust. General malaise, they'd called it in her training days. A side effect of a thousand different conditions. Maya had a severe case. It felt irreversible.

'But all you do is sleep. All day. And all night. You said we'd have a holiday, but all I've done is sit here and play on my Gameboy, or watch TV with all these old people. I'm sick of reading. It's boring,

Mum. I'd rather be back at school.'

Charlie stood in front of her, his arms straight at his sides, his hands curled into tight fists. It was as if he had all his anger contained in those two hands. If he unfurled them, who knew what might happen.

But bed was all she wanted. It was her nourishment these days, but it was a fickle diet, never quite satisfying her, always leaving her hungry for more.

It wrapped its arms around her, this bed. It rocked her, soothed her with the back of its hand against her forehead. Shh, it whispered. Its breath tickled her neck.

'Soon, buddy,' she heard herself say. No, this bed was her lover, selfish, needy, demanding its own pleasure and leaving her at the point of fulfilment before pulling back. Withdrawing. 'Mmm,' and she leaned in against its smooth skin. 'Soon. Just let me rest for a bit longer.'

'This holiday stinks.' Shouting. Hands still bunched at his sides. Shoulders harsh angles. 'The only thing that's been any fun was when that lady took me to the park. You lied about this holiday being fun, Mum.'

He turned and fled, slamming the door. It echoed, slam, and his words were trapped in the room, slam, and she wanted sleep, wanted this lover, wanted it, slam, wanted something else. Slam, slam.

She lay there in the quiet of her room (not really her room, but she would claim it for the time they were there). Maybe I should send Charlie home, she thought. It's not very fair on him, cooped up in this place twenty-four hours a day surrounded by all these sick people. That's not what a nine-year-old needs. Or deserves. And there are still four weeks to go.

Four weeks.

How would she survive? Dry crackers and bananas, night sweats, vomiting. And the tiredness that was like being encased in concrete. 'Tiredness' doesn't do it justice, she thought. There needs to be a new word for how this feels.

Only I'm too tired to think of one.

Maybe I *should* send him home. Put him on the train with his backpack and his bear, clutching a piece of paper with Unaccompanied Minor in glaring black type across the top. That was for children who were being abandoned, sent home, sent away. Given away.

But they were a team, Maya and Charlie. That was what she'd always told him. And to give him away would mean admitting that she wasn't strong enough (or mother enough, she thought, and there was pressure in her chest like a hand pushing against her).

And to give him away now would mean that if the worst happened – you know – he would already be someone else's kid and already part of someone else's family, and Maya couldn't decide if that would be better or worse.

I'll play it by ear, she thought. Go with the flow. Sounding like Rachael (and would she be the best person to have Charlie?). Was Kathy's phone call and their reconciliation a sign? Was it Meant To Be?

Que sera sera.

She had to get up, she knew. Sort this out. Find out what Charlie wanted to do. Today. And for the remainder of her time in Palmerston. Decide what was best.

But the devil at her shoulder was pulling her back into the warmth and the softness of her bed, of sleep. Worry about it later, he whispered, and his breath on her neck made her shiver. 'Bugger off,' she said and she pulled herself out of bed.

Charlie was in the lounge. He was so small, folded up in one of the chairs. 'I'm sorry, buddy. Really. We'll have an adventure. Okay?' Her hands found his and she tried to uncurl his fingers. But they were like new fern fronds, not ready to open yet. She squeezed his hand instead. She might have been trying to transfer some enthusiasm to him. She couldn't tell.

He looked up. His eyes, the colour of the sea back home, were huge and wary. 'Yeah?'

'Let's hire a car. We'll go for a drive somewhere.'

'Yeah?'

'Yeah.'

Driving. Concentrating. Mothering.

'I know, Mum, we could go to Splash Planet. We were going to go in the holidays, weren't we? We could go today. I'll get my togs.'

Splash Planet was two hours' drive. Through the Manawatu Gorge, windy and treacherous – twenty minutes of difficult, dangerous road, then across the Takapau Plains, where it was so flat and straight you were at risk of falling asleep at the wheel. Through the streets of Hastings, getting lost even though you were following the signposts, taking miles of desperately suburban streets, and finally finding the place and wrenching up the handbrake, wondering how you would manage all the activities. Any of them.

'I'm ready.' And he was. Togs in his nylon drawstring bag with a gulping fish painted on the front, Honey Bear under one arm, his Gameboy in his hand.

She had no choice. Once again she was being pulled in a direction she couldn't control. It was just a day out, though. She'd be fine. Fresh air, driving, a swim. It was just what they needed. Maybe it would help her decide what she should do. She was almost convinced.

'There's a hospital car any of the residents can use,' Mrs Edwards (call me Dulcie) said. Charlie was telling everyone, hopping, jumping around the room. Taking up too much space. Making too much noise. 'The keys are on a hook in the kitchen. Go on, enjoy yourselves. Have a nice day out. Don't think about anything.' She seemed so certain. She was right, of course. She picked up her knitting and her fingers flew over the needles.

'That's nice wool,' said Maya. She wasn't very good at small talk any more, she realised. Out of practice.

'It's for my grandson.' She held the knitting up. 'This is the back.' It was grey homespun wool, knobbly and thick. 'He's a bit smaller than you, dear. Could I try it against you? To check the length.'

Charlie stood in front of her and held his arms out, as though he had been measured for a hand-knitted jersey a thousand times. He was like a tiny scarecrow, Maya thought.

My mother would have loved to have knitted for you. Her eyes suddenly filled up with tears. She tried to blink them away but they kept coming back, betraying her with their salty sting. It was unfair that this boy had never known his grandmother. She should have spoiled him with ice-cream before dinner, phone calls (no, I don't want to talk to your mother, I just want to hear about what you've been doing, Charlie), trips to the library in the holidays, letters addressed to him that came in the post.

'You have a lovely son,' Mrs Edwards said, and she pressed her hands on Charlie's shoulders. The backs of her hands were dry and pitted, lumpy with ropey veins. Maya looked at her own hands. 'Dear?'

'I'm sorry,' Maya said, shaking her head, crossing her arms and hiding her hands under her armpits. 'Thank you.'

Was that what she was supposed to say? She couldn't remember. What had she said? Something about knitting, or sons, or hands.

'Come on, Mum.'

'We'd better go.' Maya smiled and Mrs Edwards bent her head to her needles again.

'Have a lovely time out,' she said.

'We will,' Charlie called, and he ran to the front door. Maya sighed and went to the kitchen for the car keys. She wanted more than anything to go back to bed.

She held on to the steering wheel tightly, afraid that if she loosened her grip then her concentration and her knowledge of how to drive would disappear out the open window.

'Awesome,' Charlie said. He sat in the front passenger seat but had turned his body to face out the side window.

'What, buddy?'

'Just – I dunno – everything.'

Maya smiled. This would be good medicine. If she could just stay concentrating on driving. Splash Planet would be there in no time at all.

'Can I play my Gameboy?'

'Sure. As long as you have the sound off.'

Driving felt strange after a week of being a passenger and a patient. And she was in control of someone else's car. The accelerator was heavier than she was used to. Or was it lighter?

'I'll give you the map. You can be in charge of navigating.'

'Cool. We're like a rally team.'

'We are, aren't we, chap? Okay, so you know where we're going?' She pulled over to the side of one of Palmerston North's wide streets. Everything was so flat and vast. It was as if the city had spread, like syrup poured onto a plate. It went out and out, thin, wide, filling up all the available space. 'We're here,' she said, and she pointed to a spot on the map. 'We need to get to here. That's the road out of town. To Hastings.' It slipped off the edge of the map, that skinny line.

'No problem, Mum.'

She edged into the traffic and off they went. Charlie held his index finger on the map, moving it along as they drove. Right here, left at the next corner. His voice had become important. Maya saw him hold up his left hand, extend his index finger and thumb. A capital L. L for left. An old trick, to help him remember which was left and which was right. Her mother had taught her that way, gently tucking her other fingers into her palm. Tracing a capital L over her finger and thumb. Her touch was so soft.

'Left at the end of the street.'

They headed towards the open road. Maya sped up. A hundred k's. It felt too fast. She knew she was too tired to drive at this speed, but it was what you did. Drove at the limit. The paddocks on either side of the road were wide and flat, pulled tight. The road cut through the middle of them.

'Is this right?' said Maya after a while. She squeezed one hand against the curve of the steering wheel, then the other. She was so tired. Her arms were heavy weights. She could hardly hold them up.

'Yeah, I think so.' Charlie's finger marked their progress.

I could just close my eyes for a second, she thought. To rest them. Just for a second. But wait, there was a signpost on the side of the road. Bulls, Sanson, Taupo. Do we go through Bulls? On the way to the gorge and Splash Planet? Shouldn't we be in Ashhurst soon? Oh, well, maybe Ashhurst doesn't make it onto a signpost. Maybe it's so close. Just around the next bend.

They drove, pushing miles and miles of road behind them, waiting for Ashhurst just around the next bend. Maya turned the radio up loud. She sang along. She'd stay awake that way. She curled the toes of her right foot around the accelerator pedal, scrunched up those of her left against the sole of her sandal, stretched the fingers of one hand as far as they would go, then the other hand.

'Oh, look, here comes a sign,' she said, even though it wasn't the sign that was approaching them. It was the other way around, but that was how you said it, wasn't it?

Bulls, in clean white letters against the green of the sign that was the same green as the surface of Gran's felt-topped card table. Bulls.

'God, Charlie, we're in Bulls!' She pulled the car to a stop just under the sign, as though it was necessary to see it in close-up, to make sense of it. 'Give me the map.' She snatched it from him and spread it out across the steering wheel. 'I'm too tired for this,' she said to the criss-cross of roads. 'How on earth did we end up here?'

But wanting to say – how did you get us here? How did you get us lost? 'The map doesn't go this far. It's just Palmerston. Shit.' She dropped her forehead against the map and squeezed her eyes shut to keep in the tears that were ganging up against her eyelids.

Charlie remained silent. He ran his fingers over Honey Bear's ears.

'I don't know,' she said. 'Let's just turn around and go back. We'll find a shop and I'll go and ask.' She jerked the car into gear and drove slowly until she came to a dairy. 'Wait here,' she said. She shut the car door harder than she meant to.

'Right,' she said as she got back into the car. She flung a bag of chips across to Charlie and laid a big bottle of lemonade on the floor in front of him. 'We went the wrong way back in Palmerston. Went in completely the wrong direction. But it's no problem. We'll just start again.'

'I'm sorry, Mum,' Charlie said through a small mouth. He wiped his nose against Honey Bear's shoulder.

'It's okay. It's woken me up anyway.' And they were off again, spinning the car round and heading back, covering the same ground. She lapsed into that state of sleepiness almost immediately. It was the sound of the road under them, the hum of the car's engine. The road hypnotised her. She was dulled by the broken centre line falling away beside them.

Her eyelids were giving in even before they got back to town. She wound the window down. 'Fresh air,' she announced. 'Okay, we're back where we started,' and they were, parked outside The House. Now that they were insiders, part of the system, it looked different. 'Anyone want to go to Splash Planet?'

Charlie smiled. 'Honey Bear does,' he said.

'Right then. I'll navigate this time,' and she checked the map, saying out loud the streets they were to follow. It was simple. Straight down this road, left at the first lights and go straight ahead. Stop when you get to Hastings.

Twenty

And so they drove away from Palmerston North again, from The House, past Whakarongo and towards Ashhurst.

One day a taniwha
Went swimming in the moana,
It whispered in my taringa,
Oh won't you come with me,
There's such a lot to see,
Underneath the deep blue sea.

'That's lovely, buddy,' said Maya. She had to say something to give her brain something to do so she would stay alert. 'Hey, look over there, a wind farm,' she said.

'Cool,' Charlie said, but he glanced up only briefly. He hummed the song, tapped his fingers on the door rest.

She watched the turbines turning against the wind. They stood on the top of the ridge, two dozen shiny A&P Show foil windmills. Turn turn turn. Maya blinked them away.

One day a taniwha

Went swimming in the moana . . . Charlie sang. His voice was soft like pudding. It wavered around the notes, almost finding the right places on the stave to sit.

They were at the gorge now, where to the right of them the hills climbed hundreds of feet in the air, and only sharp grasses and wild foxgloves could cling to the slopes. The road fell away to their left, to jagged rocks studded with hebes and blackberry, and down into the Manawatu River. The road immediately became windy.

Left and right, they had become a fish, pushing through the water, never swimming in a straight line but zigzagging along.

Maya's belly lurched. 'Ooh,' she said.

'Are you okay, Mum?'

'Yeah. Sorry. I just can't remember if I had breakfast.' Had she eaten today?

It whispered in my taringa . . .

The car flung them around one corner and then the next, one way and the other. A truck came at them from the other direction, sounding its horn, loud and long.

'Shit,' said Maya, and she steered the car to the left of the road, barely clinging onto the seal. She swallowed hard.

Oh won't you come with me,

There's such a lot to see . . .

Jesus. Concentrate. Her hands were sweating. She wiped one down her front, then the other. Her eyelids were heavy. She began to feel really sick now. Stop singing, would you. She breathed in slowly, exhaled, in out in out, pulling on the steering wheel to get around the bend, now hard the other way. Tired, tired.

Underneath the deep blue sea.

 One day a taniwha . . .

'Isn't there another verse to that song? With different words?'

Charlie shrugged. 'Dunno. *Went swimming in the moana . . .*'

Tired, tired.

'Shh, Charlie. I'm trying to concentrate now.' She swallowed again. There was an ocean of saliva in her mouth. Charlie's song was going round and round in her head. The stupid tune 'You are my sunshine,' the words, the irritation she felt because she knew there was a second verse but it remained out of reach, hidden somewhere in her head behind piles of everyday stuff and piles of extraordinary stuff. Way at the back, anyway, in the dark and cobwebby parts of her.

'Man, look how close we are to the edge,' Charlie said. 'I can see right down. It's nearly straight down to the river. Did you know that?'

Maya shook her head. She was afraid to speak now. Afraid to open her mouth. Swallow. Blink. Concentrate. Concentrate.

'How far down is it to the river, Mum?'

Right and left. Cars came at them from the other direction, missing them at the very last minute, it seemed, whooshing past instead. Whoosh. Whoosh. A car horn that sounded like a train whistle.

'I bet if I wound down my window and stuck my arm out I could touch that safety barrier.'

Maya's eyes found the rear-view mirror. A line of cars had built up behind them. They made a Chinese dragon – look at all the colours, how they shine in the sun.

It whispered in my taringa . . .

'Shh, I said.'

Oh won't you come with me,

There's such a lot to see,

Underneath the deep blue sea.

One day a taniwha . . .

'For fuck's sake, Charlie, would you shut up.'

She heard him gasp, and as he did, all the sounds in the car were sucked into his lungs. All the sounds outside too: the regular whoosh of the other cars as they sped past, the constant roar of the river below them, even the shrill of a million cicadas. There was no sound any more.

Oh shit, she said, and the words were loud inside her head but no sound came out of her mouth. I think I'm going to be sick.

In front of them was a widening of the shoulder of the road. A layby. A safe place to stop. The car found it, skidding on the gravel, engulfing them in road dust.

Maya flung her door open.

'What's the matter, Mum? Why have we stopped?'

'Wait here.' She scrambled to the safety rail, a flimsy ribbon of steel that was all there was between the road and the river.

'Are you going to have a pee?'

She heard him laughing. She skated down a piece of rock on her bottom, surely grazing the backs of her legs as she slid and coming to rest on a ledge only two or three metres below the road. It was all there was between her and the river. There was more than twenty metres of air and shrubs growing out of the rocks below her. She wasn't afraid. She wasn't alarmed to be there. Not even surprised.

This was just like the Waioeka Gorge. When Gran drowned Cash. It smelled the same, sounded the same, with the river – any river – pounding its way relentlessly from one place to another.

Across the other side of the gorge the train track was cut into the hill. She heard a horn sounding, like bagpipes starting up. She looked across and there was a train following the exact path of the tracks. Was it her train? she wondered. Hers and Charlie's?

She was breathing heavily and sweating. The nausea she had felt in the car was stronger now. Her mouth filled again with saliva. She spat it out and it was caught by the wind, a shiny sliver of spit floating through the air, before it snagged on a branch of gorse and hung there, an absurd icicle on a prickly green and yellow tree.

Charlie's voice floated down from the car.

Oh won't you come with me,

There's such a lot to see . . .

The words were inside her.

Underneath the deep blue sea.

Hypnotic. Entrancing.

She saw Cash, taped inside his cardboard box, turning over and over in the air until he hit the water, splash, and bobbed down the river until he was gone. Out of sight. Around the bend or under the water. She couldn't remember which.

She saw Gran brushing her hands against each other. That's that.

She saw Philip in his coffin, eyes closed, mouth in a half smile. She wanted to say, what the fuck is there to smile at?

She saw the water rushing past; it would be cold, take-your-breath-away cold, like the first swim of the season at the beach. *Come on, Maya, dive under. It'll be better once you're under the water.* And her mother with her frilled togs, flicking under, breaking the salty

257

surface with her fingers, her arms, all of her, into the water and under it. And surfacing a moment later, hair plastered to her head, water dripping off her nose, her ears, her chin. *There, Maya, if I can do it, so can you.* Young Nick's Head in the background, as real as Christmas. Salt washing her eyes, stinging in her mouth. Sand in her ears, under her small fingernails.

One day a taniwha . . .

Come on, Maya, dive under. It'll be better once you're under. It'll be better. And now seeing herself as one of a Trinity. Philip, Maya, Charlie. Mother, Maya, Charlie. Gran, Mother, Maya. Always one of three. Three three three. And always part of something else. Never quite existing alone. A child, a grandchild, a wife, a mother. Something to someone else. Wanting more than anything to be a family again. Wanting to be looked after, held. Having someone else make the decisions. Share them with her.

Feeling the wind stroke her face. Being calm now. No longer sick. No longer tired. Seeing it all. And knowing with a surety that came from the riverbed, the sea bottom, that they were a family. She and her husband and her son. Knowing it. *Went swimming in the moana, it whispered in my taringa.* Whispering now, in her ears. Around them. Words surrounding her, warming her against the wind that tunnelled through this rocky place. You're family. All of you. Mother. Husband. Son. In groups of three. Dancing. In threes. One two three, one two three, always family. All of you. And thinking, how was it for Cash after he died? And Philip? And Gran? And even her mother? How was it for them? Black, quiet, nothing. Like lying on the lawn that night. *Oh won't you come with me . . .*

Hearing the passenger door shut and the echo of it bouncing off the tree-covered face of the other side of the gorge, bouncing off, swimming back to her and settling around her. Here, take my hand. I'll help you. Look at the view. Those are our train tracks. Right across the river. Isn't it beautiful? *There's such a lot to see.* Look how the water sparkles. Smell it. Careful now. Here, stand next to me. I've got you. Can you feel the wind against your skin? Doesn't it feel as though it's grabbing you? It might push you into the water at any moment. Hold on. Isn't standing on the edge, in total danger like this, fabulous? I can feel it in every part of me. Can you? See, I won't let you go. *Underneath the deep blue sea.* I wonder how deep it is? What do you think? Your nana would have known that kind of thing. Your dad too. Not me. I've got you, chap. It's okay. I won't let you go. I'll take care of you. This is like when we go to the beach, isn't it? Or the train tracks. It's just like that, Charlie. Isn't it? I won't let you go.

'Mum.' Charlie squeezed her hand. 'I've just remembered.'

Maya turned and focused on his face. His eyes. Everything else was fuzzy. It was as though she was drunk, stoned. She swayed. He did too. She could sense his fingers curled inside hers. She could almost feel the loops and whorls of his fingerprints.

The wind played with his yellow hair. His eyes were round pebbles, blue as summer.

Keep looking at them. If she concentrated on his eyes, on the surety and truth of them, she would be safe, there, on the ledge. He would be too.

'What have you just remembered?' Her voice was a surprise to her. It was strong and even. It hovered in front of them, buffetted this way by the wind, that way, it seesawed before them.

'The second verse to the song,' said Charlie. 'Can I sing it to you?'

Why not? Singing would be fine. Here. On this small stage. Philip? Cash? Mother? Gran? Charlie's going to sing.

Are you listening?

But I said kaore kaore kaore,
I have to haere haere haere,
Although I know we could be friends . . .

He stopped for a breath. But it was as if the wind was snatching his voice away, plucking it out of his mouth with its bitter fingers. Flinging it out over the Manawatu River.

She could see his words catch on a scud of air, and they bobbed about, a jumble of letters and spaces, and then they began to sink, lured by the sparkle and shine of the slippery water below. It was intoxicating with its glitter, with its hum.

She looked out to where the gorge was gashed deep into the flank of the land. The wind continued. Around them, over her bare head, in waves, past them, on, on.

Charlie pulled out of her grasp and reached out. Maya looked down at him. She watched him grab it back – his voice – with his eyes, his open mouth. He held it to him, his arms tight across his chest.

She smiled, suddenly strong.

This voice is my child's.

You can't have it.

You can't have him. Or me.

You've got enough.

My mother's waiting for me
Under the kowhai tree,
Taniwha, haere ra.

Breathe

Jackie Davis

'Is it true that every breath contains a secret?'

As we gather for a family funeral, *Breathe* lures us cautiously into a time past. It is through the unguarded impressions of the nine-year-old narrator that we see a world of 'good girls', classical music, childhood games, longed-for dreams and make-believe. But as the story unfolds, a darker picture emerges.

'I had hoped for a miracle. They happen, don't they?'

Breathe is the highly regarded first novel by Jackie Davis.

'*A lesser writer might have wallowed in the emotional detail, but Davis pulls it off in a strangely Ronald Hugh Morrieson-ish way.*'

Gavin McLean, *Otago Daily Times*

'*Davis is a gifted storyteller with the rare ability to capture raw emotions and present them in an unsentimental yet sincere fashion.*'

Steve Scott, The Press

Paradise

Tina Shaw

Claudia Vogel lives and works in a perfect world. Paradise, the tropical resort she manages, is a high-tech heaven where everything, even the sunshine, is regulated. Owned by mysterious billionaire, Pasqua, the resort is a holidaymaker's dream.

There is, however, a large snake loose on the premises. Claudia's estranged and quizotic husband, Tony, has seen it. Or perhaps he is just being malicious. It is Claudia, after all, who has insisted on a separation, for reasons that are unclear even to herself. She is haunted by experiences as a hostage. The troubling, jungle-clad island of Jolo occupies most of her waking hours and all of her dreams.

Paradise is the story of what happened on Jolo, the ripple effects of terrorism on Claudia and the people who love her, and the elusive search for utopia

This is Tina Shaw's fourth novel. Her previous novel, City of Reeds, was published by Penguin Books (NZ) Ltd in 2000.

'Tina Shaw's status as one of the best of New Zealand's young writers is confirmed by this book.'

Molly Anderson, Otago Daily Times